ANDRENE N. LO..

# DIETVALE

SSP

ISBN: 978-0-9951416-3-6

Squabbling Sparrows Press

"When you say
you'd do anything
to lose the weight,
do you really
mean it?"

Thank god his elderly mother was over at his aunt's place and wouldn't be back until morning. He thought she'd never go – plenty of time for him to enjoy himself and clean up after.

Anticipation makes his groin tighten, something he finds harder these days without help both physical and chemical. Struggling out of the decrepit chair sitting dead-on to the large TV that overpowers the living room, he waits. Not until he's sure of his balance does he walk over to the door leading to his den in the basement.

Locking the door behind himself, he makes doubly sure he won't be disturbed by sliding a large bolt across. Were anyone to interrupt him, not only would it ruin his enjoyment, it could land him in prison, perhaps permanently.

His progress down the stairs is measured, with the handrail creaking in alarm as it takes his full weight. His concentration firmly on where he puts his feet, he only looks up after he's safely negotiated the bottom step. No point rushing. This is viewing by appointment; they'll wait for him.

The Vale logo flashes on the large screen mounted on the far wall. Excellent, Candy had come through for him, even though his request is the most extreme to date.

The Vale said it would cater to anyone's tastes, and they weren't kidding. Sure, it's expensive, but it's his money, he should be able to spend it how it likes. It's not like he pays his mom any rent.

He makes himself comfortable in the large recliner that stands sentinel in the middle of the room and retrieves the remote from down the side of the cushion. Hitting enter, he puts the device down on the small table next to his chair.

A beer and some nuts would usually keep him company, but he wasn't bothering with those tonight. Who knew how his stomach would hold up to his special request?

The screen flares into life showing him every detail is as requested and he gives into a high-pitched giggle. This, this right here, is the Holy Grail.

# 1

**D**ammit, *I can already see my epitaph*. There'll be no 'Quietly in her sleep' on the slab of marble planted above my head; 'Death by Spandex' will be listed as the cause. I've worn wetsuits that were less depilatory in their treatment of my lady bits.

Lying back on the super-king that dominates the bedroom, I fight to get my breathing under control. The iron grip of my foundation garment, added to the dread of visiting David's lawyer that afternoon, makes this impossible.

I'm hyperventilating to the point I'm in danger of blacking out.

*Come on, you stupid tart, get a grip.*

This pep talk, along with a few measured breaths, and the black spots fade back to wherever they'd come from. As calm as I'm likely to be, I attempt to stand so I can continue my search for another outfit. One in which I resemble a slimmish over-stuffed sausage is my best hope.

I can't do it.

Stuck amid my earlier wardrobe malfunctions, I'm like a cast sheep.

Flailing my legs and arms, I try to roll onto my side but my torso is a solid block of Lycra-constricted fat and bone, mammary glands and useless ovaries.

The tears that have been my constant companion in recent months spill over and roll down my cheeks and I give in to the temptation to wallow.

*Maybe if my ovaries hadn't shown themselves to be purely decorative, things would be different?*

Smacking my stomach hard in frustration does sweet FA to remedy my situation; instead, a boom echoes around the bedroom.

*Damn it. I'm bloated again.*

I hate my body with a passion, with 'disgusting' being the best way to describe it. Hell, if I find myself too gross to masturbate successfully, it's no wonder David no longer wants a bar of me.

My hand snakes down between my legs and I rip open the poppers that are hanging on for grim death and moan in pleasure. Any relief on my part is snatched away when the front crotch panel rockets up and over my tummy in a desperate bid to regain its unstretched state.

Without anything to hold it in, my stomach wobbles out of control, leaving me looking as though I'm pregnant. At least, from the spare tyre of undergarment around my waist and below it does.

"Oh, for god's sake."

Slamming my hands on the bed, I lift my hips clear of the mattress and the back part of the crotch disappears under me at a rate of knots. Thank heaven I didn't opt for the G-string version; my haemorrhoids would have been shredded by now.

On the bright side, I can bend sufficiently to get

into a sitting position and, after a short breather, I clamber to my feet.

From a morbid sense of self-hatred, I look in the full-length mirror sitting at the end of the walk-in wardrobe. Even from this distance, it isn't pretty. I would have been okay with my old glasses, but these new contacts do nothing to protect my fragile ego.

I've given up thinking back to how attractive I was when I first caught David's eye. There isn't a diet I haven't tried to regain my glory days. The merest lip curl from my husband of twenty years and there wasn't a chocolate bar without my name on it. Each fall from the diet wagon took an ever greater toll on my psyche, requiring more chocolate, or carbs, or fat, to heal it. More often than not, it took a combination of all three to restore any sense of equilibrium.

Turning side-on to the mirror, I succumb to my absolute self-loathing and, giving up any attempt to hold it in, let my gut hang out. If it weren't so sad, the result would be funny, but it does give me an idea of what will fit.

Marching across the bedroom and into the wardrobe, I continue to the very back and concentrate on rummaging through the items hanging in David's corner. Few of his clothes remain since he moved into the guest suite over the garage.

He hadn't been happy about this, but there was no way I was moving out. The divorce was his idea, even if he hadn't been in a hurry to follow through.

He'd taken his own sweet time until the call yesterday, telling me I needed to be at his lawyer's office at one-thirty today, sharp. I'd longed to tell him the time wasn't convenient but lacked the nerve to go through with it.

Only after I flick through nearly all the garments do I find what I'm after. Taking the dark blue dress off its hanger, I hold it in front of me and turn to face the mirror.

"Perfect." If I look pregnant, I may as well wear maternity, even if it's musty and full of memories of my phantom pregnancy. David's joke that the missing foetus was last seen wearing a purple jumpsuit like The Phantom of comic book fame still hurts. Even after all this time.

Sure it's dated, but at least my tummy won't need to be squished flat for the remainder of the day.

Freeing myself from the elasticated torture device isn't easy, the muscles in my arms not up to the challenges set by the boa constrictor-like bodysuit. In the end, I have to hack at it using the kitchen scissors to escape its death grip. The relief at being free is short-lived when I see my boobs are back to their sagging unperky selves. Talk about a let-down.

Shoving my hands under them, I lift, twist and rotate until I'm happy with their appearance. Pity there isn't a bra that can replicate the look. I tried a Wonder Bra once, but by the end of the evening, I – and even my boobs – was exhausted.

The girls looking twenty years younger and a couple of inches higher than they were in reality was what did us in. The disappointment voiced by David when I removed the confection of lace and industrial-strength boning left me unsure who was the biggest idiot.

Me for thinking I'd get away with it, or him for expecting a miracle.

.  .  .

The drive into the city is as stressful as expected, even though I'd left myself plenty of time for the trip. All it took to grid-lock the city was a single fender-bender or someone to think about having one.

*Liveable city, my sizeable butt.*

If it weren't for all my friends living here, I'd give serious consideration to leaving.

After parking in a car park that will require me to sell a kidney to pay the bill, I hurry to the café where I'm meeting up with Sue-Ng, the pocket-rocket divorce lawyer recommended by Lorraine. Progress is slow: my heels, while slimming, are precarious enough that if I hurry, I'll twist an ankle. I choose to be late over limping into this meeting with David.

Just how late I am becomes obvious when I spot Sue-Ng waiting outside the café. Dwarfed by the enormous briefcase, double-gripped in front of her small frame, the New Zealand-born Chinese handles its weight with ease.

"You're late, Marilyn! I wanted to brief you before the meeting. Now we'll have to wing it." She takes off up the hill and I do my best to keep up. Our destination is the tower that houses Screw, Shaft & Swizz, or whatever name David's firm of lawyers go by. Not an easy task with Sue-Ng pulling ahead with each step.

"Hold up. We aren't all wearing sensible shoes," I gasp out.

Sensible is an understatement. The woman is wearing running shoes that appear to have covered a lot of miles. They're at odds with the tailor-made burgundy skirt suit that fits her like a glove. By comparison, I'm a lumbering beast. Hippo in high heels is the description that springs to mind each time I catch my reflection as I stride by yet another honest-to-a-fault plate-glass window.

After a couple of close calls, I concentrate on putting one foot carefully in front of the other, rather than torture myself with a multitude of side glances.

Sue-Ng doesn't slow when she hits the marble floor of the large foyer at our destination. I do the same and come close to taking a cropper. Only by windmilling my arms do I remain upright, but puts real strain on my ankles.

Sue-Ng's repeated pushing of the 'up' button does nothing to hasten the arrival of the lift. By the time it dings its presence, there are half a dozen be-suited gents with us, all eyes glued to the illuminated display above the doors.

*Blast it.*

I wanted a mini briefing from Sue-Ng on our game plan and, despite our destination being the penultimate floor, we're still the first to get off. Any hope of a final catch up is blown because we exit straight into the law firm's reception area.

It doesn't take a brain surgeon to know David is furious I'm late. The overt checking of his watch and sneering in my direction are hard to miss.

So melodramatic that I'm fully expecting to hear a chorus of "She's by the lifts," like something out of an English pantomime. Well, he can screw himself if he's expecting me to apologise. As usual, I'm not game to voice this.

Sue-Ng hasn't even had time to give our names to the receptionist, when a shark in a suit pops out of nowhere and glides to David's side. The grey sheen of the predator's suit is a perfect match to the dull metallic lustre of his eyes. However, there's nothing grey about his smile. His teeth are toilet-bowl white and gleam against his tan. He reminds me of someone, or could it be I've met him before?

Apparently not, if his introducing himself is genuine and not some weird legal mind game. He ushers us into a humongous boardroom with sweeping views of the harbour and immediately slides around the end of the table, making for the far side. Not to be outmanoeuvred, Sue-Ng skips around the other end, beating him to it. She hurriedly takes a seat with her back to the windows, motioning for me to join her.

As soon as the other two sit opposite us, I grasp why my lawyer has opted for these seats. The men are blinded by the light streaming in through the floor-to-ceiling windows. That is, until The Shark takes a remote out of his pocket and drops the blinds.

Without giving anyone a chance to speak, David's lawyer starts on what is obviously a carefully prepared and well-rehearsed piece. It's akin to something from a soap opera. The upshot is that David is as poor as a church mouse's poorer cousin and in no state to support me once the divorce goes through. Also, he's tired of waiting and wanted to get this whole sorry mess over with.

*What an arsehole.*

My mouth opens but soon closes again. It's a struggle as to what shocks me most: that David has frittered away a fortune, or that he blames me for holding things up.

Sue-Ng, however, has no trouble finding the

right words, thanking The Shark for a masterful summing up. She hefts her large briefcase up onto the pristine surface of the boardroom table.

The Shark's serene countenance takes as much of a battering as the table when Sue-Ng shimmies the briefcase around until the locks are facing us. Doubtless the large domes on its bottom gouging the French polish are the reason for his horror.

After unlocking the case, the small woman lifts the lid on a mountain of paperwork that's hidden from the two men. I'm not surprised at the reams of paper in there. I'd printed most of those pages myself. Heck, I'd even had to run to the stationers halfway through because I was out of ink.

Sue-Ng takes a couple of pages off the top of this financial fire hazard and drops them on the table in front of David and his lawyer. "Perhaps the next time your client tries to conceal his true financial worth, he should change his one and only password."

This must be the report from the forensic accountant Sue-Ng convinced me was money well spent. It's excellent value if David's pallor is anything to go by.

His face now matches his lawyer's teeth.

The Shark doesn't appear affected unless you count the tic flickering next to his right eye. After turning to the second page of the report, he puts his hand up to cover this 'tell'.

He presses it into submission by putting his elbow on the table and leaning into his hand.

*Good luck with that mate, you're busted.*

"There's nothing concrete here that isn't part of public record. A good accountant will easily show a loss." The Shark's smile is once again in place.

"My forensic accountant would not agree with you on that." Sue-Ng stands and lifts the block of paper from her briefcase before slamming it on the table. "This is what we've uncovered so far, but I'm sure there's more where this came from."

The Shark makes short work of scanning the contents page, before speaking in a controlled manner. "Will you excuse us?" He's already standing.

David staggers to his feet and trails the lawyer from the room.

No sooner has the door shut than I bombard Sue-Ng with questions, but she doesn't answer. Her head bowed, she scribbles on a yellow legal pad she'd grabbed from the top pocket of her briefcase.

Eventually, she holds this up and any further questions gag deep in my throat.

*Is that even legal?*

## 2

I scribble yet another question on the crowded legal pad, and Sue-Ng replies in kind. It requires squinting at her abysmal handwriting, and saying the individual letters in my head, to decipher each word in turn. With handwriting this illegible, she could have had a promising career in medicine.

Checking I've read her final reply, Sue-Ng rips the top sheet off the pad and screws it into a tight ball. She tosses this into the briefcase, followed by the pad and pen, closing the lid with a hollow boom.

It's securely locked before David and his paid shark return.

They don't look happy, The Shark's killer smile no longer on show. His eyes are darker than when he played his friendly 'let's get along' cards.

The men barely regain their seats when Sue-Ng goes on the attack, proving everything Lorraine had said.

"Of course, we realise this report doesn't record all of David's holdings, so we'll be going to court to obtain an Order of Discovery. Or ..." The two men lean forward, eyes squinting against the sunlight hitting them full in the face. The remote The Shark left on the table is sitting in my lap, and there's not a chance I'm handing it over. The better illuminated David's squirming is, the better I like it.

"Or we can settle this now," continues Sue-Ng. She shows a deft sleight of hand by retrieving a couple of sheets of paper from underneath the briefcase. These she spins across the table to The Shark. His reactions are fast, stopping them aquaplaning off the highly polished table.

The men scan the contents with David paling even more than earlier. If anything, the lawyer's teeth, visible in a scowl, are grey by comparison.

"This is preposterous. I can't afford this!" David's face once again shows a surplus of broken capillaries.

"You have three options, gentlemen." Sue-Ng splays her hands flat on the table on either side of the briefcase.

"Three?" say The Shark and David in unison.

I fight to stop myself asking the same question.

"One." Sue-Ng holds up her left hand and taps the forefinger with her right. "You settle as we've outlined here. Two." She counts off another digit, giving the men the fingers in the process, "We go to court and secure the Order of Discovery. Or three, we send a copy of that report to the tax department and let them sort it out."

It takes a moment to register that the gurgling sounds are coming from David and not dodgy plumbing in the cavity above the floating ceiling panels. But there's no avoiding his ashen face as he slides off his chair and into a heap under the boardroom table.

The lack of reaction from The Shark makes me think he's as used to David's community theatre episodes as I am. I have to give it to David; this is his best performance to date.

*Maybe the idea of handing over half his money has spurred him onto this more Shakespearian offering?*

When it becomes obvious we can't hear breathing coming from under the slab of wood, all hell breaks loose. The way The Shark gets on with CPR suggests this isn't the first time he's revived a client. Meanwhile, Sue-Ng shouts at the receptionist to call for an ambulance. The one conscious player not participating in the melodrama is me, unable to believe David isn't faking it, again.

The paramedics arrive and dutifully take over from The Shark. However, despite all this attention, David isn't up to an encore. Shame because he'd love to receive the critical acclaim he'd undoubtedly think was due.

His time of death is recorded as 2:37 p.m. He leaves the building in a black zippered bag, well on his way to being stiffer than he's been in my presence for well over two years, if ever.

"So what happens now?" I voice the question that hovers on the faces of The Shark and Sue-Ng.

"It depends." Sue-Ng's statement hangs low and ominous over the boardroom table.

The Shark lifts a brow; he's not biting in this instance.

My lawyer huffs in annoyance, forced to take the lead. "Did your client update his will?"

"I instructed him to do so with one of my associates. Yes." The Shark's teeth are again on show.

"This could take years to sort out." I'm disturbed to see Sue-Ng is smiling as broadly.

*Money-hungry arseholes, the lot of them.*

I wait until The Shark looks in my direction. "Has your associate confirmed David actually got around to changing it?"

It's all I can do not to laugh at his confusion. No doubt he expects people to do what he tells them. Evidently, he doesn't know about David's inability to complete anything without continual, around-the-clock nagging.

It was a role I'd been happy to relinquish as soon as the waste-of-space had moved into the upper level of the garage. Constantly reminding David to take his heart medication every morning had been what I'd missed the least.

*Oops.*

"One moment." The Shark gets to his feet and disappears through the door he and David used earlier.

He's not gone for long.

He does not look happy on his return.

I, on the other hand, am ecstatic

Despite its modest size, my hotel room still looks empty, even though I've got all my worldly goods with me.

Thinking back on my instruction all those months back to Sue-Ng to, "Liquidate everything!" I still experience a surge of power in my solar plexus. Funny, those words had quite the opposite effect on David's lawyer. Perhaps down to the fact David was still in transit to the morgue at the time.

It wasn't that the seasoned legal professional would miss my hairy-backed, doughy late husband. No, it was more a case of having been done out of a hefty fee because David had forgotten to update his will. As it was, there'd been no need to contest it as I was the sole beneficiary.

Without any children or long-lost relatives waiting in the wings, it had been straightforward gaining access to the full estate. And what a heap of everything there'd proven to be. Although this didn't come to light until after the forensic accountant was given full access to all the records. Then the extent of how much David had planned on screwing me over became apparent.

*Bastard.*

The other thing that came to light was David's mistress, or the MiniMe, as I've coined her. It explains why people kept saying it was such a shame I'd put all the weight back on. They'd seen David gadding around town with a younger, slimmer version of me.

The one thing I didn't sell was the apartment David had set Mary-Lynn up in. Yes, even the bitch's name was similar, no doubt to avoid him getting confused in the sack when calling out her name.

I took great delight in sidling up next to her while she was sniffling over the open casket and whispering that I was doubling the rent. Even though dead a couple of weeks, and in receipt of a mortician's makeover, I was sure David flinched. He definitely had more colour in his cheeks than his mistress.

A knock at my door brings me back to the present. The instruction to "Liquidate everything" had been spur-of-the-moment. Down to the shock of the quickie 'divorce' David's death gifted me.

I don't regret it either. Shrugging off my old life along with all its excess baggage was liberating. Especially when all that baggage was chock-full of clothes that no longer fit my body or my life.

My wardrobe now consists of loose-fitting outfits that can cope with my weight fluctuations. If I need to dress up a little, I throw on the blue maternity frock and accessorise the hell out of it.

This is all a far cry from the style of clothing David had insisted I wear, and that Lorraine and my other friends still favour. All those years of standing next to him at events, nodding when I should, and smiling when inside I was screaming. I was the perfect corporate wife.

"Marilyn? You in there?" Sue-Ng's voice is faint through the slab door, designed to stop fires and the racket of inebriated guests as they stagger back to their rooms in the small hours.

Mentally shaking the memories free, I struggle off the luxurious bed, rush to open the door and stand to the side. Rather than take advantage of my unspoken invitation, she hands me a fat envelope, explains that she's on her way to court and races off. I haven't even had a chance to close the door when I hear her impatiently pushing the 'down' button. Sue-Ng's "Don't spend it all at once" sneaks between the metal doors as they hiss closed.

Holding the envelope against my chest, I lean my back against the door, managing to both close it and open the letter simultaneously. On seeing the number of zeros on the law firm's trust account cheque, any strength in my legs flees. I slide in a heap to the lushly carpeted floor.

Unaware I'm crying until a second tear splatters onto the trembling cheque, I have to swipe at my eyes to stop any further damage. It doesn't matter how hard I concentrate, my maths skills aren't up to the challenge of calculating my hourly rate over the course of the marriage.

I straighten the sheath of papers that hold the cheque snuggly in their bosom and make short work of skimming the contents. It takes a while to see how the crazy total for the entire estate has been calculated. "Wow, that's ridiculous!" I'd realised house prices were going through the roof, but three-point-two million is way more than the house was worth.

It had tons of land for being so close to the city, but was old and riddled with problems. Certainly enough to have even the most dedicated house flipper backing slowly away. If whoever bought it has any sense, they'll bowl it, or better yet, get the fire brigade to burn the place to the ground. The crews were always after practice like that. I'd gladly throw the first match in a reverse ribbon-cutting ceremony.

I have no wish to see my old home again. The memories it holds I can happily abandon to the fates. I'm pleased to be shot of the whole thing, even moving out before the funeral, knowing David couldn't move back in. The one reason I'd stayed before then was to ensure he didn't change the locks, something I'd beaten him to.

A pleasant afternoon passes, virtually spending my windfall.

*Scratch that, it isn't a windfall. I worked hard for every damned cent.*

Years spent performing CPR on a marriage that had suffered an irregular heartbeat from the day of the over-blown ceremony. Wasn't my fault David had drunk so much at the reception that he'd had trouble getting it up. Also not my fault he'd poured so much alcohol down my throat that I'd laughed it off as being no big deal. Unfortunately, all of that happened before the little blue pills were dished out like candy. David's only way to move on from what he claimed was his complete and utter humiliation had been counselling.

*Was that the real nail in the coffin of our marriage, and not my inability to conceive?*

Either way, David soon looked to bolster his manhood in places other than our marital bed.

The major expense I face in establishing a new life is a house. No, make that a *home*. One without memories stuffed between loosely fitting floorboards. And, much as I'd loved the large rooms of my old house, I'm thinking of something smaller for the next stage in my life.

Perhaps I should kick the MiniMe out and take over the *love nest*? I've already and had a nosy at the neighbourhood from a mix of research and morbid curiosity. Mostly to get my head around who'd screw my late husband by choice.

Of course, before I'd deign to move in there, I'd have to have the place fumigated. Something involving women dressed in purple velvet and armed with burning bunches of sage should do it.

*Does the Catholic Church undertake exorcisms these days?*

That sort of money at my disposal, I don't need to bother. Hell, I can even head overseas if I want to, although I'm unsure of where I'd go. There's a lot to be said for keeping a few familiar things around after purging myself of everything else. I haven't even seen that much of my girlfriends since David popped his clogs.

Whenever we got together, the main topic of discussion was always ripping apart our other halves, never mind that they paid for the lunches. David gone, I had little to talk to them about and they weren't particularly interested in the challenges I was facing. It's as if they preferred me when I was miserable.

*No, apart from an abundance of cash, my life is depressingly empty.*

I tap away at the calculator app on my phone, adding up ball-parks on things I'll need. I even include a few that are more 'want' than 'need', but barely make a dent. I'd had no idea David was worth as much dead.

The way he'd told it, we were merely scraping by. Technically that would have been the case if I hadn't sold off everything, sometimes at below-market prices. Asset rich, cash poor, although not anymore.

I've already talked with Sue-Ng's accountant friend in general terms about how to invest the money. The bulk will go to an off-shore trust, in Central America of all places. Somewhere the government can't get its sticky fingers on it and where I can pay little or no tax. Tax avoidance rather than evasion is how the accountant puts it, so technically legal.

This isn't the only asset protection I'm investing in. If I can't get a bra to lift and twist my boobs into something worthy of Instagram, I know of a surgeon who can help. Just as Lorraine had recommended Sue-Ng as the perfect lawyer for the job at hand, she recommended Mr Ian Stamford as the best tit man in town.

My friend's perky D-cups – with the gravity-defying properties of something produced by NASA – are a testament to this. Heaven knows she gets them out at every opportunity; she didn't even wait for the stitches to be removed to show them off for the first time. In a restaurant! And boy hadn't that lead to a Mexican wave of dropped cutlery.

The irony of implants effectively adding weight

to my body isn't lost on me. Being officially single again, I'm desperate to lose poundage. There's also the teensy issue of not wanting to settle for someone as average as David, or even me. Sadly, in my current state, it's all I'm capable of attracting these days. *Ugh*, even thinking about getting naked with a guy in my league is gag-worthy.

Yes, double standards, I know.

Of real annoyance is that even though I'm carrying a ton of extra weight, none of it has managed to find its way north of my waist. If you're into the fruit and veg morphology of body types, pear-shaped doesn't do it justice. My body tends more to the malformed butternut squash end of things.

## 4

E nsconced in the plush couch at the plastic
surgeon's, I'm tense and excited in turn. Tense
because having undergone fertility treatment, I've
been prodded, poked and explored enough for one
lifetime. The excitement is around thoughts of
having boobs perky and uplifting to my soul and my
life. Not a pair of those fridge-magnet puppies.
Perky, yes, but still natural-looking is what I'm after.

After I've read the same advertisement for the
third time, I close the Italian Vogue on my lap and
place it back on the dark mahogany coffee table. I
straighten it until it's perfectly aligned with all its
glossy neighbours. A reading selection this high-
end and up-to-date guarantees each breast will cost
a fortune. It's not like you can get them done in
instalments either.

Following a muted ding, the receptionist stands
so she can see over the reception desk. "Mr
Stamford will see you now, Mrs Channing."

The woman is in remarkably good shape for her
age, even if it's hard to determine what that is.
Maybe she works for contra instead of wages? Not a
wrinkle mars her serene countenance. If she's ever

had jowls, they've long since been incinerated in accordance with industry standards.

Struggling free from the depths of the couch, I'm glad of my loose-fitting new wardrobe. The couch is squishy and getting out of it is akin to something you'd normally do during an advanced yoga class.

Sitting in the visitor's chair across from the surgeon, I'm not surprised by how young he looks. I Googled the hell out of him, rather than take Lorraine's word for it. Anyone who's going near my girls with a scalpel needs thorough research.

He doesn't look exactly as he did in the photos I'd found of him online. Still, if you're a plastic surgeon and you play golf with plastic surgeons, it stands to reason you're getting a little work done now and then.

Perhaps a *little work* isn't the best description. From the looks of things, the surgeon has had the lot, except for a boob job, unless he's had a reduction. It's difficult to gauge with any man-boobs well hidden under the three-piece suit he's wearing like a badge to his hourly rate.

"And what can we help you with today, Mrs Channing?"

That Stamford says this while looking at me with a critical eye is unnerving. He hasn't even looked at my chest yet, having obviously found more than enough to focus on north of my neck. Sure, I'm rich, but I'm stuffed if I'm funding his next golf trip to Hawaii.

"Ah, I'd like to talk about a breast augmentation." Sure, I'm happy calling it a boob job in my head and amongst friends. But there isn't a chance I'm using that term with the man who'll be wielding the scalpel.

"Really?"

He punctuates this single word by lifting an eyebrow, something I hadn't thought possible considering the help they've already had. His tone does nothing for my confidence.

Possibly there's another surgeon available with a better bedside manner? Mind you, did I want to entrust my new tits to someone else? Knowing my luck, I'd end up with the surgeon responsible for the brow lift opposite.

"Yes, really!" I put as much force as I can into my reply, although it's still a struggle to find my voice after all the years of being muted.

Even faking it has the desired effect and the air of up-sell drops a notch. The surgeon then goes into his spiel about the pros and cons of augmentation. It's rote to the point he may as well be skimming through a handbook in his head. It's as though he's reading me the Miranda rights, but for tits and not assholes.

I can't fault the thoroughness of Stamford's examination; I haven't been groped this much since my first school ball. And just as then, so successful are my efforts to distance myself from the action that by the time he's finished, it's as though my girls belong to someone else. Much easier than dealing with unwanted and embarrassing reactions with him the first man to touch them in over a year.

Only after I'm dressed, and my breasts are my own again, do we discuss cup size, shape and options like over or under the muscle. Under the muscle, if I'm to avoid them looking like a couple of poached eggs. He buzzes the receptionist and arranges for me to undergo a few tests.

These are carried out by a nurse in a side room that's clinical in the extreme. No squishy couches in here, it's all hard, sterile surfaces and no-nonsense equipment. The first thing the nurse does is weigh me, something I've avoided for months. The last thing the nurse does is take my blood pressure. And that's where things go tits-up.

My blood pressure isn't so much high, as stoned out of its freaking gourd. My best chance of getting new boobs is to grab the implants off Mr Stamford's desk and leg it.


"Now, we can put you on statins for six months or so to help drop the blood pressure to a level where we can safely operate, or ..."

The surgeon leaves the other option tantalisingly out of reach. It doesn't matter; I already know what he'll say. I don't need him to voice it. I don't give him a chance, stuttering out, "But I've tried every diet under the sun, and none of them work."


Until I Googled it, I had no idea there were so many spas on offer in New Zealand. Places that would dispatch the thatch, trim the brows and IPL you to within an inch of your life, all without losing a gram.

Residential fat loss centres, however, were thin on the ground. You'd think *The Biggest Loser* would have people clamouring to be locked up, starved and forced to labour for hours, but no.

Personally, I've always found the show too much like a documentary about Third-World-prison systems. Not that this stops me from watching it.

I undertake a cursory search of overseas centres, starting in Australia, before working my way on to the more accessible parts of the USA and Europe. Sure, I can afford them, but the idea of being on my own on the other side of the world fills me with trepidation.

I've never been much of a traveller, preferring the comforts of home to ritzy five-star resorts. The irony that I'm presently living in such an establishment isn't wasted on me.

There's also the brand new Lexus sitting in the hotel's basement car park to consider. It's the one significant thing I've bought since receiving the mega pay out, and I'm keen on putting a few miles on the clock. That won't happen if it's rusting away in airport long-stay parking.

A sense of pride in my purchase of the vehicle envelops me, because it's the first time I've ever bought a car on my own. Initially, my parents dictated the choice of vehicle and then David.

His propensity to harp on about the resale value had meant years and years of Hondas, to the point I hated them with a passion. The Lexus was the most ostentatious, impractical thing I could find without going over the top. I couldn't navigate supermarket speed bumps in a Lamborghini.

The girls said I was mad and should have bought a Tesla. And if it hadn't been for David categorically saying no to a Lexus last time my vehicle was updated, I would have done so.

Leaving my laptop to hibernate, I swipe through the contacts on my phone until I find the one I'm after.

My call is answered on the third ring, as though my frenemy has been waiting beside the phone.

"Lorraine, have you got a second?" It never pays to assume she's free to talk; shame she doesn't extend this courtesy in return. Usually, I'll be halfway through my greeting when she bombards me with whatever crisis currently befalls her. The problem is that if anyone will know of a suitable 'fat farm' – spa to you and me, darling – it's Lorraine.

"I have!" Lorraine sounds as surprised about this as I am. It's more common to wait for her to call back at a time convenient to her.

Unprepared for this immediate audience, I stutter for a second or two, unsure how to proceed, eventually deciding that just stating what's happening is the best approach. "I, ah, went to see Mr Stamford about the boob job and unfortunately it can't go ahead."

"And ..." says Lorraine, this one word telling me that she's full of expectation about learning a juicy morsel she can share with our group.

I'd given up asking her to keep anything in confidence as it seemed to be a pathological impossibility. Tell Lorraine, you tell everyone. I've saved a lot of phone minutes over the years.

"It's my blood pressure." I stop in hopes she'll catch on.

My hopes are in vain. Either she doesn't know about the link between hypertension and excess weight or, more likely, she's being deliberately obtuse to force me to say it aloud.

"It's my weight."

"Oh, yes!"

Her glee in this short acknowledgement is evident and the rustle of wicker comes through loud and clear. Lorraine has settled into one of the chairs in their conservatory, ready for me to spill my guts.

*Damn, I should never have phoned, but to back out now would be pointless.*

"I've been told I need to lose at least fifty pounds."

I don't bother going into the whole course of statins option because I've discarded that as far too time-consuming. I want new boobs ready for next summer and that's not happening if I'm faffing about taking drugs.

"What about Weight Watchers?"

Grinding my teeth in small circles without conscious effort, I hope it's not audible at the other end.

*Is the woman being deliberately thick?*

"I was thinking of somewhere residential. So I won't be tempted."

That I'm usually tempted by Lorraine and my other friends goes unsaid. There's no need, both parties to this particular conversation are well aware of it.

"There is this one place, but ..." Lorraine peters out and I hope to hell I won't be left hanging. I'll be strung along over several days like the mouse to Lorraine's cat. Lord knows it's happened before with whatever interaction taking days, not minutes and proving frustrating as hell.

*Dammit, I don't want to lay myself bare like this. But if this is what it'll take to get her to divulge the information, so be it.*

Opening my jaw to ease the tension, I press on.

"I need this. My life is as good as on hold until I have the operation."

Her answer comes faster than I could have hoped for, or even expected.

"The Vale. Down on the Coromandel Peninsula. It's fairly full-on though. Although it's only for the elite, so you might not get in."

*In other words, I'm not elite. Thanks for the vote of confidence, Lorraine.*

There's a sudden intake of breath from the other end, before Lorraine presses on, "But I was told about the place in confidence, so you didn't hear about it from me."

"My lips are sealed." In a lifelong habit, I mime zipping them shut, even though she's not privy to the motion. "Do they have a website?"

I prefer any establishment I deal with to have a website, so I can get a sense of the place before committing to anything.

"Just a mo."

The change in Lorraine's voice confirms we're en route to another part of the large, rambling Remuera mansion, hopefully somewhere with a website address written down.

"Got a pen?"

Scrabbling for one of the multitudes sporting the hotel's logo stashed in the drawer of the small bedside table, I listen intently.

After scribbling it down, I read the website address back twice to confirm I've got it right. Rather than consisting of words that translate to the actual name of the establishment, Lorraine has dictated a random collection of letters and numbers. A Mensa chapter Christmas party would be stuck recalling this lot.

Following the usual ritual of agreeing to lunch and 'we must chat more often', I tap the call shut and open up my laptop again. I type the URL in one letter at a time, checking it's correct, making sure my zeros aren't Os and vice versa. It's convoluted and involves a few symbols giving the overall address a Cyrillic look.

The website, however, is clean and fresh. It's also professionally reassuring and offers exactly what I'm after. Fast-track weight loss under professional supervision at a location so remote that escaping would burn more calories than you could snag during a blow-out at McDonald's.

The name is the one off-putting thing about the place. The Vale at Shady Meadows makes it sound less like an upmarket spa and weight-loss centre and more like an upmarket lawn cemetery.

## 5

For once in my life, I don't hesitate. I fill in the online application form, hoping the place will take me. Apparently, it's not a given the spa will accept me as a guest, AKA, inmate.

*Hah, it doesn't matter how flash it looks, with all those professional photos and beautiful typesetting, once I'm checked in, it'll be a prison.*

Although, this is the only thing it has in common with those facilities overseen by the Corrections Department. As well as weight loss and pampering, they also have chakra balancing, massages, mani-pedis and something called an ozone sauna.

Perhaps one of the most comforting things about the place is that they have a money-back guarantee, with my credit card not being hit until after I check out.

The place is exclusively for women, which is a major relief, as I've had enough of sweaty guys labouring away next to me to last a lifetime. Lovemaking with David had always been a damp affair. A tremor skitters across my frame in response to the memories flashing soggily back.

The form completed and dispatched, I snap the computer shut and leave the rest to fate.

The wait is short. The wheels of fate positively spin and a confirmation email arrives that afternoon. In addition to confirming they'll accept my booking, they assign me an alias.

*Maisie Smith? Are they serious?*

Scrolling down, I see the reason is to maintain their clients' anonymity; they have had problems with paparazzi in the past. Now a bubble of excitement gurgles away in my tummy. Or it could be wind. Either way, I quite like the idea of mixing with celebrities over breakfast, even if I eschew the limelight myself.

I also receive a link to their online registration and dutifully fill this in. The other thing I have to trawl through is a page and a half of T&Cs, mostly related to keeping quiet about the location of the facility and that I'm actually going there. There's enough legalese attached to this that I know if I breech any of them, it's going to cost me big time. The last section I need to complete relates to my next of kin in the case of emergency.

My elderly mother couldn't cope with anything drastic from the cushioned comfort of her La-Z-Boy recliner at the rest home, down the other end of the country. Nor do I want to assign this task to any of my girlfriends. Eventually, I type in the name and contact details of Sue-Ng. She, more than anyone, should know what to do in case of anything dire occurring.

They also want to know my hair and eye colour,

height, weight, blood type, blood pressure and if I have any distinguishing marks.

Most of this I know from a lifelong association with my body. The answers to all the medical questions are on the report from my initial consultation with the boob man. The next question is one I can't answer immediately. I know I have a mole high on my back. But being able to mark it on the line drawing of a human body on the website? That's not happening without clever camera work in the bathroom.

I mark it as best I can by dragging and dropping the mole symbol from the menu at the side of the screen. I also add a few piercings and a couple of tattoos to check out what they'd look like, before deleting them and clicking the NEXT button. The request on the following page makes me second-guess the advisability of completing the booking.

*A nude selfie?*

*They cannot be serious.*

I'm in danger of the registration timing out before I can bring myself to strip. Taking a photo via the full-length mirror on the back of the bathroom door, I break out in a cold sweat. I do, however, take the precaution of ensuring my face is obscured by the camera.

Not long after I hit SUBMIT, I receive another email. This one confirms all my details as well as listing an anchor tattoo on my forearm and pierced nipples.

*No, no, no!*

I deleted those before hitting the NEXT button. I know I did.

Immediately, I hit 'reply' to put things right. An automated message states that if I want to contact management at The Vale, I need to do so via the online contact form.

This doesn't work.

Neither does the link to the original registration page.

*Damn.*

As upsetting as the management of The Vale thinking I'm a redneck, is reading the menu and finding out I'll be going vegan for the duration. Kale and I don't get along.

My visit to the fat farm set for a little over two weeks away, I see no point not to indulge a little in the interim. A back-to-back binge of lunches, dinners, decadent desserts and a LOT of chocolate ensues. The highlight of this feasting is a going-away dinner with my girlfriends at the Hilton, where I tuck into a large steak with all the trimmings.

If I'm subsisting on tofu and kale for the next six weeks, I want to boost my levels of whatever it is a large slab of meat provides. The creamy potatoes that accompany the steak are the perfect thing to top up my potassium and calcium.


Unfortunately, these 'supplements' don't sit comfortably when I do up my seat belt the following morning, ready for the drive down to the Coromandel. What had been light, fluffy and succulent the previous evening has coalesced into something that's doing me no favours. And with the waistband of my snug-fitting yoga pants close to chopping me in two, I'm anything but comfortable.

Zooming down the motorway, my overindulgence accelerates its way through my gastrointestinal tract, demanding a mercy dash into a service centre. It's this or risk besmirching my lovely new leather upholstery.

While unpleasant in the extreme, the relief is immense. Climbing back into the car, which I hadn't so much parked as abandoned, my stretch pants are no longer in danger of leaving permanent marks.

And it's sure to make a difference to that all-important first weigh-in.

In a snap decision – one of many after years of having to research everything to death to satisfy David – I decide to take the back roads. This will avoid traffic and speed traps in the process. One of the joys of a new car is seeing what it can do. That won't happen if I'm in bumper-to-bumper traffic and in fear of being done for speeding. Directed by the GPS, I'm soon out in the country and away from the city's gravitational pull.

Despite a dry summer in the city, here the fields are lush and green, rolling in gentle waves before lapping against the native bush that tops the surrounding hills. The road too is in good shape. It's time to let this new baby of mine show me what it's capable of.

Pretty quickly, I realise it's capable of more than I am, and I ease off the accelerator for fear of putting myself in a ditch. First thing I'll do when I'm back in town is sign up for advanced driving lessons. Images of myself dressed head to toe in black leathers, tailor-made to fit my new boobs, flash in a delightful slide show inside my head. That is until lights flashing in the rear-view mirror break my concentration. I'm tootling along at

70kph and have half a dozen cars queued up behind me.

Rather than speed up and deal with the pressure of keeping ahead of them all, I pull over at the next farm driveway. I'm shocked that the little old lady in the Nissan Micra at the end of the queue gives me the finger when she zips past.

In a move out of character, I return the gesture, although chances are the myopic biddy won't have seen it.

Before pulling back onto the road, I open the sunroof and turn up the volume on Coast, my favourite station. Singing like no one's listening, and seriously hoping they aren't, I get back on the road.

The rest of the drive is uneventful, but pleasant all the same. The highlight is the drive through the bush at the back of Kawakawa Bay. Here I turn the radio down and listen instead to the local birds and cicadas, with their voices filling the air. Along with the scent of the damp undergrowth, memories flood back of trips out this way when I was a teenager.

That was before I met David, when I'd been full of confidence, thin and happy. Well, happy with life; I hadn't liked my body back then either, being skinny as the proverbial rake and built more for speed than comfort.

*This boob job of mine is long overdue.*

The journey slows after I leave Thames, where I stop for a light lunch at McDonald's. The road is narrower, the corners more frequent. While the car will handle these at speed, the drop-offs ensure I drive conservatively. Even so, I've given myself ample time to get to my destination.

According to Google Earth, it's in the middle of nowhere, in dense bush. I've been instructed to park there before a 4WD vehicle that's better suited to the roads takes me the rest of the way.

I'd searched long and hard on Google Earth, hoping to spot anything that looked remotely like The Vale, at least based on the photos on their website. Despite zooming in on any open areas on the hills above Coromandel Township, I'd come up empty-handed.

Eventually, houses pop up more frequently, announcing I'm approaching civilisation and I soon locate what I'm after. The bright green signage on the petrol station catches my eye from a good distance along the road, meaning my turn into the forecourt is slow and measured.

I don't ease in next to the pumps, instead pulling in hard on the left-hand side to park well out of the way. Even if I'd wanted to, I couldn't have pulled up next to the pumps. There's a filthy 4WD hogging the space closest to the buildings, while the side closest to the road is home to a ridiculous gold Hummer. It looks like something out of a porno.

The Lexus secured, I'm about to enter the small shop that forms the basis of the petrol station when I'm forced to jump back. A tall, rangy chap with greasy shoulder-length hair storms out, his whole focus on the smartphone gripped in his grimy hand. I bite down on the pointed "excuse me" that hovers on my lips. It's best not to antagonise his sort. Any further words fail me when instead of getting into the beat-up 4WD he clambers into the 'porn-mobile'.

*He must have stolen it.*

The automatic doors start to close right behind

me, prompting me to wave my hand above my head. Only then do I enter the station's shop blindly, my eyes still glued to the Hummer.

"Can I help you, love?" says the chap standing behind the counter.

"Oh, ah, yes." I don't turn to give him my full attention until the ugly vehicle roars out of the station and off down the road. It's as though the hounds of hell, or the cops, are in pursuit.

"I wonder if I can park my vehicle here for the next six weeks? I'm happy to pay. Somewhere secure and under cover, if possible."

His mien flips from professional enquiry to small-town gossip in the blink of an eye. "And where will you be, love?"

Tempted to tell him it's none of his business, I'm conscious he's all that's between my beloved Lexus being safe and being parked in the middle of the boonies.

"I'm, ah, booked in to attend an, ah, yoga retreat." I stumble over the small lie. Better than telling a stranger I've booked in for six weeks of starvation and enemas. And all so I can get a new pair of boobs. Even thinking about it, my cheeks warm. "Someone will collect me from Flays Road."

"Really?" Gary, if he is the manager on duty as the sign above the register implies, is surprised. The tilt of his head questions the advisability of this course of action. "You must be with that lot who've set up in the old army base."

I'd argue his assertion that I'm truly setting off for boot camp. I could explain their high-end website doesn't look in the least ex-military. But the less I say about what I'm up to, the better.

Along with preserving my dignity, there's also the Vale's T&Cs I've agreed to online.

"I'd prefer to park here and get a taxi. I've booked one." I'd also tried to ring the garage to check if I could store my car with them. Despite trying several times, it was either engaged, or there was no answer.

To detour him back to my immediate problem of finding lodging for the car, I ask, "So, can you help with parking?"

"I can. There's plenty of space in the back shed and I'm sure Bill wouldn't mind."

"Bill?"

"The bloke who's shed it is. Not part of the station, you see."

"Is he around so I can ask him?"

"No, love, he's dead."

## 6

Unsure how to negotiate a price to store the Lexus with someone who's already passed on, I stand in front of the counter, dithering.

"Raewyn!" Gary shouts at the top of his voice, causing me to jump.

We wait.

"Raewyn!"

The volume has doubled, although this time I'm not taken by surprise.

There's shuffling before a girl flings aside the multi-coloured, plastic fly screen that separates the shop from the private spaces behind. She's got her music turned up so loud I recognise the song, even though the buds are firmly shoved deep inside her ears.

Her pissed-off expression of teenage angst is as loud, with its 'volume' directed at me.

Gary doesn't bother to speak further with her. He points at her and then the seat behind the counter. He repeats this when she doesn't move as fast as he'd like. It isn't until she's in place that he leads me out of the front doors. Swinging to the right, we walk down the side of the garage to a hodgepodge of tin sheds that clutter the back of the lot.

We stop outside the double sliding doors to the biggest one and he pulls a large bunch of keys from his back pocket. His pants lift as a result of their lightened load. A quick flick through the multitude on offer and Gary selects a large key. He slides this into a padlock that looks to be older than the patchwork of corrugated iron that skins the building.

The lock opens with surprising ease given the rust that coats it, but the squealing when he slides the door to one side, sets my teeth on edge. Inside the shed is much lighter than I expect with most of the roof given over to plastic sheeting rather than long-run iron.

The smell of oil, sawdust and long-forgotten projects, is one that takes me back to my dad tinkering away in the shed at my childhood home. A true workman's shed.

"Now that's odd." Gary stops so suddenly that I run into the back of him, forcing him to stagger forward a step.

With nothing other than a pristine Morris Minor parked in one corner, I ask "What is?"

"Bill's car being here. It's been missing since before those pig hunters found him down the bottom of that cliff. It wasn't in here earlier because I checked. The cops'll want to hear about this."

"The police? Should I store my car elsewhere?"

"What? No, she'll be right, love. It was pretty much an open-and-shut case. Silly old fool was out hunting by himself and must have slipped. Pigs had at him something chronic before they found him."

"Pigs?" I say weakly, the Big Macs from earlier

doing their best to be back on the menu. Make that with double fries and a sundae that mostly consisted of chocolate sauce to follow.

"Nasty things, wild boar. Did you know they can eat a sheep, bones 'n all? Couple of hours and they'll be done. And that's a healthy animal, not an old injured bloke like Bill would've been."

I didn't.

I didn't want to.

"Excuse me."

I stumble out into the fresh air, filling my lungs slowly, all while avoiding images of people being eaten alive by pigs. It's not an easy task given I'd been up-sold bacon on my burger. Gary continues with a chomp-by-chomp account of how this happened. I shove my fingers in my ears and distance myself until I'm over by the corrugated iron fence. The property truly is a shrine to iron.

As if realising I'm no longer behind him, Gary turns and, although his lips move, thankfully I can't hear anything. I wait for him to twig his gruesome account isn't gratefully accepted this time. Not until his lips stop moving do I pull my fingers out of my ears.

*I now understand why Raewyn keeps her music at full volume.*

"Sorry, love, didn't mean to upset you."

Not trusting myself to open my mouth, I wave my hand in acceptance of his apology.

"If you're happy with the shed, we can put your car in there now. No need to charge you."

Whether this charity is down to small-town kindness, or me almost barfing all over the yard, I'm unsure. Either way, I can't accept it.

"No, I'd prefer to pay. You can give the money to a worthy cause if you like."

We're back at the Lexus before Gary speaks again. "Bill was always a big supporter of the local animal shelter. We can give it to them, if you like?"

I agree, unlock the car door and climb in. It's another ten minutes before I'm safely parked next to Bill's Morrie and have dragged my bag out of the back. Progress was slow because Gary walked in front of my car like a signalman from the first days of motoring. Locking the shed door had taken on a ceremonial air.

Back out front, the forecourt is free of cars. Probably just as well with Raewyn sitting with eyes closed and music cranked up so loud that we're right next to her and she has no idea.

Not until Gary nudges her does she open her eyes. There isn't an ounce of surprise shown by the sullen teen, so perhaps she was aware of us. She jumps down off the stool and flings the fly screen to one side before skulking through. She doesn't go far, instead turning and watching us through the rippling strips of plastic.

Gary stands at the cash register and scratches his head, peering at the plethora of buttons on the state-of-art till in pride of place on the counter. "Not sure what I should put car parking under."

I don't have time for this; I'm due to be picked up around the corner in less than half an hour. I grab a packet of chewing gum from the stand next to the register. "How about I buy this and get $200 cash out? I can give that to you to pass onto the SPCA."

His relief is evident by how quickly he takes my purchase and rings it up. I duly sign the receipt to show I've received the cash and hand it straight back. All of this under Raewyn's watchful – some might say avaricious – gaze. Despite not hearing much, I doubt she misses a thing.

I'm relieved when Gary folds the money and puts it carefully into the pocket of his shirt and pats it reassuringly, the drop in the teenage girl's demeanour palpable.

Running shoes and a wheeled suitcase see me at the taxi rank in good time. I share the old-school bench seat with a woman who must be in her eighties and has a small child in tow; a grandchild, no doubt. Neither of them looks keen on conversation and I'm not one to strike it up without encouragement, so we sit quietly.

The peace is eventually broken by the beat-up 4WD from the front of the petrol station pulling up in front of us. Something that would lead to a turf war at any taxi rank in the city doesn't raise an eyebrow here. I worry that my taxi will have trouble pulling in with this grubby vehicle hogging the whole space.

The kerb-side window whirs down and the driver leans across the passenger seat. "Mrs Rogers?"

It takes a beat to twig he's talking to me and that this must be my 'taxi'. I'd forgotten I'd booked it under my maiden name in a flight of fancy at being free of David. "It's Ms, actually, but yes."

My identity confirmed, he jumps out, marches around the front and collects my bag. While the vehicle isn't taxi-standard, his outfit of walk shorts, white shirt and a pot belly, acquired from hours of sitting behind the wheel are spot on. The buttons on the front of his shirt are put to the test when he slings my bag in the back. Ditto the expensive French cosmetics I'd packed the night before.

I resist the urge to tell him to be careful, with any damage done by now. I hope when I open my toiletry bag that everything hasn't coalesced into skin-smoothing-wrinkle-beating goo. Glass bottles can be a curse.

I've already tried the handle of the back door when he marches by me and opens the front. "Lock's buggered on that door. You can ride in the front."

This doesn't sit well with me, although I demur and climb in anyway. I've not had time to get comfortable when he floors it and I'm pressed back into what is a surprisingly clean seat.

While the outside of the vehicle looks as though it's been driven through bush backwards, the interior is immaculate. There's even a box of tissues in the centre console in case of spills. The small cardboard pine tree, swinging wildly from the rear-view mirror, gives off that reassuring taxi smell. All that's missing is a meter, making me glad I'd agreed the price upfront.

Any hopes the trip will be completed in silence are soon dashed. As with all taxi drivers, Colin likes a chat, although the spew of words he keeps up for the first ten minutes of our trip hardly match the term.

Verbal diarrhoea would be a better descriptor.

He touches on the backgrounds of everyone we pass. He goes into the history of buildings, roads and anything else not nailed down. He even proves knowledgeable on the flora and fauna and modern farming methods.

We turn onto Flays Road and his diatribe changes direction, too. It's not one I'm keen on.

"Such a shame about old Bill. It was hereabouts they found him. He was a character, all right."

"What sort of ferns are these?"

My question is borne out of desperation to keep away from stories of people being eaten alive. Personally, I couldn't care less about the native plants thrashing themselves against the side of the Land Rover in an attempt to stop us passing. But if it'll shut him up, I'll summon my inner gardener.

"Oh." He seems put out at me cutting him off. "These are Dicksonia fibrosa."

In response to my blank look, he adds "Golden tree fern."

Out of distractions, unless I want to get into the grade of shingle on the road, we're back on the subject of Bill.

"The strange thing was he didn't have his pack with him, or his gun. If he'd had his gun, he could have taken pot shots at those porkers and kept them at bay. Ripped his throat clean out, they did."

"Stop!"

Colin looks at me as if I'm bonkers to interrupt his story like this.

"Stop the car! I'm going to be sick!"

The speed with which he applies the brakes has me close to having my lunch all over his dashboard. He's still not been fast enough. I'll never make it out of the vehicle in time. I open the door, lean out and introduce the McDonald's franchise to Flays Road.

Colin inches the Land Rover forwards, so I can get out without stepping in my Big Mac. I stumble from the vehicle before giving up the rest of my lunch. After each expulsion, he moves the vehicle along to a clean spot, something I'm grateful for. Eventually, I run out of ammunition and get ready to clamber back into the 4WD. A brief nod from Colin and I stop.

"I'm so sorry." I lean over the passenger seat and snatch several tissues from the box before wiping the door frantically.

*When on earth did I last eat a carrot, because it wasn't in the past couple of days?*

He checks for longer than I like before I get the nod that I've cleaned to his exacting standards. I ball the tissues and place them in the plastic bag hanging from the knob of the glove box.

Despite the occasional whiff from the dirty tissues, the little pine tree is up to the challenge of masking them from my driver.

We haven't gone more than another ten metres when Colin says, "He'd scratched 'Cooking P' into the dirt. Cops figure he must have stumbled across a cook lab."

He goes quiet, although not for as long as I'd like. "Guess writing that would have been quicker than methamphetamine." He thinks about this for a beat, before continuing. "Now isn't that funny. I wouldn't have a clue what P stands for. Do you?"

I shake my head weakly, both as a result of all that purging and knowing I don't have the nerve to tell him to shut up.

*How on earth am I supposed to know what the street name for the drug of choice stands for?*

"Yep, meth labs, the modern-day equivalent of an old-school dope patch. It's happening here too, ya know. It's not just in the big smoke, ya know."

I avoid the inevitable argument about Aucklanders being money-grubbing, house-gobbling, road-hogs and lean back into my seat, turning my head to stare, unseeing, out of the window.

Sleep is impossible, the duelling banjos not showing any sign of shutting up and allowing me to do so. I'm also conscious we must be nearing the designated pickup place.

## 7

Colin peers briefly at the coordinates on his GPS as we inch forward. "You sure this is the right place?" We're on the lookout for the tag on the tree, mentioned in the instructions emailed to me a day earlier. Another email I couldn't reply to in order to rescind my redneck credentials.

Scanning the bushes on my side of the road, I'm as unsure as he is. Civilisation is now a long way behind us. Any establishment expecting me to park my car out here seems less legit with every mile.

It confirms my decision to park in town was the right one.

"There, there!" I point excitedly at a bright pink tag nailed to a tree that overhangs the deeply rutted gravel road. "The parking spot should be around this corner, on my side."

Colin doesn't speed up, which is just as well. The optimistically named 'parking spot' is more a scruffy gap between the ferns. If we'd been going any speed at all, we'd have missed it. Given the density of the undergrowth, my car could have been safe after all. Still, I would have hated taking my brand new Lexus on the road we've driven up, the potholes and ridges more challenging than the speed bumps at the local supermarket.

Expecting Colin to swing into the space so he can turn, he doesn't; instead, he cranks on the hand brake, kills the engine and gets out. It's not until he pulls a machete out of the driver's door pocket that I grasp what he's up to.

The blade looks lethal and makes short work of the ferns that curve in on each side of the narrow gap. By the time he's finished, there's a discernible space in the bush. He doesn't stop there, but stomps all over the ground, checking for stability. It's not something I would have thought to do.

Even inching forward into the bush as far as it's safe to go, turning the Land Rover is no easy feat. I'd never have managed it in the Lexus without the removal of paint and scraping the undercarriage, or sliding off the side of the hill. We're back on the road and facing town before he speaks again.

"You sure you're meant to wait here for your ride?"

He demonstrates as much trepidation as I feel. I metaphorically pull up my big-girl pants – perhaps not so metaphoric – and convince him I'll be fine.

"I've got my mobile and the battery's full. I can phone you if they don't turn up."

He opens his mouth but before he can speak, there's a crackle of static and a woman's voice fills the cab.

"Colin, you copy?"

He retrieves a mic from under his seat, stretches on the cord and presses a big button on the side, causing it to beep. "Receiving …"

"I've got a pick up for you in ... Kennedy Bay ... Six passengers ... American ..."

The pauses have been for effect and to elicit the desired response.

He peers at me briefly, drops his gaze and replies. "I'm on my way."

He's now less concerned with leaving me in the middle of nowhere, focussed instead on exchanging me for what will surely be a massive fare given the distance alone. Add to this the reputation Americans have for being big tippers and I'm as good as on my own.

"If you're sure you'll be okay, love. I'd offer to drop you back in town, but I'll be heading in the other direction when I get to Kennedy Bay Road."

At this point, I imagine he's firmly crossed the fingers of the hand I can't see. He's hoping I don't change my mind and insist he drops me back at my car. I'm tempted, but I've come this far and with each mile travelled, those perky boobs of mine are inching ever closer.

"I'm due to be picked up in," I glance at my Rolex, "ten minutes. No harm can come to me in that short a time. It's a beautiful day." I trail off, unable to come up with any other pluses to standing on the side of a gravel road, deep in the bush.

He takes me at my word, hops out of the cab and unloads my bag from the back. Carrying it over to the recently cleared piece of bush, he plops it down on the edge of the road before striding back and opening my door. Having paid by bank transfer the day before, I swing my legs around and slide over the side of the bench seat until my feet hit gravel. I retrieve my handbag from the footwell and once I'm clear of the door, Colin slams it shut with the finality of a job well done.

Shame he leaves at a greater rate of knots than we'd arrived. Coated in a thick cloud of dust, I have to lift my arm to form a mask of sorts. Any sound of the departing taxi now purely my imagination, the stillness of the bush closes in. It's quiet, except for the local birds chattering as though they haven't seen each other in weeks.

Then, as if they've caught up on all their gossip, they fall silent; eerily so.

I turn my back on the road and peer into the bush. There are birds there, sitting in branches, stock-still. But, there's no preening, no stretching of wings, no shuffling along branches in hopes of a better view. They're frozen and quiet, as though waiting for something to pass.

I step closer to the bush.

*What's got them so spooked?*

Could it be there are wildcats up this way? The ones that politician wants to wipe off the face of the earth along with all the domesticated pets.

Folding my arms across my chest, I rub my upper arms, working at the goose bumps that have popped up unbidden. I back away from the bush, scanning its depths from left to right. I'm missing something, I'm just unsure what, but the sensation of being watched is hard to ignore.

My concentration as it is, it's the crunch of gravel underfoot that tells me I'm back at the road. I stop where I am, my gaze still trained on the bush, my ears straining to pick up on the smallest sound. And when they do it's not the local birds getting on with their day, it's the roar of an approaching vehicle.

*I must need my head examined to agree to a pickup*

*spot as remote as this. David always said I was stupid, could it be he was right?*

I'm still dithering over hiding in the bush until I'm sure it's my ride, when the gold Hummer pornmobile thunders around the corner.

*What on earth is that thing doing out here? And what if it's the same creep driving?*

I've taken a few steps back from the road, when the gold Hummer pulls up dead in front of me. The window slides down to reveal the scruffy bloke from the petrol station.

*Hell's bells, someone's had a tidy up since almost mowing me down earlier.*

Rather than look at me, he peers at a crumpled piece of paper he's holding against the steering wheel. Only then does he examine me as closely.

He may or may not have washed his hair but at least it's pulled back into a tight ponytail giving him the semblance of being clean-cut. The other thing that looks clean is his shirt, even if all I can see is the sleeve, with his arm propped out of the window. Gone is the grubby black singlet of earlier.

Wondering why he stopped, I edge towards a full-on panic attack when he shoves the grubby sheet of A4 through the window. It's a copy of my Vale registration form, fortunately without my naked selfie in evidence. "Is this you?"

"Yes, that's me." Now I know who the hell he is, I give him a small wave and my friendliest smile, hoping to soften his demeanour. He's not happy. If anything, he looks even more ticked off now than when he nearly bowled me over leaving the petrol station shop. The reason becomes apparent.

"Where's your car?"

His accent is feral, concentrating on all the bad

points of the New Zealand twang. It's not something one hears in the cities, and there's nothing polite about his enquiry. Aggressive at best. I'm extremely glad I practiced my response in the bathroom mirror of my hotel room, until I could spit it out without stuttering or blushing beet red.

Despite all the rehearsals, I still need to lubricate my mouth with my tongue before I can utter. "It ... it was playing up on the trip here, so I left it with a mechanic in town."

My response does nothing to placate him. If anything, his brow crunches down further. This becomes even more obvious when he opens the door and slides out of the ridiculous tank of a vehicle. He stands on the road, legs braced and arms crossed. If he's trying to intimidate me, he's doing a good job.

"So how did you get out here?"

Again, I revert to my prepared script. "A local was collecting his car from the mechanic and he offered to give me a ride here."

"Did you give the mechanic your real name?"

I crane my neck and squint up at him trying not to think about all the other T&Cs I've blithely ignored. My voice stuck in my throat, I shake my head. Part of me is screaming, 'I've changed my mind'. To grab my suitcase and hightail it back into town. Shame my body isn't up to the task.

"What about the person who gave you a ride?"

I shake again, more emphatically this time.

He shoves his hand in my direction, opening and closing his fingers while barking, "Where's the ID you were told to bring?"

This has me scrambling to get my drivers' licence and passport out of the zippered pocket deep inside my handbag, before handing them over to him. Only after he's scanned them does his body language drop a notch from 'I'm going to kill you for breaking the rules' to 'mildly pissed off'.

I flinch and even stumble backwards when he shoves the documents back at me. I know I'm not imagining his smirk when he grabs my suitcase, again getting closer than I'm comfortable with.

*Bastard.*

My bag is placed in the trunk of the Hummer with surprising care. I'd expected more of the luggage-handling capabilities of Colin, the taxi driver. I'm also surprised when he opens the rear door and stands back, waiting for me to enter. This is easier said than done. The step is a good half metre off the road.

The vehicle's enormous and positively shrieks 'look at me'. Thank goodness the windows are tinted and we're in the middle of nowhere. I wouldn't want to be seen dead in this thing anywhere near civilisation.

The term 'wanker' comes to mind for anyone willing to be seen in one, right up there with stretch limos. It smacks too much of 'school ball' for my liking.

It's an effort to lift my leg to step onto the footplate. I'm beyond mortified when this results in a fart so toxic my chauffeur stumbles away. He waves his hand back and forth in front of his nose, gagging.

My humiliation is complete.

Unfortunately, this isn't quite true.

There's no way my leg muscles are up to the challenge of stepping into the vehicle. I have to resort to scrambling in on my hands and knees.

Awkwardly, the driver picks the wrong time to step forward to close the door.

To a background chorus of more coughing and retching, I clamber onto the back seat, slide over as far as I can, and settle in. From force of habit, I pull the seatbelt over my shoulder and secure it. This, more than anything else, reinforces how big the seats are.

For the first time in a long while, I feel small. I could lay full length across the back seat without messing my hair or bending my legs, and at 5'8", it's not as though I'm short.

I'm not tempted in the least to try it. Bubbles of flatulence threaten to convert the Hummer into a mobile gas chamber each time we rattle across another rut in the road. I suspect this is also worrying the driver, if the number of times he looks at me in the rear-view mirror is anything to go on.

My relief must be as evident as his when the road becomes a soft dust bowl that's easier on the vehicle and my gastric symphony. It'd be a nightmare if it rained but being late summer, the road is bone dry and so he whistles tunelessly to a song no one else is privy to. Odd in itself, as the dashboard features a stereo system that's better than the one David and I'd had at home.

It looks like a case of way too many recreational drugs to me.

About twenty minutes later, I notice grass growing in the middle of the dusty road. The ferns on either side attack the pristine gold paintwork with a passion not often seen in foliage. There are even a few worrying crunches.

If it bothers the crazy man in the front, he doesn't show it. When I catch his gaze in the rear-view mirror, the calculating nature of his examination freaks me out. I'm so out of my depth here I'm close to drowning; and with good reason. Stuck in a strange vehicle, with an even stranger bloke, heading for god knows where.

## 8

I'm sure hours have passed before we drive into the open, the sunshine blinding after the dark of the bush, the tinted windows not up to the challenge presented.

While the narrow road carries on before again disappearing into the trees, we turn off and swing through large double gates that appear industrial, even military, in nature. A quick peek out the back window confirms these are shut and locked behind us. This is so not what I signed up for.

That's when I notice the tall chain-link fence.

The driveway meanders through gardens that are more cleared bush than anything featured in glossy magazines. However, when we crest the brow of the hill, the panorama spread out before us, shows me why titivating the gardens would be overkill.

The view is spectacular and of the variety often seen in high-end real estate brochures, the colours so vibrant as to appear retouched. I'm doing my best to check it out when the Hummer jerks to a hasty emergency stop, throwing me hard against my seatbelt.

I know I'm not imagining the suppressed laughter coming from the front; it looks as though my driver has needling people down to a fine art. So far, it's been annoying but nothing more. If I complain, I'll appear delusional.

The building we've stopped outside is not what I've been expecting, at all and nothing like I'd expect to see at a high-end spa.

For one thing it's relocatable, complete with large skids underneath it, making it easy to move around. Closer inspection shows it to be a shipping container, and a big one at that.

"Ah, are you sure you've brought me to the right place? It looks nothing like the images on the web—"

Any further questions die on my lips when he wrenches himself around in his seat. He leans over it and shoves that screwed-up note of his right up in my face. Close enough I can smell a combination of cheap aftershave and engine oil.

I push myself back into my seat. This distances me from his grubby fist and gives me the focal length required to read the blasted thing. However, before I can make out more than a couple of words, he snatches it back again. It would appear seeing The Vale logo at the top right-hand corner is all the answer I'm getting.

This does nothing to settle my nerves although I'm thankful when he turns back to face the steering wheel. I don't like the way he looks at me, there's something off about it.

Not waiting for him to get out and open my door, I do so myself.

Before lowering myself to the ground, I make sure to let go of any metre joules of gas left in my system, thankful this doesn't lead to anything more substantial. He explodes out of the vehicle in response to my gassing; I'm grateful the ugly thing is between us.

He stalks around to the back, throws open the trunk and wrenches my bag out with a complete disregard for the contents. It's dumped unceremoniously next to the front steps of the building.

Looking up, I'm surprised to see wide eaves, and a roof covered in native grasses, something that would have made it as good as invisible on Google Earth.

Other than this nod to an off-grid lifestyle, I'm relieved to see three large satellite dishes anchored to the roof. Given the remote location, I worried I'd be cut off from civilisation.

An 'Administration' sign sits to the right of large bi-fold doors giving a full view inside. The set up goes a long way towards explaining why I'll be paying so much on departure, with Reception like something out of a design magazine. Sure, the chairs are plastic, but they're Philippe Starck Ghost Chairs, a far cry from the stackable variety seen at barbeques the world over.

They're also not a good idea at a fat farm.

If I sit in one, I'll be stuck wearing the blasted thing like see-through underpants until the tyre irons are produced.

While I'd like to go in and register, the driver is between me and the door and I intend to keep as much distance as I can. He makes my skin crawl. Turning, I concentrate on the view, doing my best to avoid the confrontation hovering between us. His eyes are like daggers in my back and I have to fight the urge to turn and apologise. It requires me to subjugate years of compliance and doing what was deemed 'right'.

And the vista, now I can look at it properly, is one hell of a distraction. The land rolls away from us in a mix of bush and farmland, bordered by the sparkling waters of the upper Firth of Thames. Sitting amid this sea of turquoise are Ponui and Waiheke islands.

"That will be all, Lance."

My heart hammers in my chest in response to the woman's voice, coming out of nowhere. Her tone is a hard New York accent, more common on sitcoms and usually from the character that is the biggest bitch of all. The amount of scorn she injects into this simple request is impressive; the greasy twit moves far quicker than I suspect a polite request would motivate him.

He's back inside the Hummer in a flash. Coughing and barely concealed cussing emanate before all the windows whir down simultaneously. He gives me one last filthy look and floors it, coating me in dust in the process.

If the woman standing patiently just inside the large glass doors thinks anything of this insubordination, she doesn't show it. I'm not sure whether this is because she's genuinely unconcerned or has sufficient Botox on board to paralyse an elephant.

I'd describe her as monochromatic. Hair, black. Skin, white. Artificially so in both cases would be my guess. Her lipstick is a red, so dark that at first glance, I mistake it for black. The shapeless smock that hangs from her shoulders is crisp enough it could surely stay upright on its own. This slap to the face of fashion is snow-white, has overly large pockets on the front and conceals any curves she has.

*Any money you like, the damned woman is built like an ironing board.*

What is it about women who weigh 100 pounds dripping wet running these sorts of places? It's cruel, is what it is.

"You must be 'Maisie Smith'," says the woman, slowly making her way down the steps.

It takes a second to appreciate the greeting has come from her. Her lips didn't move that I saw. All she needs is to be sitting on a bloke's knee with his hand up the back of her smock and they'd be all set for vaudeville.

"Yes, that's right." I'm conscious of nodding woodenly while agreeing to this alias, even if this goes against every fibre of my usually obedient self.

She holds out her hand, leaving me no option but to step forward and shake it. I'm surprised at the warmth, something not shared by the woman herself. Despite having just met her, I know she's what my late dad would have called a 'cold fish'. Certainly, her eyes are reminiscent of some I've seen at the fishmonger's I frequent back in the city.

"I'm Candice Hawkie. Welcome to The Vale at Shady Meadows."

Her American accent makes it sound more like a lawn cemetery than ever, and I struggle against the smile that threatens. The narrowing of her eyes suggests I haven't been successful in this endeavour. At least, I think they narrowed.

If Candice thinks she's hiding her true age from me, she's out of luck. Having been on many an outing with 'the ladies who lunch' I drop my gaze and quickly examine her hands.

Yep, they're out of whack with her face and neck by around forty years. While the former belong to a twenty-something, there's nothing she can do about her wrinkled mitts. If a procedure were available, Lorraine, the Queen of Plastic Surgery, would have had it by now.

Dropping my hand abruptly, she makes her way back up the steps where she stands beside the door, signalling for me to enter. "Please, do come in."

Yet again, I wonder at the advisability of interring myself here. I know nothing about the place other than snippets from Lorraine.

And who knew how much she'd held back in her love of keeping others in the dark.

Years of being subservient first to my parents and then David mean I bend over to retrieve my suitcase.

"No need to worry about your luggage, we'll take care of it for you."

*This is more like it!*

Entering a reception area strangely bereft of personality, I search frantically around. My hope is a chair more suited to my Rubenesque figure than those fragile-looking ghost chairs. There's nothing on offer, although I do spot a door marked 'Private' to our left.

"Delia's away sick today. We can go through to my office and fill in the paperwork there." She slides the door shut, silencing the cicadas and confirming the glazing is double, or possibly even triple.

Her office, to the right of Reception, is also starkly furnished. It doesn't even benefit from the view because the windows are skinny and hug the ceiling. Guess it helps her concentrate on her work, whatever that is.

My relief is doubled when I see the visitors' chairs in Candice's office. No arms on these designer pieces, although the crossed metal bands on the Barcelona chairs will be put to the test. I'm on edge until the piece of classic design takes my full weight and any residual bounce subsides.

I notice the matching chair Candice sits in doesn't settle at all.

I also notice the clipboard on the glass table between us. *Strange there are so empty spaces considering how many questions I answered on that online form of theirs.*

Unsure of how to broach the subject, I wade right in. "I don't have an anchor tattoo or pierced nipples."

To reinforce the truth, I push back the sleeves of my top, to reveal my forearms. But I stop there. She'll have to take me at my word after this. If she needs confirmation, she can check the naked selfie I submitted.

She doesn't respond verbally and without any facial expressions, I'm in the dark about what she thinks of me adding these features to their online form. Not my fault there was something screwy going on with the software.

"But I do have the mole on my back."

Again there's no response other than her sliding the clipboard, with pen on top, over to my side of the table.

"Even though we did get you to fill in all your details online, we have to show you a hard copy of everything." She tries to lift an eyebrow before continuing. "For legal reasons."

Extremely legal reasons if the wodge of paper jammed under the clip is an indicator. While the first couple of pages repeat everything I've already completed online, the rest is dense legalese.

In a six-point font.

The type is grey.

*It's as if they don't want me to read it.*

Coupled with the utilitarian nature of the place, I have second, and maybe even third, thoughts. I'm close to handing the agreement back unsigned, until a quick gander at my chest urges me on.

*If this is what it takes to have me bikini ready for next summer, then I'm in, boots and all.*

Again all those years of David carping on about reading anything you're going to sign override all else. I'm struggling through Clause 4 when Candice sighs. It's the first real expression the woman's given since I met her. The subliminal pressure from her is worse than the internal pressure from my late husband to read the bloody thing from start to end.

"Look, I'm sure this is all fine." Abandoning any pretence of being able to see the type, let alone make sense of it, I flip straight to the back page and sign with a flourish. Interesting that here at least they want me to sign my real name. That I've done so without skimming anything in between should have David spinning in his grave.

*I hope the arsehole is getting splinters with every rotation.*

The bulky contract has barely flipped back into place on the clipboard when Candice takes it from me with a speed that hints at eagerness. She's on her feet in a flash, but I struggle to follow suit. Fearful of putting too much downward force on the Barcelona chair, I gain my feet slowly, taking as much pressure on my thighs as I can.

No easy task, as I haven't been near the gym since long before they stopped sending me reminders featuring dinosaurs.

I use the opportunity of Candice putting my signed contract in the top drawer of her obviously designer desk to shake the cramp out of my legs. I'm still doing this when she turns in my direction.

"Now, if you'll hand over your handbag, we'll put it in the safe."

"My what?"

"Your handbag. As per the contract you've signed, we need to hold on to your handbag. For security reasons."

*Damn it. I should have read the fine print, even if this had her huffing and puffing like an asthmatic in springtime.*

With nothing for it, I retrieve my E-reader, phone and charger and reluctantly hand my beloved Hermès bag over to her, hoping it'll be as safe as she assures me. It doesn't inspire confidence when she drops it on the credenza behind her chair and leaves it there.

She swings back and holds out her hand, beckoning with her fingers, and confirming what it is she's after.

"But I like to read at night. And what if I need to get hold of someone? Or they need to get hold of me?"

"We've given your contact details to your lawyer and if you need to phone anyone, you're welcome to use our landline. Cell coverage is patchy here at best." She takes my E-reader out of my left hand, flips the cover open, and looks at the device briefly before returning it.

"You may keep hold of this, but you can't download any books while you're here."

Thinking as I am about *can't* versus *not allowed*, my question is slow in forming. "But, the dishes on the roof," I point up. "Surely they mean I can download new books?"

"Unfortunately, no. They date back to when the New Zealand military was in residence. With them decommissioned, we're at the mercy of the cell tower in town for our communications."

This will make it tricky to stay in touch with my friends on Twitter and Facebook. They'll think something dire has happened to me. I hadn't planned on being entirely truthful with my tweets and posts, instead focussing on the beauty treatments.

I was hardly likely to post a selfie of me giving myself a right seeing to with a rubber tube and a bag of saline. I'm not one of those TMI social media types.

My thoughts of how bad the reception will be are interrupted when Candice takes my phone and charger out of my right hand, peeling my fingers away to do so.

She puts these inside my handbag before turning back to face me; she holds her hand out and again I'm in the dark about what she's after. There's nothing left, unless you count my jewellery and I doubt she's after that.

How wrong I am. After a bit of fumbling with catches and clasps, I hand over my earrings, necklace and even my Rolex. Apparently, there's no need to keep track of time while in here.

"Now, if you'll follow me, I'll show you to your room."

For someone as washed-out as she is, she sure rattles along. Not even those clumpy white ankle boots of hers slow her down. She'd give Sue-Ng, the pocket-rocket lawyer, a run for her money. Literally.

I've fallen back a good few feet before the tube of toothpaste in front of me comes to a stop, allowing me to catch up.

"That's the yoga studio."

Following the direction of her stiffly pointing digit, I recognise the building from photos on their website. What the website hadn't shown was the drop-dead gorgeous view beyond. You could take it in while in a Downward Dog, with your arse saluting the sun.

*Strange that the building didn't have a sedum roof in the photos on their website. It must be a new addition.*

It's a second before I twig Candice is no longer at my side. Luckily, she's not too far ahead and isn't walking as quickly as before. I catch up and she points out more of the facilities.

"Gymnasium. Dining room. Spa. Medical centre."

She rattles these off in a monotone that matches her persona, indicating each building as though they're emergency exits. I'm pleased we're walking on a wooden boardwalk with the open ground uneven and peppered with outcrops of tussock and bracken.

At least scooting along on the walkway, I'm less likely to trip as I swing my head from side to side. The one thing all the buildings have in common is their eco-friendly roofs and an array of surprisingly modern-looking satellite dishes.

"And whereabouts is the swimming pool?" Despite it being ages since I've been out in public in a swimming costume, the pool looked heavenly from what I saw of it on their website.

"It's at the top of the property. Sadly, the filtration system isn't working properly. So the pool's closed for maintenance." She remains close-lipped about when it will be up and running again and I conclude it won't be while I'm staying here.

I'm still contemplating the direction she vaguely pointed in and thinking how nice a dip would have been, when she announces we've arrived at my room.

Swinging my gaze back, I'm gobsmacked.

The building looks to be as utilitarian and relocatable as that housing Administration. There's nothing designer and expensive about that board and batten cladding. Steps lead to a narrow veranda, with a large window to the left of the door.

As well as a small satellite dish, and the ubiquitous native grasses, the roof is peppered with solar panels and the spouting finishes in a large water butt. Strange the website said nothing about the place being this 'green'. I've been expecting high-end, not low impact.

*This can't be right.*

This room is nothing like that shown on the website.

*There's been a horrible mistake?*

## 9

I'm sucking up the nerve to voice concerns that my room is nothing like they've advertised when Candice opens the door, enters and waits for me to follow her in. Her toe-tapping signalling I need to get a move on.

Ever obedient, I hasten to enter. Appraising the crisp, clean finish to the inside, my ruffled feathers are smoothed. They're now as soft as those in the plump duvet that sits on the king-sized bed. Here, at least, the room matches up to the photos on their website.

"There's an information pack in the top drawer of the bedside cabinet."

The last thing she does is open the wardrobe next to the door and pass me a sterile pack that contains a small bucket, assorted tubing and spouts.

"This is an enema kit. You'll need to complete your cleanse early in the morning to be ready for your sunrise yoga session."

The words enema and sunrise yoga fight for supremacy over what horrifies me most; I'm speechless. She's already out on the small deck in front of my room, before I realise something. "Ah, you forgot to give me my room key." I hold my hand out in readiness.

"Maisie, you hardly need worry." Her use of that stupid alias means it takes a second to register she's speaking to me. "We take security very seriously. The perimeter fence is there for your protection. It's not just to keep out the wild pigs, you know."

After this bombshell, she leaves, pulling the door shut and imbuing me with some small sense of safety. Still, it's not as though anyone can break in here and hope to make a clean getaway. Besides, anything valuable of mine is sitting in her office or concealed in the false bottom of my suitcase.

*Thank you, Lorraine, for the heads up on the no-phones policy.*

Taped alongside my new phone are a couple of blocks of Dark Ghana and a spare credit card. Candice won't twig the phone in my handbag is a dummy unless she works out the PIN and for once, I haven't opted for 0000. I'd impressed myself with how well I'd faked handing everything over.

Putting the bucket back in the wardrobe where it can't taunt me, I take a more leisurely look around my room. I'm pleased to see the quality of the furniture and fittings is top-notch. Less impressive is that there isn't a TV atop the dresser, just a glass and jug of water with a couple of slices of lemon floating aimlessly.

The other thing conspicuously absent is any colour, pinpointing who was in charge of the interior design.

*If the woman stood against a wall, she'd disappear.*

Next to the wardrobe is a pocket door for what I'm hoping is a bathroom. This had been promised in the brochure, but with so many other things being different to what I've been led to expect, I'm not holding my breath.

I slide the heavy wooden door to the side to reveal a cave-like bathroom. Stepping into the gloom, I'm surprised when the room is immediately flooded with light. Stepping backwards into the room, the light switches back off again.

While this is okay during the day, it'll be blinding going for a pee in the middle of the night. Closer examination of the door frame shows a discreet electric eye at knee height. With any luck, I can step over it in the dark without doing a Tonya Harding.

There's no grey in the bathroom unless you count stainless steel. White subway tiles cover every surface other than the ceiling and a metre deep strip above the double vanity. This space is taken up by an enormous mirror that will make me want to wear a blindfold before getting naked. It's either that or running the shower first to fog the damned thing up.

Hearing the whirr of an extractor fan, I look up, squinting against the brightness of the large bulb. The fan is part of this light fixture and also automatic by the look of things. It's a necessary feature given the absence of windows in the bathroom.

Waiting for my bag to appear, I retrieve the instruction manual Candice told me about and plonk myself down on the bed. A couple of bounces confirms it to be in the 'Goldilocks' zone. Slipping off my shoes, I lift my legs onto the bed and settle in to check what's on offer. Could there be other things they've neglected to put on their website? If nothing else, checking everything out will fill in the time left until dinner.

*At least, I hope we get dinner, because the website was vague regarding the number of meals each day.*

I hoped it was more than one because I'd tried the 5/2 diet and couldn't hack it. The girls all raved about how easy it was. For me, it wasn't so. Ten o'clock on the first day and my stomach thought my throat had been cut. And this didn't go away, despite their assertions it would. If anything, it got worse as time went on, leaving me light-headed and nauseated.

While the manual outwardly looks like one you'd get at a chain motel, there any similarities end. No rules here about the opening hours of a handkerchief-sized pool and how much the porn costs. It's about what time you give yourself your daily enema. The line drawing of a large woman on her hands and knees with tubing disappearing between her butt cheeks makes mine clench involuntarily.

The need to carry this out at four-thirty in the freaking morning wasn't mentioned on their website. Anything before six is the middle of the sodding night and not the 'early in the morning' Candice casually mentioned before leaving.

To add to my pain, I'll be hunkered down on the tiled floor in the bathroom. Here's hoping the damned thing is heated.

It takes ten minutes to skim through everything on offer. Some of it I'm looking forward to, other bits, not so much. The ozone sauna sounds interesting, and with this many benefits, I'm surprised it hasn't achieved world peace while we were all squabbling.

The basic premise is the sauna heats up, and then carbon dioxide is pumped in, extracted, and then replaced with ozone gas. Not unlike being stuck in city traffic at the height of summer, except you're stark naked. Well, that and being stuck in traffic does nothing in the beauty stakes.

The manual smacks me on the nose, alerting me to having nodded off. It's been a long day, with more action than I'm used to.

*I'll just shut my eyes. Not for long.*


*Looking up at the clear blue sky, I'm confused. The thunder is getting louder and yet there isn't a cloud in sight.*

"Maisie, wake up, or you'll miss dinner."

Someone shakes me gently.

Pulling free of the delightful dream where I was dancing on David's grave isn't easy. I've got a lot of dancing, and even stomping, left in me. Not until I'm fully conscious, do things right themselves. The thunder must have been the fifty-something woman standing next to my bed knocking on the door, and Maisie is my assigned alias.

My response isn't immediate; I'm too busy taking in her snug-fitting outfit. No, make that the ridiculously tight, activewear she's shoehorned into. It's black like a ninja's, but there any eastern influence stops. If you were to scale a wall in this get-up, you'd risk nasty chaffing.

To add to the ugliness of the ensemble, there are Vale logos embroidered on the front of the top and side of the pants. The stitches on these are being put to the test with breasts and thighs the designer hadn't envisaged when working on the design.

Shaking my head to clear it of images of myself dressed similarly, I stop to consider her greeting.

*Surely I don't need to use it now I'm checked in?*

"It's Marilyn."

"I'm 'Belinda', formerly known as Beverley, but you can call me Bev so I know you're talking to me. Damned, stupid idea."

The woman is right; the whole alias thing is a tad over the top for a fat farm.

"Perhaps you should call me M?"

Bev laughs and holds her hand out to help me to my feet. "We sound more like a Bond film all the time."

She does so with ease, telling me she's way fitter than she looks. As soon as I stand next to her, I realise how large she is. Sure, she's carrying extra pounds, but it's her height that staggers me. She must be crowding six feet. I'm short next to her. Not petite exactly, just smaller than when I'm next to my girlfriends while waiting to be seated for lunch.

Lorraine, in particular, is a short-arse and borderline cadaverous, despite her assertions that one can never be too rich or too thin. If it weren't for those false boobs of hers, she'd be lucky to hit one hundred pounds.

Walking over to the dining room, Bev brings me up to speed on the daily routine, the meals, or lack of them, and the personalities. She also does a complete hatchet job on the centre manager.

"We all call her Chalky behind her back."

"Chalky?"

"Yeah, C. Hawkie equals Chalky. Plus, the woman looks like a stick of the stuff and has the emotions to match."

"You think she's had Botox?"

Stopping in her tracks, Bev looks at me with eyes wide. "I've had better reactions from cinder blocks."

Because we're close to the dining room, she gives me the condensed version of her life up to this point. Coming from a remote farm, she was at boarding school from age seven. By the time she'd left at eighteen, she was well on her way to being obese, from a combination of comfort eating because she was miserable and a menu that was below basement level on the food pyramid. The one thing that stopped her being bullied was her size and being 'the best damned shot putter that school had ever seen'.

She's been married to Sid for five years and with the way her eyes light up, happily. She deems herself lucky to have snagged a chap who can see past her weight. Her confidence in herself and in her man fills me with envy.

"But if Sid is happy with you as you are, why are you here?"

She looks sideways at me, continuing to march to the dining room. "Because I want to live until I'm old and crotchety so I can be a nuisance to his kids."

I get this. The extra weight is so often seen as bad in terms of appearance, or not being Insta-friendly. Rather, the real damage is buried within – or with – the subject themselves, and definitely in the majority of women's magazines. This isn't to say scrawny equals healthy either.

Bev opens the doors to the dining room with a flourish, standing aside to let me walk in first. I'd prefer it was the other way around. While not socially inept, I'm more of a follower.

Stepping into the room, I see nothing. The whole wall opposite the one we entered is floor-to-ceiling glass. It's as though it's brighter in here than it was outside.

"Sorry, should have warned you to keep your sunglasses on." Bev taps her own.

I slide them back down off my forehead and wait until I can make out the other people in the room. There are three tables, each holding four places and testament to the boutique nature of the establishment. One table is empty, while at another, there are four women who wouldn't recognise a steak if it bit them on the arse. They have the colouring of those for whom the sun and protein are anathemas.

Perhaps the biggest disappointment is that I don't recognise any of them, and I know my celebrities courtesy of the women's magazines. The way Chalky had gone on about confidentiality, I expected at the very least to see someone off the B-List.

There isn't even an early disqualification from *Dancing with the Stars*. The poor sod with a lagging career and two left feet that the production team always contrives to include for giggles. It's a pity, as I'd been looking forward to catching up on showbiz gossip over meals.

The remaining table has two larger ladies sitting there, intent on their conversation and both dressed in double-wide ninja outfits that match Bev's. I suspect it won't long before I join them in the wardrobe malfunction department.

The lack of reaction from those seated renders us invisible, a state I'm happy to maintain. Bev has no such issues, making her presence known by walking directly over to the table of two, pulling out a chair and slumping into it. Unsure whether I should join them or take a seat at the empty table, I don't move. I'm dithering, when Bev tells me to get my skinny butt in the spare seat.

*Skinny, she called me skinny! I haven't been called that in a long time. Comparison is a wonderful thing.*

I waste no time in doing as she suggested. No, that wasn't a suggestion; it was an order.

"Marilyn, I'd like you to meet Tee and 'A' your fellow 'Agents of Fat'."

Much laughter from the other two meets this introduction, and I can't help but chuckle myself. It's so refreshing not to constantly avoid the elephant in the room, usually me.

"It's 'Tallulah'," says the woman introduced as Tee, quoting in the air with her fingers, to indicate this is her alias. "Problem is, when people call me by it, half the time I don't know they're talking to me. Still, it's better than my real name."

It wouldn't take MI5 to spot that all the aliases start with the same initial as our real names, at least, so far as I've heard up until now. Keeping my voice down, I ask, "What's your real name."

Tee looks briefly over her shoulder at the table of pale women and then through the hatch to the kitchen before eyeballing me. "Promise you won't laugh?"

I nod instead of voicing my agreement. *What's more unusual than Tallulah?*

"Teophania."

I can't stop the snort that escapes. "Sorry. You must have copped heaps about it at school."

"You have no idea."

Tee is also from the country, although not from farming stock. Rather her parents had opted for the commune life, which goes some way towards explained her off-the-wall name. Maybe it was the name-calling at school that drove her to seek solace in food, or that her appetite was rampant and food readily available; either way, she's a big girl. There, any similarities to Bev end.

Bev glows with good health, and there's also evidence of muscle underneath her cushiony covering. Tee, on the other hand, looks unhealthy. Her skin is blotchy, her breathing laboured and her breath tells of food having hung around in her system far longer than is necessary for normal digestion.

She also has the air of crazy cat lady about her, doing nothing to bolster the picture she paints of saving herself for the right bloke. I suspect they've all come out of hiding while she's in here.

*God help me, I'd do anything to avoid ending up like that.*

Turning to the fourth woman at the table, I lift an eyebrow.

It's enough. More than enough. Angela, known as Angel – an alias so similar why bother – is a motor-mouth. Ange to her friends. She doesn't waste time with full sentences. Speaks in fragments. Forty-five. Nurse. Four kids. Out in the world. Sick of clothes not fitting. Divorced. On Tinder.

She doesn't breathe once during this data dump, leaving me short of air and thankful we're not in shared accommodation. Mealtimes will be more than a challenge.

After a quick peek at the occupants of the other table, I lean forward. "Where are all the celebrities? I thought there'd be one or two in residence."

Tee bursts out in laughter. "Hah, celebrities. Yeah, fat chance of seeing one of them. They're kept well away from us riffraff. I've been here five weeks and the only stars I've seen have been up there." She jabs her forefinger skywards, before continuing. "Hell, they even sneak them in through the back somehow."

*Five weeks?*

I can't work out what horrifies me most. That she's still this size after being here for that long. Or worse, that she hasn't lost any weight at all. I hope it's the former.

She fills her lungs to speak again when the tinkling of small bells fills the room, the upmarket version of your bog-standard gong.

For someone as big as she is, Tee can haul butt. She's the first to collect her tray at the kitchen hatch. I check out what's on offer when she passes me on her way back to our table.

I'm horrified. The last time I saw that much kale was in the fruit and veg section at my local supermarket. I might cope if it were doused in oil, oven baked and sprinkled with sea salt.

Unfortunately, in its current state it's as nature, and the compost heap, prefer it.

## 10

Even aware this would be the case, confirmation the menu is vegan fills me with disappointment all the same. After the scouring at the service station and the technicolour yawn of McDonald's and random carrots halfway up Flays Road, my last proper meal was a long ways back.

Carrying my tray back to our table, I have to give the kitchen crew credit; the rabbit food is beautifully displayed. Pity I know from experience it'll do nothing to quell my raging hunger. Eating it, I long for a creamy dressing. The lemon juice and balsamic vinaigrette errs on the side of citrus, with my lips resembling a cat's arse after the first mouthful.

Any hopes this is a starter are dashed when the bells ring again and a disembodied voice from the kitchen announces our dessert protein shakes are ready. We dutifully gather our plates and cutlery and file back to the hatch. If anything, Tee is even faster to collect this part of her meal.

All this self-service is odd, given how much I'll be paying to stay here. I expected waitress service.

Perhaps that's reserved for the A-Listers, wherever they're hiding.

I slide my tray across the counter to a small weasel-like – and way past retirement age – chap who's collecting them for washing. His job is an easy one, our plates as good as licked clean.

Shuffling along, I take the tall, brown shake that the next weasel slides over the counter in my direction. At first, I think I'm seeing double. A quick peek back at weasel number one confirms they're twins. So unusual to see older twins, I've always thought of them as something that happens purely at primary school.

On the return trip to the table, I sniff my protein shake experimentally, latching onto the aroma of chocolate like a pig searching out truffles. A second sniff and I pick up on undertones of roast pork.

It just goes to show how hungry I am that I don't care if the drink is a crazy blend of chocolate and meat. If the Mexicans are able to pull off that combo, who am I to argue?

I don't get how this can be deemed low calorie. However, the speed with which Tee, Bev and Ange are sucking down their drinks conveys that it tastes okay. A tentative sip confirms this for me.

It's delicious, surprisingly so.

Smooth, creamy and sure as hell not like any diet food I've tried. For one thing, it has more substance than I expected, something that's been sadly lacking with any meal replacement I've had to date. "What's in it, apart from chocolate?" While waiting for an answer, I stand my straw up in the middle of the glass. I'm not surprised when it stays upright unaided. The damned shake is as firm as my belly fat.

There's a gurgling of dregs being inhaled through an extra-wide straw before Tee answers me. "We have no idea, and we've given up asking. I'd kill to get my hands on what goes into it."

Next morning I'm woken before sun-up by an Om chant – well past this side of annoying – coming from speakers in the ceiling of my room. An overtly soothing voice follows this, instructing me that I should be preparing for my 'cleansing'.

The voice is so soothing, I find myself nodding off again, at least until the word 'coffee' tunes me back in. Thinking about breakfast, I realise how hungry I am. I haven't been this empty in living memory, if ever.

Because I'd unplugged the bedside clock radio during the night – the glowing red numbers keeping me awake – I have no idea what the time is. I'd check the time on my phone, but I've made a pact not to break out my stash until I get desperate. As it is, merely thinking about looking at the device will be draining the battery.

Unable to ring room service for a full-English, this might be the emergency I've been waiting for. Those blocks of Dark Ghana are tantalisingly close.

*Just one square.*

*To take off the edge.*

My bag was delivered to my room the night before while I was at dinner. Other than removing my thankfully intact toiletry bag and pyjamas, everything else is where it was when I packed.

There's a hard rap at the door while I'm on my hands and knees in front of my case. The clothes drop from my grasp and I shut the lid for fear of discovery by whoever is standing less than a metre away. Even with a wall between us, I'm not risking my stash for anything.

Before I have a chance to get up and open the door, Chalky barges in, a surprise both from a manners point of view and given the hour.

"You should have finished your cleanse and be fully evacuated, ready for yoga. You're not even dressed."

At last, I get a reaction from the woman – a dressing-down for running late.

Flustered by the first reprimand since David shuffled off, my Pavlovian response kicks in. "I'm so very sorry, I usually set the alarm on my phone."

This does nothing to calm the waters, Chalky's nostrils flare even wider. "And what, may I ask, is wrong with the alarm clock next to your bed."

While her tone is calm, she looks supremely pissed off when she takes in its lifeless state. Now is not the time to remind her that she said there was no need to keep track of time while in here.

Shrinking into myself, I stutter out, "The light was keeping me awake. I suffer from insomnia."

"I want you in that bathroom as soon as you're able. It's not fair to hold up others because of your beauty sleep, now is it?"

Dropping my head, I whisper, "No."

My arms fly out defensively when she shoves a plastic-wrapped bucket at me without warning. On realising I'm not in danger, I wrap my arms around it.

The atmosphere in the room doesn't warm with her departure.

*Damn it, the last thing I need is to rush my first enema.*

My sphincter muscles are already knotted, without performance anxiety added to the mix.

I concentrate on relaxing my shoulders, close my eyes and try hard to imagine myself walking down a white-sand beach and into sparkling blue water. My bikini is tiny; my tits are not. A couple more breaths and I enjoy a virtual frolic in the surf. I'm with a guy who strangely has no face but the type of body often seen in *Men's Health*. Leaving him to his swim, I get up and walk into the bathroom, ready to get on with my new life.

The floor is still warm beneath my bare feet, allaying my fears that as the unit is solar powered; the heating wouldn't be on all the time. I rip the plastic wrap from the enema kit shoving it into a pathetically small wastebasket under the vanity unit. The components of the kit sitting in a row on the counter, it's as if I'm preparing for surgery.

I have a quick pee and hope for something more solid to minimise the enema action. Nothing's forthcoming: that session at the motorway service station really did a job on me.

The kit has everything. A lubricated soft vinyl tube, a clamp for one-handed operation, a red rubber tube and lastly a sachet of coffee; it's organic and grind #7.

*I hope the bloody stuff isn't decaf.*

A skim through the instructions surprises me by how simple it all looks, although this doesn't calm my nerves. I get the hot water running, confident in the knowledge this is pre-set to the correct temperature, taking one responsibility away from me. Next, I empty the sachet of coffee into the bucket and top it up with water from the tap. Any dreams of lattes drain away when I connect the hoses to the bucket as per the instructions.

Only when I read the next bullet point, do I become aware of a series of hooks down the back of the bathroom door. The top one holds the supplied bathrobe, the others marked at various heights are for an altogether different purpose. I peer closely to see which one I'm supposed to use.

*This crap just got real.*

*Well, it soon will.*

Five minutes and half a tube of lube later, I regret all those yoga classes I've avoided over the years. The brunches and coffee mornings I attended in their stead have done nothing for my flexibility. Something else that's making it hard to concentrate is the sound of the extractor fan whirring periodically.

It sounds too much like the zoom lens on a camera for my paranoia to subside to levels that will make the exercise easy. My imagination conjures an image of me kneeling like this on the boardroom table at David's lawyers.

*Why does my mind come up with these humiliating scenarios? Do I really hate myself that much?*

After this, the coffee isn't even good for drinking. Although I'm tempted.

I struggle to my feet, wondering if toilet paper would work as a filter when a soothing voice fills the room. 'Remember, ladies, the red tube connects to the bucket, the PVC tube connects to the douche nozzle.'

*Are you freaking kidding me?*

Rereading the instructions, I stop my cussing about black and white instruction sheets. Looking at the diagram properly, I see it is clear. That is, if you aren't freaking out about feeding a litre and a half of good Columbian in through your back door. Dumping the coffee down the toilet, I bin the rest.

Thoughts of phoning and asking Chalky for a replacement cool my blood. I'm still frozen in space and time in the middle of the bathroom when the soothing voice again filters through the speaker. This time it reminds me there are more kits in the wardrobe.

New bucket in hand, I hunker back down on all fours on the bathroom floor. This time I've got a towel under my knees because although the floor is warm, it's not soft. Following the instructions to the letter, this session is successful and not as bad as I'd imagined, although I won't be avoiding yoga while I'm here. Flexibility is the key.

The little tap is easy to turn on and off, allowing me to control how many espressos I get through in the half-hour the session is supposed to take.

*Hmmmph, last time I saw a tap like that was on a cheap cask of wine back in my Uni days. Imagine the bladder from one of those hanging from the back of the door.*

I snort.

This turns into full-on guffaws.

This jet-propels the douche nozzle from my rear end.

I spray coffee all over the bathroom before I can get the damned thing under control.

After this, my main concern is parking on the toilet before this 'short black' incident turns into a coffee with 'Grande' in the name.

*So much for thinking I was empty. Goes to show you how long a backlog of fine dining and chocolate can stick with a girl.*

I mutter away to myself as I stand outside the bathroom door, waiting to see if it's worth getting dressed when static emanates from the speakers. Quieting my breathing, I wait for the next instruction from hell. Nothing is forthcoming.

The sunrise yoga session is a distant memory before my arse has stopped doubling as a manure spreader and it's safe for me to leave my room. On the plus side, other than when I'm lying on my back, my stomach has never looked flatter.

*This is more like it.*

Walking to the dining room, I run my hand over my tummy softly. I shouldn't have. Spinning on my heel, I walk stiff-legged back to my room, all while giving my sphincter the workout from hell.

I don't make it in time.

At this rate, I'll be out of clean clothes by the end of the day. Thoughts of parading around in one of those butt-ugly Vale ninja outfits aren't happy ones. I'll wash my clothes in the shower and dry them on the towel rail before I submit to that indignity.

In the end, I have no choice. Any clothes I rinse out during the day are whisked away whenever I turn my back. Despite part of the package being getting my laundry done, there's not a chance I'll hand over my soiled clothing so someone can scrub away at my enema-induced skid marks.

Ridding myself of a piece of carrot cake I'd scoffed at least eighteen months prior, messes my last pair of clean yoga pants. I'm running low in the underwear department, too. My bras and tops have escaped mostly unscathed, but that's it.

Cleaning myself off in the shower, my tears join the water sluicing down my body. They rain down on my crappy yoga pants, huddled in a heap on the floor of the shower stall. This is not what I signed up for. No matter how hard I try, I can't envisage myself back on that imaginary beach without the handsome hunk bent double with laughter.

Six months of statins is looking better, all the time.

I don't bother rinsing the pants, rather leaving them in a filthy heap on the shower floor. Let the phantom clothes collector deal with them as they are. I complained to Chalky that I was running out of clothes. She assured me my clothes were being disinfected and that they would be returned to me when clean. She made me feel like a toddler who'd failed toilet training. But that was three days ago. Long enough they could have been boiled in disinfectant and line-dried by now.

## 11

My tears and body dried, my quandary is what on earth to wear. Yes, the place is a woman-only establishment but there are men on the staff who I'm not happy to flash any bits at; especially not the cretin who drove me here. I empty my suitcase article by article, and it's not until I'm at the very bottom that I find a solution. It wasn't on the list of required clothing, something that took me straight back to school camp days, but I'd packed it, anyway.

Marching over to the administration building feels odd. My sarong-yoga-top combination means I feel naked from the waist down. Hardly the right apparel in which to tell Chalky I've had a gutful of having my insides turned inside out and that I'm going home. It will be Weight Watchers and horse-strength statins for me from now on.

"We can't do that. I'm sorry, Maisie." Her tone says she's anything but.

"I beg your pardon?" I say this not because I

didn't hear her but because I don't comprehend what the hell she means.

"As per Clause 97 of the agreement you signed mere days ago, you've committed to staying with us for the full six weeks. We take your rehabilitation seriously, even if you don't."

*Rehabilitation? Is she kidding? It's chocolate, not crack cocaine.*

I'm trying to assemble a reply, when she swings around in her seat and collects a pile of plastic-wrapped packages from the credenza behind her. She slides these across her desk, and my heart drops. That damned Vale logo is easy to read, the outfits inside folded in such a way it as to have this dead centre.

"What about my own clothes? They should be clean by now."

"Yes, about those. We find it best if all our guests dress the same as it puts everyone on an even footing. We'll keep hold of your garments until such time as you check out."

I open my mouth to complain, but she stops me with a look. "Clause 37."

*Damn, damn, damn, I should have read that blasted contract before signing it.*


My anger escalates with every step of the return trip back. It's an emotion I've suppressed for a very long time but finding my suitcase open and pretty much gutted, anger turns to fury in a nanosecond. Any clean tops I had left have been removed. The only things left in my suitcase are my lacy bras.

I dump my plastic-wrapped Vale outfits on the bed and drop to my knees in front of the case.

Running my hands frantically over the inside, I find what I'm looking for. My head drops back while I voice a silent prayer to the gods of electronica and cacao.

*God, I could do with some chocolate right about now, lots of it, and the darker, the better.*

Static from the speakers, followed by the whirring of the extractor fan in the bathroom, and I freeze. My hands drop away from the Velcro-sealed pocket and I look over my shoulder. I'm surprised to find no one behind me.

The temptation to self-medicate is strong, and the whiff of 70% proof chocolate when I drop the lid on my suitcase is nearly my undoing. If not for the strange sensation of being watched, I'd give in. The ninja outfits awaiting my presence are cause enough to scoff both blocks.

I struggle up and onto the bed where I flick through the assorted items of clothing. I can't work out if I'm relieved or not when I find a multi-pack of underwear. I'd been wondering about that, not keen on going commando when Downward Dogs were on the menu.

*Misery, thy name be Candida.*

I don't bother with dinner that night, instead giving into my abject misery of being stuck in this place for the next five-odd weeks. *What on earth have I gotten myself into?*

The image in the full-length mirror after I struggle into the assorted items of Vale gear the following morning consolidates my despair. Great, at last I score free gear and it's as ugly as sin and several sizes too small.

Can I force myself to leave the room looking like this? On the plus side, The Vale logo sitting over my left boob isn't stretched beyond recognition like it is for the others. Shame the same can't be said for the waistband of the ninja-equivalent of yoga pants.

Hunger is what drives me out; that and a blood-sugar level hovering around zero. This will also be the first time I've made breakfast. At least I hope we get breakfast. The thought of another one of those chocolate shakes and I unconsciously speed up. I can't hear myself think over the scratching of the fabric rubbing together between my thighs.

I open the door slowly, unsure of what sort of reaction I'll garner.

It's not what I expect.

Bev looks annoyed before picking up a piece of toast and slamming it down on Tee's plate.

Ange looks ticked off, too.

By the time I grab my breakfast at the serving hatch and sit down, Tee is the proud owner of two extra pieces of toast. They're so thin that gobbling them would risk lacerations to your throat.

*What on earth? Bread has a street value in this place?*

Tee wastes no time in gloating about the fact she's won the sweep on how many days I could hold out before being stuffed into The Vale uniform. "You must have been backed up to hell to get through your gear this quickly."

It's a challenge as to what shocks me most. That she's discussing my bowel functions at breakfast, or that she's doing it on purpose to put me off my two wafer-thin slices of whole grain. Woe betides anyone who gets between me and food when I'm this *hangry*.

I keep eye contact with her and take a deliberate and overly large bite of toast, immediately bemoaning the fact it's free of spread of any kind. Ange and Bev laugh delightedly, although it's Bev who comments first.

"Hah, she's got you, Tee. You're not gonna put her off her tucker that easily."

*So I didn't imagine it.*

I dwell on this while chewing my toast.

And chewing.

And chewing.

*My god, the stuff has the consistency of cardboard, although I suspect cardboard has more flavour.*

It's a while before I can safely swallow without risking a spontaneous tonsillectomy. It goes down like a golf ball, before dropping solidly into my empty stomach. I know the booming echo sound is purely my vivid imagination. Still, it's appropriate.

I drop the piece and it clatters about on the plate before settling next to its mate.

*Hell's bells, I hope my jaw is up to taking care of this lot.*

Chewing the stuff would surely burn more calories than it contained.

*Still, if it's this or nothing, I'm pushing on.*

A sip of green tea, bursting with antioxidants but totally lacking in flavour, clears my throat of any residual gravel. There's no way you could describe them as crumbs. I grab my piece of toast for another bite.

Before I can do so, Ange picks up her one remaining piece of toast and slams it down on Tee's plate.

"Damn it, I didn't expect you to manage more than one bite." Ange looks down at her empty plate, before licking her finger and clearing up any remaining crumbs.

Bev looks at me with admiration and even a tinge of pride. "I told you she's made of sterner stuff."

By the time I've chewed my way through a whole slice of cardboard, Tee is down to one slice and Bev has three on her plate. Some down to carbohydrate wagers being won and lost, others because they'd managed to chew their way through a slice or two. Ange, whose plate is pristine, looks longingly at the piece left on my plate and I take pity on her. It's not like my jaw is up to gnawing through another slice and the idea of two slices exiting after tomorrow's enema has my sphincter clenching in terror.

Piles?

What piles?

Breakfast, such as it is, is over and we're left to our own devices for an hour or two until a pre-lunch yoga session, something I'm hoping to attend. Between trips to the bathroom and rolling around on my bed dealing with stomach cramps, this will be my first session. At least, I hope I make it.

Bev slides her tray across to one of the kitchen twins. "You want to go for a walk around the property, M?"

I can't look at either twin without Bowie's 'Laughing Gnome' jingling in my head. They're too weedy to be labelled Tweedle Dum and Tweedle Dee and they are gnome-like in appearance. Give them each a fishing rod and a pointy hat and you'd be in possession of the perfect garden ornaments.

"A walk sounds nice." Fresh air will also make a welcome change from the stench of antiseptic spray backed up by more organic undertones.

"Mind if I tag along?" says Ange, dashing any hopes of a quiet commune with nature.

"The more the merrier." Bev doesn't show any signs that Ange's presence isn't welcome. "Tee, you up for a stroll?"

The large woman is quick in her refusal, hurling rapid-fire reasons to the point Ange holds her hand up to stop the ever-growing list. "Chill, not our loss if you get caught breaking the rules."

Despite the website boasting that the resort covers twenty acres, most of them are off-limits. This is a combination of the impenetrable bush that backs the property and the drop-offs along the front.

These are such that my stomach does somersaults every time we get near them. This could be down to vertigo or the toast beating the hell out of my stomach acid. Either way, it's not a pleasant experience and I keep well back from them. Even so I have to fight their magnetic gravitational pull with every step.

I slow my steps. "What was that about Tee breaking the rules?"

"Chalky doesn't like it if we stay in the dining room, says it leads to temptation," says Bev, her laughter eventually getting the better of her.

"Temptation?"

*Is she for real?*

My digestive tract wouldn't cope with any more of that plywood masquerading as toast, let alone be tempted by it.

"Yeah, temptation. Someone broke into the kitchen. At night. Drank all the chocolate protein drink. A whole bucket of the stuff." Ange's tone is one of incredulity at whoever managed this feat.

"What? Wait? A whole bucket of it? As in a bucket, bucket?"

Ange nods emphatically. "Chalky's been strict about security ever since. It doesn't take a rocket scientist to work out who it was."

Bev shakes her head and I wonder if her disappointment is aimed at Tee for the break-in, or Chalky for not fingering the woman for the crime.

"It's a bugger. It's put a stop to any late night incursions. I've been hungry ever since." Ange's pout following this list of complaints wouldn't be out of place on a two-year-old.

So Tee wasn't alone in raiding the kitchen? It's a wonder Ange could keep quiet long enough to sneak in anywhere undetected. My gaze catches Bev's and her shrug confirms she's been in on the raids, too. This place is more like school camp all the time.

Continuing our walk, no make that stroll, I perceive what my days will be like over the next five and a half weeks. One good thing is that, like a brightly burning flame, Ange's staccato chatter soon splutters and dies and we're left to enjoy the birdsong.

We work our way around the back of the accommodation units, following the tree line before crunching our way into the bush along a narrow path. Mesmerised by the rhythmic sound of our steps and the beauty of the dark bush on either side, when Bev stops, I bump into her.

"Sorry, wasn't watching where I was going."

Bev spins on her heel with military prowess, facing me. "This is as far as we can go."

Peeping around her, I can see why. A two-metre high hurricane wire fence, topped with razor wire, stretches tight across the path in front of us. Although the path continues to meander its way through the bush, we're stuck right where we are.

"That's strange?" I say, my head cocked to the side.

"Maybe it's part of the old army base that's supposed to be up here," says Ange, who must have heard the same story as I had.

Bev jerks her head at the wire barrier. "It's for security. Keeps the pigs out. Nasty things, they are."

I shake my head before speaking. "Not the fence, Chalky told me about that. I'm talking about the birdsong."

The other two join me, listening intently. Bev even closes her eyes to concentrate and I follow suit, focussing on my hearing. It confirms I hadn't imagined it.

It's as though someone has hit Mother Nature's mute button. Not even the smallest of cheeps is audible. The swishing of the ferns and the occasional creak of a branch are all that come back at us. It takes a second to remember where I'd experienced this before: the day I waited on the edge of the bush for Lance to collect me.

*Could it be him who silences the birds? Or something else entirely?*

Opening my eyes, I take in the surprised expressions of the other two and know I'm not alone in thinking it's strange. We're still staring at each other when a scream shatters the unearthly quiet.

My scalp does its best to scuttle off my scull at the eerie quality.

"What the hell was that?" Scrubbing at my skull, I try to rid it of the awful crawling sensation. Spinning on the spot, I do my best to locate the source of the shriek, waiting for a follow-up, but none is forthcoming.

Straining for a repeat, I become aware of a deathly cold swirling around my ankles and creeping up my legs.

"I don't like it. That didn't sound like any bird I've ever heard." Ange wastes no time in turning and stumbling back down the path as though pursued. In a heartbeat, I'm on her heels, followed closely by Bev.

Bursting out into the open, I swing to face the bush, kicking wildly to rid myself of the evil that's latched onto me. "What the hell was that?"

Bev is pale, the fine sheen of sweat on her forehead out of kilter with our stroll. "I'm not sure. It could have been a Long-Tailed Cuckoo?" Her words are tentative, unconvincing.

"Creepy as hell is what it was." Ange is shivering like a dog that should have been dried off hours ago.

"Not the scream, the other thing." As if in answer to my question, the presence I'd picked up leeches out of the bush. It wastes no time crossing the ground to swirl again around my ankles. I kick my feet out at it again before moving faster than I have in a hell of a long time.

Ange and Bev show themselves to be up for a burst of speed, too, with none of us slowing until we're safely back in the dining room. Tee doesn't appear to have moved since our departure. She looks guilty because we've caught her still lounging.

While a stonking big brandy is what I want, green tea will have to suffice.

"*Sheesh*, what's up?" After this, Tee's mumbling gets so bad, I move closer in hopes of catching more. Then I spot the toast crumbs caught at the corner of her mouth. Her tongue flicks them away so rapidly, I think I must have imagined them.

"Tee, what have you done?"

Bev's shout gets my heart chattering double time.

"You promised!" Ange also has her volume cranked right up.

The guilty party's face turns from an unbecoming mushroom to the rhubarb side of florid before she gulps deeply and crumples under the scrutiny of the others. "I know, I know. But it was just one piece."

*One piece, that's not so bad. Is it?*

I look at Tee as the other two give her a dressing-down. I'm genuinely sorry for the woman until I spot her ninja top isn't sitting as smoothly as it should. "What's that?"

While the others don't hear me over their haranguing, Tee does, hunching her shoulders in an effort to hide her carbohydrate contraband. I don't say anything else. It's not my job to police toast consumption in the place. If rations are as scarce as they appear to be, I'll be in a similar position in a day or two.

Tee slams her hand over her heart – and the hidden toast – before stumbling to her feet and fleeing. The one remaining sign she's been there is a single slice of wholegrain cardboard on the floor. Bloody hell, how many slices did she have stuffed inside her bra?

"Three-second rule!" Ange drops to the ground and nabs the piece of toast before Bev, who looks as though she's harbouring the same thought, can react.

Sheesh, *how desperate do you have to be to eat off the floor?*

## 12

The yoga class is a shock on a couple of levels. The first is that Anton, our yoga instructor, thinks I'm capable of folding myself into the positions he demonstrates. The second is his being overly blessed in the anatomical department.

His singlet is so loose and so thin that I don't know why he bothers. Meanwhile, his Lycra pants are form-fitting to the point he wouldn't need to remove them for a prostate exam.

*If he's wearing undies, I'll eat mine.*

A snort escapes at the notion of munching through the utilitarian pair I'm wearing. He swings in my direction and I don't need a mirror to know I'm an unbecoming shade of pink.

There you have it, the one thing between me and a naked bloke for the first time in a year is elastin in nature, like the man himself. He walks in my direction and I tense. Which leads to wobbling: I'm nowhere near ready to process the ton of testosterone he has on board. And it doesn't matter that he plays for the home team.

My relief when Tee demands help in achieving the posture is immense. My relief is short-lived.

Anton bends her into the correct position, being none too gentle about it. She over-balances, crashing in a heap, taking him down in the process.

Then it's all I can do to avoid a 'code yellow'.

Ange isn't so lucky.

Free of Tee's embrace, Anton demonstrates the next position as though nothing has happened. Seeing how complex the pose is, it's obvious he's taken our laughter at his tumble to heart. That'll teach us to get the giggles, although watching him extricate himself from under Tee was funny. Even the vegans had trouble keeping their mirth under control.

I'm halfway through rolling and folding myself into the pose when I nasty skittering sensation works its way up the back of my neck.

I look up, expecting to see Anton glaring at me for my non-existent yoga abilities.

It's not him.

It's Lance.

Standing just the other side of the large picture window, there's no censure in his eyes as he looks at me, rather something much darker. It's amplified when he runs his tongue over his bottom lip.

Not wanting to keep eye contact, I drop my gaze, mortified to see his hands are shoved deep into the pockets of his filthy jeans. He's groping around for something, and I doubt it's the keys to the Hummer.

I spend the rest of the day avoiding thoughts of Lance ogling me during yoga, and food in general. While delicious, the vegetable broth served up in lieu of lunch hadn't hit the spot, or even come close.

More than this, it didn't even hit the sides as it rocketed through my empty digestive tract. My belly button and spine haven't been this close to each other since I was in the womb.

The other thing that's been hard to park is the scene in the bush. It's easy to think it was a flight of fancy, but I have my doubts. I've always prided myself on being pragmatic, down to earth, not given to the vapours. And yet I'd given in to all three just that morning.

Mid-afternoon and Bev suggests another walk, but I decline. Despite it being a beautiful sunny day, I'm shaky and cold, with my blood-sugar levels destined to drop as the afternoon progresses. Huddled under my duvet, I try for sleep to pass the time. It's a pointless exercise with the gurgling of my gut and hunger gnawing away at my insides, making it impossible.

It's an awfully long time before dinner rolls around.

Except there are no dinner rolls, just more sodding kale salad followed by another chocolate shake. A lack of hot dishes does nothing to help rid me of the shivers that roll through my system at regular intervals.

I finish chewing another piece of kale to the point I look as though my ancestors were rabbits. I want to drag this out for as long as I can. Surely this will fool my body into thinking it's had more sustenance than it has in reality?

Therefore, I'm not even halfway through my minuscule salad when the bells ring announcing that our protein drinks are up and ready to go.

I have to finish pulverising a mouthful of kale and celery before I'm able to speak. "Can one of you grab mine when you're up there?"

"Not allowed," says Ange, looking down at me pityingly.

"For goodness sake." I drop my fork amid the detritus of salad and stand.

Tee shakes her head. "You have to return your plate before you collect the second course."

"Are you kidding me?" I say to her departing back.

Bev doesn't answer before also wandering over to the kitchen hatch.

Sitting back down, I fork another mouthful of green into my mouth and get on with chewing. I can stick to their stupid rules, but if they think I'm bolting the rest of this child's portion, they can think again.

Tee has seated herself and is already halfway through her drink before she speaks. "I'd hurry if I was you."

"Why?"

Ange siphons the remainder of her drink up the extra-wide straw. "Because, if you don't collect your shake pronto, they'll bin it." She sucks on her straw again, ensuring she's got everything on offer out of the glass.

This is the first I've heard about this. Guess I'd been as keen as they are to guzzle it before now. "How long have I got?"

Bev likewise vacuums up her dregs. "Two minutes tops."

I don't bother with any further discussion. I shovel the rest of my salad down as if kale is on the brink of extinction. Something I wish was true. Even if I don't chew it as much as I'd like, there's no way I'm missing out on the chocolate drink.

I'm still working on the final mouthful when I

slam the plate down on the kitchen counter. My hand closes around the glass at the same time as one of the laughing gnomes, presumably so he can dispose of it.

*My god, is that growling coming from me?*

It must be, if the speed with which the gnome snatches his hand away from the rest of my dinner is any measure.

I'm about to slurp the first delicious mouthful up the straw when Tee puts her hand on my shoulder. "Better mix it up first. It's started to separate."

"Separate?" I tilt my head to the side to see if I can ascertain the constituent parts in hopes of being able to replicate the recipe at home. The top layer is darker than it was moments before, while the sludge at the bottom has a distinctly yellow cast to it.

*Yum, there must be banana in there somewhere.*

A favourite of mine, I slide my straw to the very bottom of the glass and take a tentative sip. Nope, my theory is all wrong.

*If I didn't know better, I'd say it was pure fat, and bacon fat at that. How in the hell am I supposed to lose weight if I'm subsisting on what equates to chocolate-flavoured gravy?*

After dinner, we wander over to the yoga studio, although not for another session with the half-naked Anton. No, tonight is movie night and I'm hoping for a RomCom, or something light. Even the four women from the corner table join us. They do so without uttering a word, which is weirder than weird.

Falling back beside Bev, I slow my steps to match hers. "What's with that lot? They haven't spoken once since I got here."

"Idiots have taken a vow of silence." Ange snorts over her shoulder, indicating I haven't spoken as quietly as I'd thought. She hasn't bothered to whisper herself.

"Something to do with that barkin' meditation retreat they're on." Bev doesn't bother keeping her voice low either, as if the hearing of the group in front is somehow impaired along with their speech.

A glower thrown in our direction tells me she's so very wrong.

Tee's booming laughter slices through the twilight like a laser. "Careful, Bev, I reckon they're hungry."

This teasing of the mute crew doesn't sit well with me. Call it what you will, it's bullying pure and simple. Of course, I think they're stupid for keeping quiet for however many weeks it is they've signed up for. Am I giving them a hard time about it? Well, not to their faces.

*What's the collective term for mute vegans? A Mugan? A Mutgan? A Megan? The Megans! That'll do perfectly, and it's not like they can tell us their real names.*

I'm pleasantly surprised at the transformation in the yoga studio. While not exactly Gold Class Cinema, the bean bags scattered in haphazard rows across the bamboo floor appear comfortable. The large screen, previously hidden behind shoji panels, is state-of-the-art.

Tee struggles to get herself down into a bean bag

in the back row and I question the appropriateness of the 'seating' on offer. It's as though Chalky has deliberately chosen furniture to emphasise how overweight we are. First the ghost chairs and now these.

I'm careful when I drop into the bean bag next to her. The last thing I need is for the blasted thing to burst leaving me covered in polystyrene balls and looking like that tyre company's mascot. After this, I try to keep as still as I can, something that negates any comfort offered by the squishy thing. Waiting for the movie to start, I twist my head to the side so I can speak to Tee.

"There must have been a heap of people through the place while you've been here." Part of me still clings to the hope of mingling with a famous guest. Even someone from the C-List would suffice.

Tee doesn't turn to me when she answers, keeping her eyes glued to the still-blank screen. It's as if she's afraid of missing a single second of whatever's on offer in the way of entertainment. "Sure, there've been a stack of them." She puffs before continuing. "Bloody lightweights couldn't hack the pace. And I didn't even get the chance to give 'em hell about it."

I speculate on the toast-stealing nerve of the woman for a moment. I'm beginning to understand why The Vale chooses to keep their elite clients separate from the likes of us. With Tee's disappointment as large as she is, I wonder what's stopped her from haranguing anyone checking-out early. "Why's that?"

"They all left in the middle of the bloody night, every single one of them."

A very familiar intro bursts from the large speakers standing at attention on either side of the television, denying me the chance to grill her further. So much for something light and fluffy; in lieu of actual entertainment, we'll be watching back-to-back episodes of *The Biggest Loser*.

The evening's a wash-out for me. It's not that I don't like the show. It's more that I usually watch it with wine and chocolate on hand, comforted that I'm not as big as the poor shmucks being put through hell week after week.

It always makes me feel slimmer, although this isn't the case tonight. Needing to roll onto all fours before I can get to my feet, I'm more conscious than ever of the gravity-defying pounds I'm lugging around.

Sleep doesn't come easily. Stitch that, it doesn't come at all. Each time I'm about to drop off, my mind swirls with images of me at the fat camp from hell in a strange half-awake nightmare. It's one where I'm forced to exercise endlessly in workout clothes that have The Vale uniform looking runway-ready in comparison.

Turning on the light, I grab my E-reader off the bedside table. I suspect the only reason Chalky's let me keep hold of this is because it's the most basic model.

Luckily for me, I'd ordered twenty books online before leaving the hotel. It's a shame only fifteen had downloaded safely, the other five lost somewhere in the ether. As well as these, there are numerous old favourites I can resort to if I run out of new material. Sometimes, even if I haven't, I enjoy that sense of peace from rereading a book that's like an old friend.

A loud knock on my door coincides perfectly with this very action in the Stephen King I'm reading. I shriek, my heart rate goes through the stratosphere and my E-reader is last seen flying over the side of the bed.

*Get a grip!*

Opening the drawer in the bedside cabinet, the radio alarm glares balefully, showing me it's just after midnight and hardly an appropriate time for visitors. The horror story still haunting me, and undecided on whether I want to answer the door, it opens.

It's Chalky, dressed as always in her demon dental assistant's get-up.

*Lord, doesn't the woman ever sleep? Or more to the point, doesn't she need to wait to be invited in?*

I know this is the accepted practice with vampires.

"Trouble sleeping?"

She doesn't wait for a reply and walks across the room, putting the tray she's holding down on my bedside table. This holds a very small plunger of herbal tea that's the colour of three-day-old pee and that will doubtless taste the same.

"An important part of weight loss is ensuring you have quality sleep. This should help." She plunges the tea and then pours a cup for me, holding it out so I have no option but to struggle into a sitting position and take it from her.

Wetting my lips confirms any tasting notes on the packet should include the word 'urine'. While it looks as if I've taken a sip, there's no way in hell I'm drinking this muck. I fake a couple more sips before she's happy.

She pauses in the doorway, holding the handle in readiness to shut the door. Her gaze travels to the floor next to my bed. "Best you turn your device and the lights off."

I don't argue the point, worried she'll confiscate my E-reader; there's more than a smack of House Mistress about this woman. Under her watchful gaze I put the cup down on my bedside table and retrieve the device.

I'm hurriedly turning it off when I notice the bar at the top states 'items downloaded'. I don't dare check to see what they are, instead shoving the device in the top drawer and shutting it.

Only then does Chalky leave, pulling the door to behind her, but not shutting in properly. I dwell on this while lying in the dark, waiting for her to walk away. It's a full five minutes before she does so.

## 13

An hour later and I'm no closer to sleep. As tempting as it would be to drink the cup of urine Chalky delivered earlier, I can't bring myself to do so. I'm doing deep breathing exercises in an effort to calm my mind, when I'm aware of movement outside my unit door.

The door handle turns gradually – whoever it is, they're trying to be quiet.

*Damn it, why don't they have chains on the door like they do at motels and hotels?*

It's all I can do not to laugh aloud when whoever it is trying to sneak in into the room fails miserably.

I'm still not sure why I shoved the desk chair under the door handle after closing it following Chalky's late night visit. I'm glad of it now.

There follows a stage-whispered exchange and while I'm not surprised to detect Chalky's American twang, when Lance, the chauffeur, responds, I'm stunned.

"Can't you break in?"

"You think those knock-out drops of yours are up to that sorta ruckus?"

*Knock-out drops?*

*The tea!*

I sense movement outside the window by the headboard. Did I close it? It's too late if I didn't. The last thing I want them to know is that I'm onto them trying to drug me. The window behind me slides open a fraction, and then stops.

Without the glass to muffle him, Lance's curses are loud; whatever is in that tea is meant to incapacitate me in a big way.

It takes a moment before I remember the lovely piece of bleached wood I found the day before and that looked nice on the windowsill. My hope now is that it will work in the same way as a broom handle in the frame of a sliding door and stop it from opening wide enough for him to climb in.

My eyes open wide. It wouldn't be hard for him to put his hand in the window and move it.

Hearing movement on the other side of the black-out curtains I cough, and am pleased when it ceases.

*To hell with them knowing I'm awake.*

I make a good show of turning from side to side, mumbling as though trying to find a comfortable spot and thumping my pillow for good measure.

Even though I don't detect anyone moving away from the window, I sense Lance is no longer there. Snaking my hand up underneath the curtain, I slide the window quietly closed and am relieved when the catch snaps tight. God knows what would have happened if the beautiful bone-shaped piece of wood hadn't been sitting on the sill.

My heart engaged in a weird polka, complete with missed steps and dips, there's fat chance of me sleeping after this. Slipping from bed, I take the plunger of tea off the tray, step carefully over the beam in the bathroom doorway, and pour the contents down the toilet.

*Best Chalky believes I drank the damned stuff.*

I can't face yoga the following morning. Not on an hour of sleep. I feel like hell and from the reactions of the others at breakfast, I know I look like it, too. I wait until we're all on our second slice of plywood before broaching the subject.

"Has Chalky tried to drug any of you?"

"Drug!" Tee says, energetically and spraying me liberally with toast crumbs.

A peek in the direction of the kitchen shows the laughing gnomes have turned to look at us.

*"Shhhh!"*

My warning comes too late, but I can't help but worry she'll blather on without thinking. To reinforce this, I furtively place my finger over my lips and look at each of the others in turn. They all nod imperceptibly.

Leaning over the table, I speak as quietly as I can. "Late last night, I was reading when I got a visit from Chalky."

"No surprises there. Woman's nocturnal." Ange's lips barely move during this assertion, the volume of her words as hard to discern.

Luckily, she too is leaning well over the middle of the table. Something Tee and Bev are quick to copy.

"She came armed with a pot of tea. Said I should drink it because sleep was important in achieving weight loss. I barely tasted it, but it was awful."

Bev looks first over one shoulder and then her other. "Awful is how you feel in the morning, too."

Bev's paranoia ramps up my own; I pop my head up, my eyes darting nervously around the room. "What do you mean?"

After giving into a full body-shudder, I look in Bev's direction again.

"It's like you've been running for hours. And everywhere hurts." Her colour intensifies before she whispers. "And I mean everywhere."

If I was in any doubt, she points subtlety through the table in the direction of her crotch, confirming she really does mean everywhere.

*Gross!*

"You think that's weird. Once, I woke up to find the sheets had been changed. Don't remember an effing thing." Ange looks impressed and disgruntled in turn.

My gaze darts between the three faces. "How many times has it happened?"

"Seems to be every second or third night for me." Bev's whisper is hoarse.

"Same for me," nods Ange.

"Only a couple of times for me." For once Tee looks relieved to have had less of something than the others.

"Why do you keep drinking the tea?"

"And risk the wrath of Chalky by leaving it? Don't think so," says Ange, through a muffling mouthful of toast. "I was ready to up sticks and leave because of that, but she waved that bloody contract in my face."

"Yeah, me too," adds Bev. "Kept going on about Clause 37B, like I knew what the hell that was. The bitch halves your rations if you don't drink that godawful tea." Bev follows this up by finishing her second piece of toast quickly, as though Chalky will sneak up and snatch it away.

"Hang on, if you weren't drugged, how did you get away without drinking it?" Ange looks intrigued at my avoiding the nasty brew and yet still being the proud recipient of two planks of toast.

"After they left, I stepped over the beam in the bathroom door and chucked it down the toilet."

Tee's face drops in disappointment. "Damn, I was hoping it was something we could do."

It's then I comprehend these ladies can't clear the beam because of their weight.

"Oh, sorry. But hang on, why don't you chuck it out of the window?"

"Tried that once," says Tee. "Opened the curtains to find Chalky staring back at me. Scared the crap outta me."

Ange and Bev's solemn nodding confirms they've experienced the same.

Fearing interruption, I make quick work of telling them how I'd shoved my desk chair under the door handle. "Lance would have got in the window if I hadn't jammed a piece of wood in there."

The colour drains from Ange's face, leaving her looking ready to pass out. "He was there, too?" Her words are as weak and pale as her face. "Excuse me." She staggers to her feet and totters out of the room.

"What's got into her?" I turn to the other two, hoping for clues.

Tee slaps her hand over her mouth before she too stumbles to her feet. If I didn't know better, I'd think she was about to puke. She's gone before I can ask if she's all right. The sounds of retching from outside confirms she's not okay.

Bev stays where she is, but she's not happy, either. "At least we know why we all wake up feeling like we've taken part in a marathon sex session."

I don't bother to ask what she means; I roll my hand in the air, urging her to press on. She nods and leans forward. I follow suit until our heads are millimetres apart. The more she tells me, the happier I am that I barricaded myself in my room last night.

As tempting as it had been to scream holy murder when Lance tried to get in through the window, I'm happy as hell I didn't. At least this way I can maintain the pretence of having consumed the tea and been unaware of Chalky and Lance's attempted break-in.

*I have got to get out of this place. And soon.*


Immediately, on entering my room after breakfast, I notice the desk chair is missing.

*Damn!*

A glance shows my beautiful wooden souvenir from the window sill has also vanished. It confirms two things for me.

One, they're trying again tonight.

Two, I need to join the others on their walk.

Drained after my sleepless night, I'd opted out of this. I hope they've taken the same route as last time, sans the eerie path into the bush. I do a quick mental calculation to figure out where the best spot is to intercept them.

I don't close the door behind me. What's the point? I aim for the far corner of the compound, bypassing the raised boardwalks in favour of going cross-country. It takes ten minutes of serious trudging for me to find them, and when I do, they're far too close to the haunted path for my liking.

"Hi, guys, I ... had ... to tell ... you ..."

*Hell, I'm out of shape. Shouldn't be this knackered after a brisk walk.*

"Oh, crap!" Ange spins in my direction, her hand clutching her crotch, in lieu of pelvic floor muscles.

"Jesus!" Bev seems as shocked, although she's clutching her throat.

I'm surprised. It wasn't as though I snuck up on them.

*Didn't they hear me coming?*

I hadn't been quiet when walking through the ankle-high grass that had done its best to trip me at every opportunity.

"You scared the crap out of us." Ange doesn't remove her hand from between her legs, suggesting her preventative measure has been in vain.

"Sorry, I wasn't trying to be quiet."

"Something moved." Bev's hand drops from her throat to her side. "Deep in the bush."

Ange briefly sniffs her fingers and shrugs, before adding, "On *this* side of the fence."

"Really? I didn't think there was anything out this way." The map in the welcome pack showed this part of the property as dense bush – no buildings and no paths. "I hope it's not a pig."

Bev never takes her eyes off the bush, her gaze intent, like that of a hunter. "I bloody hope not. Nasty beasts they are." Her voice isn't much above a whisper.

"There!" says Ange, managing to keep her voice low, despite her excitement.

I see it, but only because Ange has pointed me in the right direction. It's not a pig, unless the local population is human-sized and has taken up wearing camo. Thanks to my contact lenses giving me something north of 20:20 vision, if I squint, I can even make out the smears of paint on his face. Another thing I just make out is a diagonal strap across his chest and the barrel of a gun towering over one shoulder.

To see someone armed with what appears to be a military assault rifle shocks me to the core. Is Chalky really that worried about one of us doing a runner to supplement the Spartan diet? And surely it's illegal to have a gun like that after the laws changed following the Christchurch Mosque atrocity? Shouldn't that kind of gun be exclusive to the military?

And anyway, didn't Colin, my chatty taxi driver, say the army decommissioned the base yonks ago? He did, didn't he? Lord knows he'd told me everything else.

Bev stiffens. Has she spotted him, too? Or is she readying herself to face down an enemy of the porcine variety? Her backing away while whispering, "Let's get the hell out of here before he realises we've spotted him," says she's seen what I have.

I agree. Anyone trying this hard to stay out of sight doesn't want us waving and saying "hi". And after last night's potential intrusion, I'm gun-shy on the gung-ho. The three of us stick to an unspoken pact to keep mum until we're well away from camo-boy and there's a building between him and us. For once even Ange keeps quiet.

Only then do we slow. Not until we're on the far

side of the compound and hidden from admin by a copse of trees, do Bev and I tell Ange what we'd seen. They're both as concerned as I am that the guards patrolling the perimeter are armed to the teeth. Despite analysing this discovery from all angles, we don't come to a conclusion, or even a decision.

We sure as heck can't go to Chalky about this, because the chances of her not knowing about it are slim to none. Could it be that because she's from the states, she's happy having guns on the property?

It wouldn't surprise me. It'd be a different thing altogether if he were on the other side of the wire fence. His presence on the property tells us a lot, although not as much as we'd like.

We've gone from being rooted to the spot, to wandering aimlessly before I remember why I'd come out here to find them. And, now that I know what lurks in the native bush, the mission to protect myself from unwanted nocturnal visitors is more important than ever.

"They confiscated my chair. And the lovely piece of aged wood I had on my windowsill. I came out here to replace them." Without them, my room is as secure as your average pup tent.

Ange looks at me for a heartbeat. "Hate to break it to you, but I don't think you'll find a chair out here."

Bev nods in agreement. "She's right."

"I know that, but there's no reason I can't find a piece of wood to keep the window closed and a smaller bit that I can jam under the door to stop them opening it."

Bev scans the bush in front of us, looking for likely spots, and more armed guards. Her body language says she hasn't spotted either. She looks back at me over one shoulder. "Where did you find the last bit?"

Shading my eyes from the sun, I scan the bushes that cloak the perimeter of The Vale. Sighting the Rata tree that marks the beginning of the narrow path, I start tentatively forward. I'm relieved it's nowhere near where the guard was patrolling earlier.

"This way!"

## 14

We scurry over to the Rata, its scarlet flowers scenting the air with their unusual perfume. After a quick scan to check there's no one else around, I inch forward.

Close to the fence line, I find another piece of wood perfect for securing the window. Flooded with relief, I hold it up in a victory salute, before looking back down to find something to use as a doorstop.

"Ah, Marilyn, I hate to break it to you, but that's not wood." For once, Bev's voice is reedy.

Ange looks up from kicking the undergrowth. "Holy crap!"

I drop my find, before frantically wiping my hand on the leg of my Vale uniform.

Ange isn't as squeamish; thanks to her nursing background, retrieving it before it has a chance to settle back amongst the ferns. "Part of a femur, I'd say."

Bev murmurs, 'Hmmm hmmm,' in agreement. "And it's too thin to be bovine."

. . .

Buried deep in the ferns, all we can see of Ange is her backside. She's rummaging through the bone pile as if she's at a Black Friday sale. "I'd say they're all female."

She's a nurse; I don't question this assertion. The other thing I know for sure is that it was no Long-Tailed Cuckoo we heard screaming the day before. It was a woman, and she was in pain. A lot of it.

Bev scans the depths of the bush, before leaning over to speak to Ange in such a way she can keep her voice low. "How many do you reckon there are?" Before Ange can answer, Bev speaks again. "Holy shit. Look at that." She points frantically at something I'm unable to see. Something I don't want to see by the sounds of things.

Ange is now peering as intently. "What is it?"

"You see those regular marks on the bone? That's evidence of knife work. Last time I saw something like that was after we had a beast at the farm home killed." Despite Bev's words being measured, the disbelief at what she's saying is evident.

"Oh, god." Ange stumbles out of the ferns, crashing in a heap in the middle of the non-existent path. She flicks her hands around wildly.

"Gross, I'm not used to the bodies I handle wriggling with maggots."

Revulsion floods my system. Maggots freak me out in a big way. And if a nurse looks green, there's no hope for me. I get the hell out of there, with Bev hot footing it behind me.

"But why would they shove the bodies here?" I think for a beat. "If they threw them over the cliff, the pigs would take care of them, wouldn't they?" I turn to Bev, suspecting she's more up to speed on porcine behaviour than I am.

"That they would, but they'd also make one hell of a racket while they were about it. That must be why they've shoved them on this side of the fence."

Ange joins us and she's not happy, crouching down and repeatedly wiping her hands on the grass to rid them of any remaining gunk. After examining them thoroughly to check they're clean, she takes a deep breath before speaking. "We can't say anything."

"What? We have to!" I can't believe she wants to sweep this under the ferns.

"And who will you tell?" says Bev. "Whether they died of starvation or something else, Chalky surely knows about it. The fact they've been butchered has me bloody glad this place is vegan. We have to keep quiet until we're out of here."

*Dammit, she's right.*

In unspoken agreement, we beat a hasty retreat, getting ourselves as far away from the spot as we can. We slow our pace when we're well away from any buildings or trees, finally free to talk. Even then we keep our voices low, indulging in the occasional burst of rapid-fire laughter in an attempt to throw anyone who's watching us.

I, for one, have read far too many horror stories to know that looking on edge won't do us any good. Yet again, my hand strays to the back on my neck to smooth the fine baby hairs. Yet again, the gesture fails.

Ange wrings her hands together in a virtual scrub. "I guess this explains their 100% success rate."

"Stop doing that." Bev's voice is low when she

whacks Ange's hands hard, stopping the scrubbing motion in an instant.

I look casually over my shoulder. "How much longer do you two have to go?" I'm well aware five long weeks stretch ahead of me before I'm allowed back through the metal gates.

"Three weeks for me." Bev looks relieved at being halfway through her stint.

"Three and a half for me." Ange too looks to be counting the days.

*Great, I'll be here on my own for a couple of weeks, unless new inmates arrive.* "And I guess Tee will be gone in just over a week?"

Bev rolls her eyes and shakes her head before responding. "She's here for the duration."

"The duration?"

After a burst of nervous laughter, Ange answers for Bev. "Not leaving until she's lost 200 pounds."

*Okay, so I won't be on my own.*

At the rate Tee is inveigling extra rations out of the laughing gnomes in the kitchen; she'll be here for life. The question now is, how long will that be?

*What was it they scrawled on those chalkboards outside cafes? That's right. 'Skinny people are easier to kidnap. Stay safe. Eat cake.'*

Not so sure it'd keep you safe from being murdered, but it'd sure as hell make it harder to dispose of your body.


The rest of the morning crawls by, with Bev, Ange and me acting the part of the relaxed and carefree, which involves more effort than you'd think. We keep ourselves busy fitting in an extra yoga session and completing further loops of the property.

Our loops are foreshortened by us studiously avoiding rotting corpses, disquieting paths, and that armed guard. This has us passing the sheer drop-off more times than I'm comfortable with. In the end, I decide I'd much rather face this than the other obstacles on offer.

It's at lunch that we hit a snag.

It's bone broth, a dish that has no place appearing on a vegan menu. If they'd served this up before we stumbled across the human remains, I'd have beaten Tee to the serving hatch. As it is, I mutter something about fasting and leg it. Bev and Ange are close behind.

Thanks to Tee's habit of blurting everything out at volume, we can't even warn the poor woman not to touch it. And seeing how desperately she was chugging that mug of bone broth down, if we'd tried to take it away from her, one of us would have lost a finger.

After a thankfully kale-based dinner, I'm getting ready for bed before I realise I never did get a wedge for under my door. The window's not a problem because I can make sure the catch is securely caught. Without a key, I haven't got a clue how I'll keep the door from opening.

Nine o'clock and there's a knock. It's not entirely unexpected, but I'm still loath to answer it. Not a problem because Chalky walks in uninvited, holding a tray with another plunger of pee masquerading as herbal tea.

"Oh, how lovely."

My opening gambit throws her off her stride. It's as though she's expected me to argue about drinking more of the drug-laced urine.

"I slept so deeply last night." I briefly cast my

eyes skyward, because if you can get struck down for out-and-out lies, there's a bolt of lightning with my name on it.

Her eyes narrow imperceptibly, most likely a combination of my passable acting skills and an udder's worth of botulism toxin swirling around inside her face. Walking across my room and placing the tray on my bedside table, she continues her examination of me.

She straightens and stands with arms folded, waiting for me to drink the toxic brew.

"It looks lovely. As soon as I've had a quick shower, and let it steep, I'll drink it tucked up in bed."

Her mouth opens as though to argue this course of action. "Don't let it get cold, it doesn't work, ah, taste as good then."

I fight my reaction to her slip, busying myself with pulling the covers back in readiness before bed. "I'll just have a quick sluice off." I smooth the covers and plump the pillows, all the while stalling. "It should still be hot by the time I hit the hay."

*Hit the hay, sheesh, when have I ever said anything that hokey?*

Turning, I'm surprised to find her gone. Those ankle boots, while clunky, allow her to move without a sound, giving me yet another thing to be wary of. She hasn't bothered to shut the door, leaving me to do so and wonder how the hell I'll make it Lance-proof.

A moment's deliberation and the answer is staring me right in the face. By jamming one of my flip-flops under the door and then wedging the other under that, I've got a passable door stop.

Whether it'll be capable of holding the greasy cretin at bay, I'll soon know.

Ablutions and dumping of the disgusting brew over, I climb into bed. A quick flick of the curtains behind the headboard confirms the window is fully closed and looks to be securely locked.

But when I touch the clip to make doubly sure, it's clear someone has tampered with it. It wouldn't keep a cockroach out, let alone Lance, the biggest cockroach of them all. At this point, I'd even be happy with a femur on the sill to stop the window opening fully. Short of using my own, there doesn't appear to be anything else to hand.

Biting on my thumbnail, I scan the contents of my room, hoping for inspiration for how to keep the window shut. Or booby-trapped sufficiently so that if Lance tries to open it, all hell will break loose.

I stare at the desk for what feels like a minute before the perfect solution strikes me. That is, if the drawer comes out completely.

*There are fresh flowers on David's grave. No doubt put there by the MiniMe. I stop myself jumping for a moment to kick the vase. That's weird. It shouldn't have made that much noise.*

I can't stop the scream. My plan to pretend to sleep through any racket, buggered. This time Lance's exit isn't as quiet, but even though I hear his muttered 'Fuck', there's still an element of stealth about it. I've got two options: I can turn on the light and let them know I'm awake, or I can keep it off and feign a nightmare.

In the end, the need for light wins out. If Chalky storms in, I'll say I was woken by a bad dream.

. . .

"Hell, girlfriend, you look like crap." Tee's assertion is as audible to me as it is to everyone else within a twenty-metre radius. Her loud persona is particularly grating this morning. "Anton wanted to know where you were."

*Anton? Oh right, the half-naked yogi.*

This is the second morning I've missed yoga and imagine my breakfast rations will reflect this. While not a fan of that cardboard toast, having seen what happens to those who don't eat, I'll happily chow down on it; even if it means a visit to the dentist when I escape.

I slump in my chair for a moment before responding. "Thanks, Tee. I feel like crap, too."

Bev drops her elbows on the table and leans in. "What happened?"

Ange too has shimmied forward in her seat to get closer.

I start to fill them in, but the words dry in my throat. Chalky stands inside the doors to the dining room, her gaze firmly glued to me. I drop my head to stare at the table, but I'm all too aware she's walking in our direction. She stands by my side, her foot tapping in a manner I can't ignore.

I peek up at her. "Good morning Ch— Candice."

*Hell, that was close.*

No need to piss her off more than she already is, if her body language is anything to go by.

"*Maisie*, I'd like a word with you. In my office."

It takes concentration to get rid of the golf ball stuck in my throat before I can speak. Even so, my "Now?" has a strangled quality to it.

"No, after breakfast will suffice."

None of us speaks until she's left the room, and then it's all at once, with everyone, except Tee, keeping their voices down.

Tee wants to know what it's all about; she's still in the dark about our grisly discovery the day before. Ange, Bev and I opted not to tell her; mostly because of her booming voice. This would make it next to impossible for her to keep a secret, no matter how hard she tried.

A quick peek at Ange and Bev and their slight head shakes, and I steer clear of the topic. Instead, I mutter about not being able to get back to sleep after Lance had tried yet again to get into my room at two a.m. The lateness of the hour presumably to give the drug time to work.

"But why would Chalky want to speak to you about that?"

Tee has trouble getting her words out around the large mouthful of toast she's working away at. It makes me realise I haven't yet collected mine.

Knowing I can't dodge my visit to Chalky, I nip up to the counter and grab my toast and a mug of peppermint tea. I've barely parked my rear end before Ange speaks.

"Tee's got a point. Why would Chalky want to bring that up at all?"

Bev's cogitation keeps her quiet for a moment before she too questions the reason for the visit. "Yeah, it doesn't make sense."

"Maybe it's because I've missed yoga for two days in a row?"

Tee taps my plate with its two slices of toast. "Can't be that, otherwise you'd be down to one slice."

"Maybe she knows about that, ah, other thing?"

Bev's face creases in concern. "It's got to be serious to warrant a visit to the principal's office."

Hearing this term, I experience a flashback to my first day of school. Another girl had pulled my hair hard, and I'd been sent to the principal's office for smacking her around the head in retaliation. It was my first and only visit. Any thoughts of standing up for myself in the future, had been truly smothered by the fear I suffered while waiting. The officious man kept me sitting there for an hour, my legs numb from hanging over the edge of the hard chair, my teeth chattering from the wind whistling down the empty corridor.

It was the loneliest place in the world for a five-year-old.

## 15

I n short shrift, I'm over at the main office, unable to finish my two slices of toast, my throat anaphylactic in nature, any swallowing a chore. My toast hadn't gone to waste; Bev and Ange went halves on it.

Tee hadn't been happy about this, but they quashed her argument that she had more body to sustain. They pointed out that she'd wait around until after breakfast and get extras from the gnomes in the same way she usually did. That shut her up good and proper.

I don't know whether I'm relieved or not when I open the sliding door to the main office to find Chalky waiting for me. No sitting in the cold to think about my sins with this visit to the principal. This time I gain an immediate audience.

Careful theatre design guarantees I am uncomfortable. Gone are the Barcelona chairs with their crisscrossed metal frames. This time I sit on a straight-backed model. It faces Chalky's desk, its smooth surface all that separates me from her and my fate. It's the chair that until recently sat in front of the desk in my room.

Chalky makes a real production of flipping through my notes, tapping the pages with a pen to highlight my lack of progress on the weight-loss front. She hasn't said a word when one of the laughing gnomes arrives with a tray. Clocking the contents of the plunger, my eyes dilate.

*Coffee! Surely not?*

*Bet the bloody stuff is caffeine-free.*

No sooner has he placed the tray on Chalky's desk than she gives a curt, "That will be all, Simon." It's no secret her brusque wave irks him, although only if you're looking at him as I am.

Chalky looks up, examining me minutely, her eyes full of speculation while she pushes the plunger down slowly. The aroma of dark Columbian fills the room and my mouth waters in anticipation. I know I'm getting a cup because there are two on the tray.

"Hmmm, your progress hasn't quite been what we'd hope for."

She's right. Even in possession of the world's cleanest colon and having ingested more kale than would be required to make a bunny nauseous, I've lost a measly five pounds. And I suspect most of this is down to backed-up lunches. And as if that wasn't insult enough, my damned blood pressure is even higher than on check-in.

I'm stuck with the boobs of a twelve-year-old boy for the foreseeable future.

"You'd be a perfect candidate."

I hear her perfectly. My "I beg your pardon?" has more to do with what she means than what she's said.

Making me wait, she pours two cups of coffee, pushing one in my direction. I savour the first mouthful but have guzzled the rest before she's even finished stirring two heaped teaspoons of sugar into hers.

"It's something we usually offer to our celebrity guests."

*Still in the dark here. I'm not playing her stupid game.*

I keep quiet, forcing her to do all the work.

"We have a special programme."

Again, I say nothing.

"It's the Sleeping Beauty Programme." As if understanding I won't respond, she presses on. "Yes, well. You keep saying in your daily weigh-ins that you'd do anything to lose the weight. The question is, do you really mean it?"

My answer to this question in the past would always have been a resounding 'yes'. Now I'm not so sure. What if being thin meant being dead?

*Hardly likely to need new boobs then, am I?*

I hedge my bets. "Within reason."

Normally, I'd be in full agreement. However, my survival instinct hammering away in my chest at full throttle is making me exceptionally fond of my few extra pounds.

She does her best to lift an eyebrow before pressing on.

"When you're a guest in the Sleeping Beauty Suites, you're lightly sedated. This means we can cut right back on your calories, with you sleeping blissfully through any hunger pangs. There are daily massages, and we use neuromuscular electrical stimulation to keep your body in shape. Our celebrity clients love it."

Until two days ago, this would have been my idea of bliss. As it is, there isn't a snowball's chance in hell I'd put myself in her hands like that. "Can I think about it?"

She smirks at me. "Unfortunately not."

I soon comprehend it's me tilting to the side and not the room.

## 16

I don't so much wake up as claw my way back to consciousness. On arrival, I wish I'd stayed where I was, the comfort of the blackness winning hands down.

Whatever Chalky slipped me was strong. I have not the faintest recollection of the trip from her office to wherever the hell I am now. My money is on being somewhere in the ex-army base rather than anywhere you'd find a celebrity.

Indeed, the linens on the large bed are more akin to rubber than 1000 thread count Egyptian cotton, as I'd expect. The lights illuminating my body are as bright as any seen in an operating theatre. Sadly, they're not so blinding that I can't see a multitude of cameras on the periphery of the room.

I know without lifting my head that I'm starkers. I know without trying to move my arms and legs that I'm tied down. I know my legs being spread wide doesn't bode well.

"Lance!"

This one-word command is nasal and 'Noo Yawk' announcing, without the need to twist my head around, who issued this command. I'd assumed the headboard would be against the wall, but this doesn't appear to be the case.

Consciously slowing my breathing, I fight the urge to panic. This stillness allows me to appreciate that while the voice had come from behind me, I'm alone in the room.

Unfortunately, not for long.

While Lance's clothes are deplorable, seeing him at the end of the bed and harder than my ex on his way to the morgue, I'd be happy for him to be wearing anything. Even the most hideous of outfits from his wardrobe would be better than nothing.

I concentrate on the ceiling to obscure my view of him. The mattress dips under my legs, my worst fears realised. Unable to stop myself, my gaze drops, meeting his. There isn't even a spark of compassion there.

I try to speak, to tell him no, but the words jam in my throat. When they do escape, they make no sense, even to me. He stills, poised above me, waiting for something. Words failing me, I resort to pleading with my eyes. A silent 'please, no' on my lips.

The only thing I can hear now is my heartbeat thundering away, faster and faster. I struggle against my restraints and my pulse increases, my breaths now ragged gasps.

None of this does anything to free me.

"It'll make a change to pork a live one," he hisses, while poking at me experimentally.

"Please don't do this," I manage to snotter out, my sinuses evacuating in sympathy with my tear ducts. "I can pay. I have money, lots of it." I make eye contact with him, mouthing *please* to avoid my voice being picked up by one of the microphones. He stills, and a small beacon of hope flickers to life in my chest.

"Lance, the client is waiting. You have your instructions!"

*Client*?

He smiles broadly at me before continuing to crawl up the bed.

There's nothing gentle about how he enters me. He buries himself to the hilt, ripping my insides as he does so. No foreplay, no lubricant, just raw anger. His withdrawal hurts even more, and I can do nothing about my screams of pain.

The laughter that meets my cries, from somewhere above me, barely registers as I pant trying to cope with the agony. Lance's next thrust isn't any easier on me and from a stinging hot core, pain throbs in waves, filling me body and soul.

After this, no matter how hard I call on my church-going roots with prayers and then entreaties, he doesn't stop, at least not until I'm hollow and my insides feel ripped to shreds. My tears ceased when, even with self-help, he could no longer get it up.

Then he amuses himself, or an unseen client, by twisting my nipples and girly bits hard enough that I again scream out in pain.

Over and over he repeats this brutality, until all sensation is gone and I lay there staring at the ceiling.

"Cut!"

I whimper again before understanding this was a directorial command from Chalky and not an instruction to Lance to get the knives out.

A stream of cold water shocks me into full sentience, the final insult. I open my eyes but soon close them when I'm sprayed full in the face, the water filling my mouth and nose, choking me.

Sluiced down like a side of beef in an abattoir, Lance gives my private parts more attention than they deserve after the last hour. I try for oblivion, but it remains as out of reach as ever.

"No passing out, you're on again now!" An unfamiliar male, whose clipped accent firmly marks him as South African, barks at me.

"Piers, you have your instructions," comes from the speaker above my head. There's a small pause before Chalky continues. "Annnnnd, action!"

Despite my continued prayers, relief doesn't come. Only Piers, the South African does, covering my face in a noxious stream, that has me gagging and choking in turn.

The hours turn into what I think might be days, blending into a living nightmare with barely enough sleep and nourishment to survive. There's neither rhyme nor rhythm to when the studio lights flare into life. The accents coming from the speaker above my head as varied as the time zones they must represent.

I'm not fed any solids for fear this will interfere with the more bizarre client requests, instead subsisting on those chocolate shakes. Even their delicious flavour turns my stomach to the point I spew up as much as they can force-feed me, with yet more icy hose-downs to follow.

Everything stops. It's as though I've been voted off the island and they've moved on to torture another contestant. As much as I want to feel sorry for whoever it is, I'm relieved to no longer be the centre of attention. The chocolate shakes stop, leaving me faint, even though I'm lying down.

I think I'm imagining things when I detect scratching from somewhere off to my left. Dropping my head to the side, I face the Venetian blinds I'd assumed covered an interior window. I listen carefully.

*There it is again.*

Even knowing the consequences, I yell for help as loudly as I'm able. This isn't any great shakes with my voice unused for days and nothing to drink for at least one of those. But it's done the trick. I make out the words 'get help' before quiet returns.

The relative peace is short-lived, with Lance, and then Piers, thundering into my room. Both of them are naked.

*Oh, crap.*

I don't have long to think.

"Cockroach, there's a monster cockroach!" I throw as much energy into this declaration as possible, adding to my apparent terror by twisting against my bindings in a vain attempt at escape.

"You stupid bitch, you fucking interrupted a triple." Piers follows this up by backhanding me across the mouth. It's so hard I see stars and have those little birds tweeting around my head.

Lance twists my clit so viciously, I pass out.

## 17

Maybe it's the sense of malevolent evil that inveigles its way into my dream that rouses me, ruining the solitude where I'm frolicking on that golden beach of mine. My eyelids flutter open and I see Chalky next to the bed looking down at me, her gaze unsettling, full of speculation.

I don't know what to make of it when she holds a cup with a straw next to my mouth so I can take a drink. I don't care what it is in the plastic cup; anything that will help rid my mouth of the gum accumulated from a lack of fluids will suffice.

I take several deep swigs of what tastes like water before she takes the cup away. I'm not sure if she's done this to stop me overloading myself, or she's being her usual bitchy self.

I opt for the second and before I can stop myself, let fly with a satisfying gob of spit that's just this side of tenacious. My reward is that it sticks to the front of her pristine smock in a satisfying manner. Not so gratifying is her look of pure venom that spears me.

*But what the hell, it's not like I'm getting out of here alive.*

Unless, that is, whoever it was at the window arrives with the cavalry pretty damn smartly.

"You'll regret that, Marilyn."

"Hah, you don't scare me!" Despite my bravado, this is complete bollocks: the fact she's used my real name does not bode well.

"Did you think we'd just let you slip away?" The laughter that follows has that same tinkling quality often associated with fundraising events. Fake to the core. Her voice has none of this subterfuge: it's raw and unfiltered. "It's amazing what our clients enjoy watching, and how much they'll pay."

There's no need for her to go into detail, my imagination more than taking care of what I still have to face. Knowing my subsequent death will be neither easy nor cheap, impels me to shut my eyes to the room.

The ropes scraping my wrists and ankles raw stop me. Opening my eyes, I find I'm on my own again, with only my thoughts for company.

These are reaching Stephen-King-level crazy when Lance stomps back into my room; he's dressed and doesn't look happy. He pulls a gigantic knife out of a sheath strapped to his leg and I whimper in terror. My demise isn't far off and I'm about to find out if David made it to heaven, or hell where he deserved.

I squeeze my eyes shut. I can't watch my own dispatch. Therefore, I'm stunned when, rather than disembowelling me, Lance hacks through my bindings. He throws me like a sack of grain over one shoulder and makes short work of striding out of the room.

After trudging down a long corridor, we enter

another room. Even viewed upside down, I can see this is set up for one thing and one thing only.

There's nothing gentle about how he drops me onto the hard concrete floor. My muscles have atrophied to noodle status, and there's nothing I can do to soften the blow. My cries of agony bounce off the concrete walls and ceiling. Rather than tip my head back and cut my throat, Lance shoves me with his foot and I sprawl on my back next to a grate in the floor.

My startled gaze latches onto a series of meat hooks hanging from the ceiling, letting me know my time is up. I'm therefore surprised when rather than bend over and casually dispatch me; Lance makes a performance of unzipping his filthy jeans and dragging his penis free.

This is a surprise; he's usually show-ready, pre-fluffed and ready to go. My eyes widen in horror; the way he's holding his old fellow having more to do with accuracy than stimulation.

I jam my eyes and mouth shut before turning my head to the side as far as it'll go, but I still cop an ear full of urine that reeks of asparagus. This splatters up at me from the cold concrete. But it could have been worse. My relief is short-lived when I turn back as Lance steps aside, replaced by Piers.

*To hell with this*!

"Pencil dick, pencil dick, can't get hard without a stick. Pencil dick, pencil dick, can't get laid without a trick." I sing-song this stupid rhyme at the top of my voice, rewarded with a sharp intake of breath coming from the speaker in the ceiling.

Piers looks confused, thinks my singing is directed at him, but there's no point emasculating him. Better to go to work on the pay-per-view jerk, living in his mum's basement, who's forking out for the performance. "Pencil dick, pencil dick, can't get hard without a stick!"

I'm working through yet another refrain when a burst of static from the speaker is followed by Chalky speaking, her tone clipped and dripping with wrath. "That will be all, thank you, Piers."

He's leaving when Chalky storms in. She doesn't slow as she crosses the room and without warning kicks me hard in the kidneys. "That's for us having to give a refund!"

The pain is excruciating. I dry-retch, with even those hideous shakes refusing to make a comeback. Throwing up all over the cold-hearted bitch is out of the question. I make do with screaming at her with as much volume as I can muster. "You frigid, skinny OLD bitch!"

This time she kicks me between the legs hard, making accidentally smashing into your bike seat child's play by comparison. It doesn't shut me up though, even if my words are forced.

"Frigid, skinny OLD bitch! Frigid, skinny OLD bitch!"

I don't stop until Chalky bends over and punches me in the nose hard, spraying blood in all directions. My mouth full of O positive, I take delight in spitting it out as hard as I can, ruining a crisp, white smock that looks fresh on.

I'm laughing maniacally when Pencil Dick starts screaming "Get rid of her," over and over before snarling, "I'll watch."

Cold water assaults me: Lance taking the opportunity to hose down the room at the same time as me. Lifted dripping wet, he throws me over his shoulder for the return trip to what I think of as *my* room.

No sooner has he flung me back on the bed than a tinny voice says, "I want to see that bitch fucked until she snuffs it." Presumably, this is Pencil Dick himself looking for another go-round.

I'm readying myself to start singing when Chalky storms into the room, holding a power drill aloft like it's an Oscar's statue.

*Oh hell.*

"Hurry, hurry," says Pencil Dick, obviously having worked himself into quite the lather over what's about to happen.

Thoughts of him distract me sufficiently that Lance has tied me down with new ropes before I fully comprehend what's going on. Then all I can focus on is Chalky making a production number out of putting a spade bit into the power drill.

I know I'm hysterical when I start laughing about thoughts of that sort of drill bit more commonly being used to put holes in than take them out.

Chalky's running commentary guarantees I'm fully cognisant of what she intends doing, although I think this it is more for Pencil Dick's edification than mine.

"Not getting any younger, here," comes a snippy instruction from the speaker, spurring Chalky to give up the theatrics and get on with proceedings.

Expecting Lance to take care of this task, I'm surprised when he slips out of the room quietly; leaving Chalky unaware he's even gone. Not until she swings to where he last stood does she show any surprise, or as much surprise as she can muster.

She doesn't bother calling for him as I expect. Rather, she shrugs and turns in my direction, whirring the drill for maximum terror ... or is that pleasure?

She's positioning herself between my feet when the Hummer roars into life outside. This is followed by the unmistakable sound of gravel being scattered courtesy of a quick departure.

Chalky's brows knot as if she's trying to give birth to last night's nut burger. It doesn't last; once again, she shrugs to convey 'if I must, I must' and 'the show must go on' and other drivel.

I do everything I can to distance myself from what's about to happen to me. I try for my happy place, which unfortunately remains elusive. The drill's so close there's a breeze on the inside of my thighs.

Tied up as tightly as I am, I can't get even a millimetre farther away. I whimper like a beaten puppy, but there's nothing I can do. Closing my eyes, I wait for the pain, thinking of babies I'll never hold.

"Cut, cut!" screams Pencil Dick, his voice more high-pitched than ever.

I relax, knowing this is it. It'll all be over soon and I can lie on that beautiful beach for eternity. The breeze cooling my very core, I know Chalky is close to gutting me, or whatever the gynecological equivalent is of that.

"Dammit! *Arrrgh*. Stop!"

Chalky's so close with the drill bit that if they'd left me any pubes, I'd have lost the lot by now. As it is, the drill stops, my relief coming early.

Apparently, it's the same for Pencil Dick, who is busy rescheduling for the same time tomorrow. Presumably when his mother is out at the shops.

## 18

A hand slapped over my mouth stops me from screaming. At the sight of Bev, tears of relief spring unbidden.

"We need to be incredibly quiet. This place is crawling with scum."

Even whispering directly into my ear, Bev's words are loud, although not as loud as a *bong* from the hallway. Without bothering to check what it is, she makes short work of my restraints thanks to a serrated bread knife she's picked up from somewhere.

She slowly eases me into a sitting position, but it's still too fast. Faintness swamps me and I have to lie back immediately to avoid passing out.

Bev speaks right into my ear. "When did you last eat?"

I shrug because I have no idea how much time has passed. It could be days or even months.

*Okay, not months. If it had been months, I'd be a maggoty all-you-can-eat buffet in the bush by now.*

Bev shoves a muesli bar into my hand. "Eat!"

I take a small bite and my taste buds explode

with gratitude before the hastily-chewed mouthful lands like a brick in my stomach.

Not until I know the food is staying put do I ask her the question that's buzzed around in my brain since I heard the knock on the window. "How on earth did you find me? How did you even know to look?"

Bev looks over her shoulder towards the door before turning back to me. "We knew you would have said goodbye if you were leaving. We followed Chalky. Nasty bitch was being sneaky as all get out, so we knew something was up."

The second bite of muesli bar tastes as good as the first and despite the desire to bolt it down, I take my time, not needing to choke or puke right now.

"I'll be back in a second."

Bev moves from my side and panic claws at my throat straightaway.

*Don't leave me!*

It's all I can do to stop myself from calling out. However, she doesn't go far, stopping in the doorway to peek out into the corridor, first one way and then the other. She disappears, and the sense of abandonment is excruciating.

The muesli bar half-finished, I painfully drag myself into a sitting position. I wait for the wooziness to disappear, before struggling to my feet. Initially, I need the headboard for support, but eventually find my equilibrium, standing unaided.

This is how Bev finds me when she returns with her arms full of clothing in a bright green often seen in medical dramas. She drops a pair of poo-coloured Crocs on the floor and then lays the surgical scrubs on the bed. I need her help to dress, occasionally having to sit and put my head between my knees to avoid passing out.

"You ready?" She looks at me and I can tell she thinks she'll need to heft me over her shoulder at some point. I'm sure she's more than capable.

No sooner have I nodded confirmation at being as ready as I ever will when there's another loud *bong* from out in the hallway.

Ange is in the doorway a second later. She's holding a large, heavy-duty roasting pan above her head in readiness but lowers it when she sees Bev and me. My stomach rumbles loudly in eagerness when the aroma of recently roasted meat hits my nostrils.

Ange doesn't question this, just hands the pan over to me. There are a few large dents in it, but the meat scrapings and pieces of crispy potato glistening tantalisingly in the bottom appear untouched by any human cranium. I make short work of them before handing Ange's weapon of choice back to her.

"Come on, let's get you outta here," Bev whispers, before throwing one arm around my middle and dragging me into a supportive embrace. Without this, I wouldn't be going anywhere.

Moments later, we find ourselves in a big industrial kitchen. Bev grabs a cast-iron frying pan from the top of the stove with her free hand while Ange keeps hold of the heavy-duty roasting dish. Unarmed, my vulnerability intensifies when Ange quietly opens an outside door and we face a large gravel parking area. It's one we need to navigate, along with a driveway that's also gravel, before we reach the cover of the bush.

Never has gravel underfoot sounded so loud to

me, meaning that rather than sneaking across, we traverse as fast as we're able. I know I'm slowing down the others, making me eternally grateful that they stick to my side. They help me move quicker than I could have on my own.

We don't get more than a few metres into the bush before it becomes obvious we aren't prepared for vegetation this thick. We don't have the equipment and we sure as hell don't have the knowledge to keep ourselves safe.

As tempting as it would be to rush down the driveway, this would also leave us vulnerable to recapture. Despite how unprepared we are for bush like this, there is no way I'm heading back into the open. Our decision is confirmed when spotlights burst into life on all sides of the building.

It isn't fully dark yet, but their effect on my fight-or-flight reflex is instant. This quadruples when a couple of dozen men in camouflage gear burst out of the door we'd so recently used.

*Where the hell did they come from?*

These are the first I've seen apart from the one guy Ange, Bev and I had seen in camo in the bush that time. And even he was mild in comparison to the battle-hardened men spreading out and walking towards the bush in an ever-widening arc. They carry assault rifles across their fronts, at the ready.

Lance and Piers make up two of their number, easily identifiable by their smaller stature.

What starts as a small tremor develops into full body-shakes, with my teeth chattering and no amount of hugging from the other two able to stop it.

Ange looks over her shoulder at the men. "We need to get the hell out of here," she gasps out.

I shake my head at this suggestion. While I don't disagree with her, I don't know if I'm up to walking yet, and certainly not as fast as will be required.

Bev grabs my head, forcing me to look at her. "You have to do this. If we go back there, we die." Her hissed words break through the terror engulfing me.

Following her scary-as-crap pep talk, she drags me to my feet and points me in the direction Ange has already started to take through the bush.

"Put your feet where she puts hers," whispers Bev. "Don't think, walk."

It's a sound strategy, even if on a couple of occasions I trip when Ange does. As long as we're tripping in the right direction, I don't care.

We haven't stumbled far when we encounter the pig fence.

"I'd rather face the pigs than those murderous thugs behind us." Ange drops to her knees and digs terrier-style under the fence. Bev joins her and in moments, they've ruined their nails but have created a good-size gap.

I fall on my knees next to them, not because I'm capable of helping with the excavation, but because my legs have given out. "I think the gap's too small."

"You are going through."

## 19

I can't see Bev's face properly in the relative dark of the bush, but her voice is a clarion call that this isn't up for discussion. Her hand on the back of my neck, shoving me towards the gap, confirms her eagerness to get me moving, and I face-plant the undergrowth.

Getting down to my level, she pats the back. "Sorry, love, but they're getting closer."

This, more than her comforting touches, mobilises me. Bev is right; we can't go back, knowing what we'd face.

I slither under the fence and roll down the hill on the other side, making a hell of a racket in the process. The other two aren't far behind; all of us land in a tumble at the bottom of the ravine, up to our waists in freezing water.

Ange is on her feet in a heartbeat, making short work of flinging the roasting dish into the bush on the other side. "Come on, move ya butt." She slides a hand into each of my armpits from behind, urging me to stand.

Bev moves in front of me and between them, they hoist me upright. I'm so tired, I'm hallucinating. A wild pig approaches us. It's walking upright, like a man. It's too much, and Bev has to slap me hard to stop my screaming.

No sooner have I stopped than Ange takes up, earning her a smack of her own from Bev.

Ange points and Bev turns, the pig well within striking distance. She doesn't bother yelling as I expect: she smacks it hard across the snout with the frying pan she's held onto all this time.

Rather than knocking it out, the pig flies through the air and lands with a big splash in the creek. But it doesn't attack us. Instead it speaks.

"Will you fuckin' crazy bitches shut the fuck up?"

While not exactly a knight in shining armour, the blood-encrusted bloke glaring at us through the half-light will do nicely. Happy in the knowledge we've been rescued, I allow the darkness that's nudging at my consciousness to take over.


The stench interrupts my dreams. If I didn't know better, I'd think I was sharing my bed with a large block of Stilton cheese; and Stilton well past its best-by date. I cough, hoping to clear my airways of the noxious presence, but it's no good, and I wake fully, opening my eyes to see how I can escape.

Right in front of my face is a pair of size elevens, wrapped securely in wet wool socks moulded to arches and ankles alike. I yank my head backwards in search of clean air and smash it into a wall. A couple of items hanging precariously on rusty nails above me fall and thwack me on the side of my head.

"*Owww!*" My yelp of pain is loud in the small

shack, but not so loud that I rouse the large man who I'm topping and tailing with.

A quick look at my new surroundings shows a basic hunting shelter, cobbled together out of punga logs and bits of scrap wood. The bright-blue plastic tarpaulin that is all that tops the structure, gives the space an eerie glow and turns our rescuer's blond hair a bright blue, although there's nothing Smurf-like about the guy from what I can remember of last night.

Ange and Bev are sleeping top and tail in a bed on the other side of the hut and I take solace in how relaxed they appear. They're not tied down, which also adds to my peace of mind.

Unable to get up without climbing over our erstwhile rescuer, I take the easy option and roll over to face the wall. A small breeze sneaks its way between the ill-fitting logs, and this freshness encourages me to sink back into sleep's sweet stranglehold.

Next time I wake, it's because I need to pee and there's no ignoring it; it works better than any alarm clock. I roll over, pleased to see the cheesy socks have gone, along with the size elevens that owned them, making it easier for me to get out of bed.

"Look who's awake." Bev smiles at me before tending to what smells like bacon in the frying pan. The pan is the same one she'd armed herself with yesterday. At least I think it was yesterday. Funny, but thoughts of eating leave me cold.

Ange bustles in with a billy, sloshing water onto the packed dirt floor of the hut in the process. She places the battered aluminium container on the small woodburner alongside the frying pan.

"Where's ...?" I ask, struggling into a sitting position.

"Johnno? He's out on a scouting mission to see what's up with the neighbours."

The casual way Ange says this would make you think the neighbours were merely guilty of over-zealous trimming of boundary trees. Or growing dope in their backyard rather than torture and potentially lethal pay-per-view.

Before I can ask more, Johnno storms into the hut. "Kill the fire!"

I'm questioning this seemingly random instruction when Ange opens the front of the small woodburner. She chucks the contents of the billy in there and closes the door. No doubt a plume of smoke shoots up the chimney, but nothing more. If we're lucky.

"You," says Johnno, pointing in my direction, "On your feet! Now!"

So forceful is Johnno's command that I stand before I'm even aware of getting up. He's not the sort of guy you'd argue with, him being what my mum would describe as rough around the edges. And if someone like this is tense, by rights I should be, too. A minute later, we've crossed a small stream and are trotting single file down a narrow track. Bev is in the lead, with Johnno at the rear. He's armed with a knife that would make Crocodile Dundee look like a pansy.

The pig is slung over his shoulders like a bloody, hairy backpack; its feet tied together to form shoulder straps.

Scared as I am, I'm unable to stop a strained smile when I see Bev has maintained a firm hold on the cast-iron frying pan. And, because of retained heat, the bacon is still sizzling. Thankfully, the breeze is strong. Our pursuers won't get a bead on our location, although I get a waft now and then.

*Nope, still doesn't appeal.*

Could it be my full bladder putting pressure on my stomach that's taken the edge off my hunger? Appetite has never been an issue in the past.

"Stop here!" hisses Johnno from behind me. Bev, Ange and me don't so much freeze, as solidify, not daring to as much as blink.

He, however, keeps up his pace, storming past us, and coating me liberally with boar bits in the process. If I had anything in my stomach, I'd be barfing for sure. Luckily for us, Ange's 'Gross', has Bev turning to see what's up. Her reactions are better than mine would be. She whips the frying pan well away from pork products of a fresher variety; saving our breakfast from a splattering of blood and gore.

Prising my gaze away from the frying pan, I don't immediately grasp what's missing. How the hell can a hulking big bloke with a pig on his back disappear like that? It's at least twenty metres before the track turns a corner and he wasn't moving that fast.

"Move it!"

A blink later, I work out the direction of this terse instruction, mainly because I see Bev advance on what looks like a solid wall of green. She parts this with the frying pan and disappears. Ange follows in her stead, and I waste no time staggering in their wake.

On the other side is a different world. The foliage forms a tunnel, which Johnno is marching resolutely down, leaving us to keep up as best we can. My blood-sugar levels protest ever louder, and I know I'm not alone when I see Ange whack herself on the side of the head. The light-headedness is getting to me, too, with more and more shaking required to clear my vision.

Soon, even this isn't working, and it's all I can do to place one foot in front of the other and keep up. My relief is immense when Johnno ducks into a cave off to the side of the track. I arrive in time to witness the boar hit the floor of this sanctuary with a sickening squelch and blood seeping out of every orifice.

No amount of gulping can keep the bile in my stomach, and I dart outside to get rid of it in the bushes. Even spitting and I'm close to having an accident.

I stagger behind the nearest tree, all fingers and thumbs in my desperation to untie the knot on the drawstring that holds my borrowed pants up. I only just make it, my relief a mix of emptying my bladder and not weeing myself in the process.

I arrive back at the cave in time to see Johnno departing.

"You lot wait here while I cover our tracks," he throws over his shoulder as he marches back the way we've come. Not weighed down by an afternoon's work for a butcher – or us – he covers the ground in long strides.

I slide to the floor of the cave, well away from the carcass. I'm comatose, but soon rouse when the cast-iron frying pan waves in front of my face.

I force myself to eat a rasher, which tastes like sawdust. The second isn't much better. If anyone had told me a month ago that I'd be eating so soon after spiting up all that bile, I'd never have believed them.

"Any more?" Ange's words rouse me from my semi-coma, both with their volume in the cave and the hope that springs into my stomach that the answer will be no.

"Two rashers," says Bev, "and I'm saving those for Johnno. We owe him big time."

Ange isn't given the opportunity to complain; Johnno storms into the cave, picks up the boar and throws it over his shoulders as though it weighs nothing. His actions speak louder than words; he puts his finger to his lips, there's a reason for his haste.

Both Bev and Ange's assistance is required for me to regain my feet. Upright, I'm anything but steady, with head spins in the realms of those experienced after a real bender. At first, I baulk when they lead me deeper into the cave. They're surely heading in the wrong direction? But then I hear Johnno moving ahead of us.

The deeper we go, the darker it is, to the point I doubt there's any light reaching us at all.

The more stygian it gets, the better my sense of hearing, until I'm more bat than human. Ange, Bev and I hold onto each other in unspoken agreement, sliding our feet along the floor of the cave to avoid unseen obstacles.

Now and then a husky 'left', 'right' or 'middle' will filter back to us from the black beyond. Without Johnno's instructions, we'd be lost for sure.

Minutes feel like hours. Our eyes latch onto the slightest increase in light and my irises contract in response to sunshine filtering through foliage covering the opening ahead. I can't see what's beyond that, but one thing is certain, Johnno and Piggy are no longer in the cavern with us.

"I hope he hasn't done a runner!" Bev's voice is loud, bouncing off the walls and battering us from all angles. The echoes are in their death throes when a sibilant, "Shut the fuck up!" is added to the mix from the other side of the green curtain. Our guide is still with us.

*Maybe because Bev has his share of the bacon?*

The closer we get to the exit, the faster the three of us walk, no longer bothering to slide our feet along the ground. If Johnno is still concerned about us making noise, then our escape isn't fait accompli. For all we know, those pursuing us could have torches.

The pain of a stubbed toe registers only as I slam into the floor of the cave, winding myself in the process. Stunned, I know my fall wasn't quiet and neither is my desperate fight to get air into my lungs. I'm struggling to breathe when Johnno man-handles me off the ground, slings me over his shoulder and jogs for the exit, with Bev and Ange in tow.

The one positive from the rough handling, is that I get more air back in my lungs. However, I come close to losing the bacon when I see how close my face is to Johnno's gore-encrusted back. Before I get a chance, I'm unceremoniously dumped next to the pig he'd abandoned to come back and grab me.

We're outside the cave on a ledge that's a couple of metres wide. Beyond that, it's a sea of treetops and open sky, with an uninterrupted view to the coastline in the distance. If the ledge were wider, you can be sure someone would have built a holiday home on it by now. One with what would be considered million-dollar views.

Helped back to my feet, I'm no more prepared

now than I was in the cave earlier. Focussing on Johnno taking the frying pan from Bev helps me to remain upright. He gobbles down the last two rashers of bacon and then sends the pan wide out into the open like a cast-iron Frisbee.

A very porcine squealing radiates from far below us. The local pig population doesn't stand a chance with Johnno in their midst. His latest victim hoisted back over his shoulders, he bolts up the track, pulling its makeshift shoulder straps into place.

Bev and Ange take off after him, but quickly appreciate I'm stuck where I am.

Standing is a challenge: there isn't a hope in hell I can keep up with the others. As unsteady as I am, my chances of keeping to the track are scarily slender.

Swaying gently, I'm a couple of steps away from the edge, a couple of steps from oblivion and the horrors facing me.

It would be so easy, so simple, and so peaceful.

Even my life back in Auckland sucked. No friends, only frenemies. Too old to have kids. No love life. Rich, for sure, but happy? No.

I've committed myself to a leap of faith when Bev shatters my dark reverie. Grabbing my shoulders, she spins me away from the drop-off and bends in front of me. My world view turns upside down. Yet again, she shows me how strong she is, possibly down to her rural lifestyle. Reverse our positions and I wouldn't have a hope of carrying her.

What follows is a stomach-churning forced march along the track that skirts the cliff face. One I'd never have managed without Bev's intervention.

If I'd had my way, it would all be over now bar the memorial service, the wild pigs voiding the need for an actual burial.

Eventually, we reach the safety of the bush. The unmistakable sounds of pig meeting dirt indicate we're allowed to rest and I lie snuggling up to the carcass.

"Why can't that useless bitch walk for herself?" Johnno looks down at me with disgust previously exclusive to my late husband.

## 20

If Ange is worried about losing our guide, she hides it well, getting right up in Johnno's face. "Because she's been systematically raped, tortured and starved for two weeks, that's why, you prick."

"You're shitting joking me? I thought you lot were on the run so you could go grab some takeaways?"

"I wasn't serious when I said that last night." Bev's expression has 'you Muppet' writ large across it.

Johnno opens his mouth to respond, but closes it again before eventually saying, "We've gotta get moving again if we wanna stay ahead of those arseholes." Johnno stares out through the bush at the track that bisects the cliff face all the way back to the cave exit. While his stance is relaxed, his gaze is alert for anyone exiting the cave through the trail of vines that conceal it.

It's obvious the second he's seen something and I force myself – painfully – to roll over onto my hands and knees in readiness to stand. It's as far as I get before he grabs me from behind and swings me to my feet so fast I nearly black out. He hooks my hands around his neck and says "Climb on."

Much as I want to escape, I recoil at repeating 'up close and personal' with that much blood and sweaty bloke.

"I'll take her, you grab the pig." Bev shoves him out of the way and with indescribable gratitude, I clamber onto her back.

Johnno's relief at not having to abandon Piggy is funny, but any smirk I'm working on is wiped clean. There are six guys in army fatigues jogging in sync along the cliff track, rifles at the ready. In an instant, I feel like Piggy must have yesterday when Johnno stalked her through the bush.

Of more concern is where the rest of the guys are that we'd seen spewing out of the Sleeping Beauty Suites the night before. There have to be at least fourteen or fifteen others around somewhere. Are we going to run into them coming from the other direction?

Right now though, our main concern has to be those we can see and we waste no time in setting off again. Not far along, the track splits and we fork left, then right, and a couple more lefts. Everyone with their feet on the ground has been studiously walking on the side of the track, allowing the leaf litter to absorb footprints. Ange who's at the back is even dragging a Nikau frond behind her, obliterating any unwanted evidence.

Without warning, Johnno takes a hard right and walks into the bush itself. But it's an illusion; the main track leads straight on and we travel down an offshoot, so little used that unless you knew about it, you'd never see it. Looking back, I see Ange walking heavily up the track for a couple of metres to create a false trail. She then cuts the corner, joining up with us again.

She shrugs at my look of enquiry. "I saw it in a movie once."

This time I do manage to smile, even if half-heartedly.


The more the bush conceals us, the safer I feel. Safe to the point I'm lulled by the rocking motion, drooling on Bev's shoulder. My deep breathing rouses me from my half-state.

"Oh, I'm so sorry." Dabbing ineffectively at her shoulder, all I get in response is a grunt. "You can put me down now." She doesn't, nor does she slow until Johnno does. At the sight of the hut, my relief is immense.

*Any luck and there'll be beds and food on offer.*

"Welcome to Hemi's place. It's crap, but better than ..." Johnno's words peter out. "Actually, it's just crap, but we can rest here for the night."

*Night?*

I guess it had to happen, but it's still snuck up on me. Bev lowers me gently to my feet, not letting go until I've steadied myself. "You need food, but not too much, or you'll be sick," she says.

There's no need to answer; my stomach does it for me, lending truth to her words even if I don't feel hungry in the slightest. By rights, even the pig should be looking good. My appetite of old, you could have put an apple in its mouth and I'd be gnawing at its rump by now.

I take in the small hut in front of me. *What is it about people around here building stuff out of corrugated iron*? Was it because this was the easiest material for them to lug up here?

Ramshackle it might be, but a perfect place to crash for the night when you're out hunting for a couple of days, or even if you're being hunted yourself.

Johnno wastes no time getting stuck into the carcass with that lethal knife of his and all thoughts of eating run for cover. Moments later, Piggy is missing part of a shoulder strap.

Johnno wipes his knife clean by running it across the leg of his jeans, first on one side and then the other, leaving tram-tracks of blood in evidence. "Hell, lady, sit down before you fall down, will ya? There's a bed of sorts in the hut."

The smell of roast pork cuts through my nightmare, unleashing me from my bed in the Sleeping Beauty Suites. The image of Lance driving himself into me at the behest of a jerk glued to a laptop, while trying to stay hard, is shattered. The one thing worse than being able to see him was when I couldn't, his sweat dripping on my back.

It'll be a good long time before I have sex again, if ever. I quake at the memories of Lance and Piers shuddering all those times, before the aroma of pork floods the hut to the point I'm freed from the remnants of my nightmare.

Even rested as I am, I take my time getting to my feet. My blood-sugar level is deserving of a 5-star rating, although not so low that roast pork is appealing, especially having seen it in its raw state so recently.

Imagine my relief when I sit next to the fire and

Ange hands me a bowl of porridge. "You can start with that and see how your tummy copes with it."

The porridge is lumpy and there isn't any cream, it does, however, have a thick crust of sugar coating the surface. It's about as unappealing as food can get, but I know I need something in my system if I'm to keep up with the others tomorrow.

Reluctantly, I dip the battered camping spoon into the gloop and taste it, expecting more cardboard. It's far better than I expect, if you don't count the ants.

After ingesting a couple, I tilt my bowl to the firelight, and pick them free of the sugar, flicking them off into the undergrowth.

The others chew contentedly on roast pork while I work my way through the porridge, nectar now that my tastes buds have reawakened. In between mouthfuls, we bring Johnno up to speed on what's been happening at The Vale. I'm pleased the others don't ask me too much about my own experiences, instead sticking to our being drugged and finding the bodies in the bush.

"But that's my land. They can't kill people on my land."

"Your land?"

I ask this in tandem with Ange and Bev, with our scepticism obvious to even the most obtuse.

Johnno has to finish a mouthful of pork before he responds. "Hey, I pay tax, which makes it mine as much as the next bloke's."

Bev puts voice to the very question I've been thinking on myself. "We're on government land? You've got a hunting permit, right?"

Johnno shrugs, with this answer enough.

This has to be the reason he's hunting only

using a knife and feral cunning, doesn't it? A quick glance at the roughly butchered pig doesn't show any bullet holes. I'm no closer to a decision when I hear rustling from the bushes on the other side of the clearing.

"Hah! They'll run outta chicken at KFC before that one forks out for a licence," booms out from the dark of the bush, eliciting cries of alarm from all but Johnno.

He's remarkably relaxed, as though he's been expecting someone, unlike Ange and Bev, who hold up lumps of smouldering firewood. They look to be ready to deck anyone who so much as looks at them funny.

After lots of crashing, hacking and foul language, a mountain of a man stumbles into the clearing. A smaller bloke wanders casually through the wide swathe created by his mate.

Without preamble, the big man throws himself down next to the fire. "Name's Hemi," says the new arrival from his position beside me. Relaxing into his pose, his gut flops out from under his worn bush singlet and spills onto the ground with a soft wobble. The armhole of his singlet gapes when he leans forward to snag himself a hunk of roast pork, and I feel more flat-chested than ever.

His companion couldn't be more different. He's squeezed himself in between Bev and Ange, showing he's not so little after all, just small in comparison to Hemi.

*Hell's bells, a tank would look small next to Hemi.*

"So what's this about people being killed around here? Name's Horse, by the way."

It's all I can do not to spit my mouthful of porridge back into the bowl. God knows what he's done to deserve that nickname, but I decide I'd rather not know.

Bev, Ange and I repeat what's been going on at The Vale for the benefit of Hemi and Horse, with each retelling making it sound even more unbelievable. Again I keep mum on my starring role in the pay per view side of the operation. I doubt I'll ever be ready to share details of that.

"The blokes chasing you have made themselves at home down at South Junction Hut," says Hemi, around a greasy mouthful of pork.

I check to see how Ange and Bev have reacted to this before putting voice to my main concern. "How many were there?"

Horse looks off into middle distance as he thinks back on their earlier encounter. "Around half a dozen, I guess. Couple of scrawny blokes and four or so big mothers."

"Hah!" bursts out Hemi. "They were all scrawny so far as I'm concerned."

I look to Bev to see that she too looks to be carrying out a bit of mental arithmetic.

She has another slurp of her billy tea, before speaking. "Better keep your eyes peeled. When we scarpered, there were at least twenty of those jerk wads on our tail."

"Twenty! Fuck me." Despite Johnno's sentiment being crass, I can't help but share it.

Hemi pushes himself into a sitting position and cuts himself another slice of meat, apparently uncaring that there are bristles still sticking out in places. "Any luck and the lot we saw will get lost in the tracks down that way. Place is a bloody rabbit warren unless you know your way around."

"Still, I wish we'd known what those arseholes

were up to, when we were passing. We could have made sure they got *lost*." Horse chomps on a large piece of pork, with any further words or clarification on what he means by *lost* disappearing with the mouthful.

Johnno looks at Horse, a huge grin on his face. "Sheesh mate, what's with the clobber, you look like something outta the centrespread in a *Hunting & Fishing* catalogue?"

Only then do I notice that everything Horse is wearing appears to be brand new, to the point there are still creases down the front of his shirt. Likewise, his khaki trousers sport creases at regular intervals from where they'd been sitting on a shelf.

"Yeah, yeah. Whatever, ya arsehole. Bloody Sharon bitched about me having my hunting stuff at the apartment. I had to hire a storage locker. When Hemi invited me along, I ripped the bloody locker to bits and couldn't find anything, just a shitload of her dodgy online purchases. Reckon she snuck in there when I was down in Wellington for a meeting and biffed the lot." He rips a mouthful of meat from the hunk he's holding and chews on it while still managing to spit out. "Not keen on me hunting."

Of interest is that he looks at Johnno when he says this, giving the impression Sharon is okay with Horse hunting, just not with Johnno.

Johnno laughs hard. "Man, she's got you under her thumb well and truly. I said this would happen when you got yourself all educated and moved to the city. Never thought I'd see the day when a staunch bro like you would be domesticated."

Hemi likewise looks across at his newly-minted hunting buddy. "*Hunting & Fishing* catalogue, yep, he's pegged you mate." His deep laughter fills the clearing, his eyes twinkling in the firelight, and I smile in return.

Johnno throws a bit of something he hasn't been able to chew into the fire before looking at Bev, Ange and me in turn. "We'll get you lot back out to town tomorra."

Bev sits tall and crosses her arms tight. "We can't leave yet."

"Not without Tee," affirms Ange.

*Oh my god.*

Wallowing so profoundly in misery, I'd forgotten about Tee. "They're right. We can't leave her behind. She'll be in danger because we've done a runner."

Thoughts of Tee being tortured flood my mind, ridding me of what appetite I have. I doubt I could force even a sliver of pork down now. Even so, I know I'll need every bit of strength I can garner come tomorrow. I pull a big piece of meat from the bone and stash it in my bowl for later.

"Could be fun," says Johnno, looking at no one in particular.

Hemi nods. "Yeah, I'm in."

Unable to speak, Horse waves a half-eaten slab of pork around, confirming he's up for it.

"Great, we should leave at first light," says Ange, channelling her inner girl guide again.

Hemi throws the bone he's been gnawing on deep into the bush before getting to his feet with astonishing ease. "Na fucking way, we leave now!"

Despite what amounts to a direct order, I stay where I am, holding tight to my bowl of pork and porridge, like a culinary security blanket of sorts.

It isn't one I enjoy for long.

Big hands shoved snuggly into my armpits lift me so quickly, I don't have a chance to yelp. The heat from the food seeping through my now-filthy surgical scrubs reassures me I haven't dropped any of my stash. Although hard up against my chest, if I move the bowl, I'll lose everything. I carefully lean forward until I feel the food drop back into the bowl. I straighten and await further instructions from Hemi.

The large man moves around the campsite, his every action measured. There's no wasted energy on his part, as though he's rehearsed for this very thing.

After rattling around in the hut, Hemi re-joins us. He's carrying a small axe, a machete and a cricket bat, all of which he dumps on the ground next to the fire. "Ladies, choose your weapons."

A chortle escapes me. This morphs into high-pitched laughter that continues until Ange slaps me, hard, shocking a final hyena impression from me in a gurgled choke.

"Sorry, love, I needed to stop that in its tracks." She rubs my face to relieve the sting before picking up the small axe, gingerly.

The upside of my minor case of hysterics is that I'm left holding the cricket bat. No chance of self-harm with that, unless I decide to scone myself.

"Right, we all good to go?" Hemi's addressed everyone standing around the campfire but he focusses on Bev, Ange and me. I try to nod as emphatically as the other two, but in truth, I'd prefer to stay here by myself in the bush than head back to The Vale voluntarily.

I know I've passed muster when Hemi pulls a machete from the sheath on his leg and flips it up in the air. He just as casually catches it again without losing any fingers. "Let's go have us a little fun."

*A little fun?*

I peer at the machete Hemi is twirling like a juggling baton and doubt being on the receiving end of it would be a giggle. Sure, the blade might be in bad shape and liberally dotted with rust, but with Hemi's brute strength behind it, that wouldn't matter.

I check to see if Bev and Ange look concerned that things might get to that point. On the face of it, they're not worried, other than over our situation in general. They remain stoic even when Horse puts his hand casually over his shoulder and retrieves a wickedly sharp machete. The weapon's pristine condition firmly identifies it as another recent purchase. New or old, I don't know if the men's weaponry makes me feel safer, or not.

*Surely things won't be so hairy that they'll need to use their playthings?*

I haven't decided when Hemi douses the fire, no doubt the same way as countless times before. A whiff of long-neglected public toilets fills the campsite, and plunges us into darkness.

For a moment I'm blinded, my vision still matched to the brightness of the fire. Gradually, my sight adjusts to the filtered moonlight sneaking through the treetops. Bev and Ange are standing stock-still, too.

Meanwhile, the men are moving around as though it's midday and not the dead of night. I'd always heard puha, that leafy green the Maori are so keen on eating, was great for night vision. It looks like it works even better than British carrots, although wasn't that story put about to hide the fact the British had invented radar?

## 21

We don't leave the campsite the same way we arrived, or indeed via the route used by Hemi and Horse. We file around the side of the hut and along another pig track into the dark bush. Hemi is in the lead, I'm behind him, followed by Bev, Ange and Horse. Johnno, and what's left of Piggy, plays Tail End Charlie.

Even with porridge on board, I can't keep up with Hemi. This proves beyond all doubt that his fat is held in place with a hell of a lot of muscle.

Aware I'm no longer right behind him, he stops and I stumble along, hampered by my bowl and the cricket bat until I catch up.

"You gonna hold us up all sodding night?"

Unable to see his face clearly and given his neutral tone, I don't know if he's angry or not. Before I can formulate a response, Bev gets stuck into him, reminding him of what we've been through, before hinting at my own personal hell.

"Why the hell didn't ya say?" Hemi grabs the cricket bat, turns his back to me and squats down. "On ya get."

This time I don't quibble about blokey odours

and it helps that his singlet while old, smells of soap and sunshine. I clamber onto his enormous back as best I can, my legs sticking out to the sides like a three-year-old playing horsey with their dad. I shove the bowl against my chest and hold it in place by leaning into his back. I can't get my arms around his neck properly and make do with hanging onto his shoulders.

I squawk when his hands, together with the cricket bat, slide under my backside like a makeshift seat. I keep quiet after that. I need his support.

To my tired eyes, our journey through the bush has a surreal Edward and Bella quality to it. There is no way I could have kept pace with the speed set by Hemi. The one thing slowing him is my out-spread feet getting caught in creepers or whacking into trees. Eventually, I tuck them back, under the cricket bat.

I have no idea how long we've been going when Hemi suddenly stops as though he's hit a wall of sorts. He removes the cricket bat and squats down so I can slide off his back to the ground. I grab the bat off him, feeling safer in possession of it.

Conscious of the bowl of food still jammed against my chest I bend forward allowing the contents to settle. We stand quietly in the small clearing for four or five minutes before the sound of the others comes from the deathly quiet of the bush.

Ange and Bev are suffering. Their faces are indistinct, but their laboured breathing says it all.

"We've got another five minutes or so before we get there." Hemi's voice is surprisingly low. "We better rest up, eat some more tucker, then we go in."

"But we're staying in the bush, aren't we?" I tap the small bowl against my chest before jabbing it in

Ange and Bev's direction. Even being this close to The Vale is doing weird things to my stomach. No way do I want to face Chalky and revisit the site of my torture and potential hysterectomy again, even if armed with a nice slab of willow.

Horse snorts. "You're safer in there than you are out here." If his ominous tone weren't enough, his staring out into the dark bush convinces me.

Other than the noise generated by the six of us, the bush is on mute. Nothing scurries, nothing squawks, even the leaves are motionless. Hemi joins Horse in staring out into the bush, head cocked to the side, listening intently. A quick jerk of his head and I know he's picked up on what I have. Something I'd prefer to be wrong about.

"We're going in the back way, aren't we?"

He doesn't answer, continuing to stare into the bush, his eyes narrowed as if this will somehow help him to see in the dark. I glue myself to his side, hiding from the malevolent presence lurking nearby.

Likewise, Ange and Bev have crowded next to Horse, Johnno and Piggy, the group taking up far less square footage than a minute earlier.

I find myself mouth-breathing in the technique of childhood games of hide-and-seek to make myself as quiet as possible. The others follow suit, the ensuing hush smothering us with an absence of sound not achievable in nature.

"Screw this, I'm not staying here and dealing with that crazy bitch!" Johnno ditches Piggy into the nearest clump of ferns. "Let's get the hell outta here." He's off up the track at a speed even Hemi will be hard-pressed to match. Ange, Bev and Horse follow suit.

Hemi doesn't need to invite me to climb on his back. I toss the cricket bat in his direction and fling my bowl into the bush. He proves me wrong that he won't keep up with the others, the unseen presence proving an accelerant.

Against Hemi's broad back, my chest is warm, bordering on hot. My back is cold and getting colder. I want to know what's behind us, but there's no way I'm peeling my face away from Hemi's comforting bulk to see what.

*If I jam myself against him, surely this will keep the evil at bay?*

The cold, not content with my skin, penetrates to my very core, settling in my abdomen. A shudder wracks my frame, receiving an instant response from Hemi.

"Na, ya sodding don't!"

He twists violently first to one side, then the other, all without any loss of forward momentum. It as though my guts have been ripped out, leaving me as empty as I'd been before my small bowl of porridge earlier.

The presence is with me again, this time seeping through my lower back, filling my womb with the only life form it will ever see. Trembling overwhelms me, slow to start, escalating until I'm unable to hold on to Hemi's shoulders. I curl in on myself in a futile attempt at protection.

Hemi surges past the others and I'm vaguely aware of him bursting out into the open, the moonlight bright after the dark of the bush. Rather than be in the parking lot, we've crossed a narrow strip of open ground, and are hard up against a building. It's one that errs towards bunker, with no windows breaking its expanse.

Unable to hold on any longer, I slide to the ground in a boneless heap. Rolling onto my side, I curl into a protective ball.

He forcibly pushes me onto my back. Before I can assume the foetal position again, he kisses me.

*No, wait. This isn't a kiss. It's a kiss of life.*

He breathes into me, slowly and surely flooding my body with warmth and strength. The presence in my womb shrinks like a pregnancy in reverse until it disappears with a pop.

Hemi lifts his head, grunts, and awkwardly pats me on the shoulder.

"Bloody hell, get a room you two," mutters Johnno looking down at us before shaking his head and tutting.

Hemi stands and smacks him around the back of the head hard, and Johnno staggers forward a couple of steps.

"You shoulda kept hold of the pig and stayed at the back." Hemi's voice drops even lower when he adds, "Elizabeth had her, ya fucking moron."

*Elizabeth? That thing has a name? And it's female?*

Bev drops to her knees beside me, jamming her machete into the soft ground in the process. Whether this is so she can get closer to me or as a result of pure exhaustion isn't clear, but I'm grateful for her presence all the same. "Are you okay?"

Ange hunkers on the other side, surreptitiously taking my pulse. "How do you feel?"

Until she asks, I haven't given it any thought, content to be free of that awful dark coldness.

"I-I—" I stutter to a halt, unable to voice my automatic response. "I feel incredible." I can't keep the amazement out of my voice; if we didn't have to keep quiet, I'd shout it to the treetops. "Who, or what, the hell is he?" Sitting up, I look at Hemi with it taking longer to make eye contact than it should.

He shakes his head before returning to my side and hunkering down so he can keep his words low. "Nothing mystical or magical about it, just my magnetic personality is all." His broad smile and wiggling of his eyebrows does nothing to lessen the impact of what he's just done.

Ange and Bev help me to my feet. Fully upright and balanced, I twitch my head in Hemi's direction, before raising my eyebrows in a silent version of 'do you believe that tripe he just spouted?'

The two women can neither confirm nor deny, but then they've only just met him as well. He must spot my expression, because he comes clean.

"Okay, fine. If you gotta know, it's something about male energy that sends that crazy bitch packing."

I'm still not sure if he's telling the truth, but for now it's going to have to do. Taking in the solid concrete structure next to us, I'm puzzled. "Where exactly are we?" I know it's not the building Ange, Bev and me had escaped from. "Are we still on the other side of the fence?"

Johnno jerks his head towards the bush. "We're just further around from where you lot crashed into me. Fence only goes so far."

Even tucked around the back of the buildings as we are, it's a good thing we didn't wait until the morning. If we'd exploded out of the bush like we have, we'd surely have had a welcoming committee. A quick peek around the corner reveals the parking lot and gravel driveway. There isn't a sign of life. The question is where exactly are all the militia? I doubt they're far away.

It must be something Ange is also wondering. Her head craned around the corner, she peers intently at the Sleeping Beauty Suites before turning back and whispering, "Should we be sitting out here like this?"

I nod emphatically toward the bush. "I am not going back in there, not with that thing lurking about." Much as I said I'd never step back inside The Vale, right now, it's looking pretty damned safe, by comparison.

I wait to catch Hemi's gaze before speaking. "What the hell is that thing? Elizabeth?" For anything this dark and menacing to have so mundane a name, is as weird as finding out the Devil's first name is Brian, or Donald, or something equally innocuous.

Hemi grunts before he explains Elizabeth Collins was an early pioneer in the area. "Half a dozen of our women were raped and murdered by her husband and his mates, when they were on a bender." He makes sure I'm looking at him before he continues. "Elizabeth got taken out by my ancestors in return."

Well, that explains her reaction to male energy. If she died as retribution for the disgusting behaviour of her long-dead husband, it's no wonder she wants to steer well clear of men, even at an energetic level.

Hemi's expression saddens. "She was pregnant at the time." At my look of horror, he rumbles on. "Hey, I'm not saying what happened was right on either side, I'm just telling ya how it was."

Part of me isn't surprised. Tit-for-tat killings were common in the early days of the colony. However, historical accuracy does nothing to lessen my repulsion over women being raped and murdered. Never mind a pregnant woman having her life, and that of her baby, snatched away brutally.

My hands settle protectively over my lower abdomen. "But, why me ...?" I'm unable to articulate further.

Horse takes up the story. "Because she's gonna have that baby. Doesn't care who hosts it. It's why none of our women come up here. Unless they're older than dirt."

*Great, an evil entity that targets other women. Like men can't handle that on their own.*

It does give me pause, though.

*Does Elizabeth's ghostly examination of my reproductive organs mean I can have kids after all? Could this be why Bev hasn't been bothered? I know Ange has already had kids, but surely she can have more?*

*Is Liz after a pristine and presumably fertile womb, like mine?*

A broad smile covers my face, although this soon falters.

Ange chops at the grass with the small axe, before studying the still eerily quiet Sleeping Beauty Suites. "So, what happens now?"

"We're not doing anything until we've got a plan." Bev's tone has a ring of authority to it, with even Hemi, the alpha male, reluctantly nodding in agreement.

"We need to check the lower buildings first. See if we can find Tee." Bev stands, yanks her machete free from the dirt and hoists it in readiness to strike out. "Damn, I wish I still had my frying pan. I hate sharp things." She looks accusingly at Johnno.

"How the hell was I s'posed to know ya were decking people with it?"

"Is there a kitchen?" says Horse.

Ange points to the third door along with her axe. "In there."

"Back in a mo."

Horse makes short work of the open area. He's not wearing boots, something I hadn't noticed earlier. Did he ditch them somewhere along the way? As new as they likely were, perhaps they were squeaking, or causing blisters? His movements are fluid, silent and blend with the shadows, a Rorschach quality to them. As hackneyed as it sounds, I blink and he's gone.

"Will he be long?" Bev looks at her machete again, as if deciding whether waiting is her best option.

"Nope." Johnno throws himself down next to the building, reclines and supports his head with his hands; making a lie of the assertion his mate will be quick about it.

*Should I be as relaxed as he, Hemi and Horse appear to be?*

I know what we're facing and they don't.

*Perhaps they're supremely confident in their abilities to beat the crap out of anyone we encounter?*

*I hope so.*

I'm mulling this over when I'm startled by a Jamie Oliver non-stick frying pan and a rolling pin being dropped at my feet. I'm pondering the choice when Ange buries her small axe in the dirt and helps herself to the rolling pin. "I'll take this. I don't even like scalpels."

Meantime, Bev grabs the frying pan. "Hmm, it's not cast iron, but if I brain anyone, at least they won't stick." She twirls the large pan by the handle. "And it's easier to swing."

I'm pleased to be still armed with the bat. I was on the cricket team at high school but failed cooking classes miserably and am much more at ease with the heft and shape of the bat.

My weapon of choice is forgotten when Horse drops a bulging plastic bag of bread rolls and a large jar of peanut butter in front of us. I'm ravenous.

The rolls are fresh, and in possession of enough gluten to shut down some inner city suburbs. Combined with the sticky, fatty goodness of the peanut butter, it's ambrosia after all those weeks of nothing but kale and chocolate shakes.

Who cares if the rolls are ripped open and smeared with peanut butter courtesy of a none-too-clean hunting knife? Not yours truly, if the speed with which I devour the first roll is anything to go by. A second follows straightaway, leaving me replete and fuller than I've been in a long time. Before this, hunger was always my constant companion, no matter how much food I threw at it.

"So Bev, what's this plan of yours?" Hemi raises an eyebrow, challenging her to come up with the goods after she quashed his idea of 'smacking some heads together and having some fun'.

Bev waits until she has everyone's attention before outlining a plan that is simple in the extreme. "We find Tee and anyone else still around, and then we get the hell out of here."

Hemi opens his mouth, closes it, then says, "And if we run into any of those murderous pricks? What then?"

It's Ange who answers, not Bev. "Avoid them. Otherwise, we're no better than they are."

Johnno and Hemi roll their eyes; even Horse struggles to maintain a straight face. Having seen the enemy up close, I agree that we should go in with all guns blazing.

After this thought skips across my brain, I twig that none of the guys is in possession of a firearm. What good are knives against what I believe are automatic weapons? Not much in my limited experience of being forced to sit through action movies with David.

I wave to get Horse's attention – I don't want to call out to him. He's standing apart and I wait until he moves closer before speaking. "Apart from kitchen stuff, did you see any guns when you were in there?" Despite Ange shying away from violence, my preference is to be armed to the teeth.

"Yeah, stacks, but we don't need 'em."

Bev's head pops up, and she unclasps the recently acquired frying pan from her chest. "I wouldn't mind one. Stainless steel is okay, but it's better when it's backed up by lead."

"Not for me," says Ange, slapping the rolling pin against the palm of her free hand.

Horse shrugs in response. "Too late, I fucked any I could find."

"I wondered why you took so soddin' long," says Johnno, who's prone again, his head supported by his crossed arms.

Bev shakes her head before glaring at Horse. "We could have used those against them. I suppose you removed the firing pins?"

"Nah, too obvious. Funnier to watch 'em try to shoot us and have the guns blow up their faces."

Hemi and Johnno chortle quietly at this, as does Bev. Not in on the joke, Ange and I look at each other, and then the others, as if hoping for clarification.

"I think he means he's stuffed the barrels on every gun he laid his hands on." Bev looks at Horse and gets a brief nod in response.

"Besides, guns make ya too much of a target," says Hemi. "Knives are quiet. Hell, even frying pans and cricket bats are quieter than guns."

As soon as he says this, it dawns on me that I'll have to hit someone with the piece of willow I'm stroking. I don't know if I've got it in me, unless, that is, I run into Lance. If I do, he's going to be recipient of the first Gray-Nicolls-sponsored castration in the history of the world. There's also a boundary shot with Chalky's name on it. It'd be nice to see her with an expression for once.

Hemi signals our break is done by over-arming the remains of the peanut butter deep into the bush. "Let's go mess 'em up." He doesn't biff the empty plastic bag into the undergrowth as I've expected, he scrunches it up and shoves it deep in the front pocket of his faded jeans.

Gaining my feet, I swing the cricket bat around, getting a sense of its weight, and striking out at imaginary balls and foes alike. It feels good in my hands, and I wonder why I'd given up the game I loved so much all those years ago.

*That's right, David said it wasn't feminine.*

*Perfect! Any baddies I run across, I'll think of David and how I let him screw me over.*

*There'll be no trouble hitting them for a six after this.*

*I might even enjoy it.*

## 22

Progress to the bottom of the property is slow, with Horse, the stealthiest among us, in front. We dash from hiding spot to hiding spot, waiting on a nod from him before moving forward.

These manoeuvres are either pointless or they're spectacularly successful, because we don't run into anyone. Are the guys right and the mercenaries are settled for the night, or lost in the bush? Both options work for me.

Just as conspicuous by her absence is Chalky, with the place a spa version of the *Mary Celeste.*

That is, until we hear furniture-rattling snoring emanating from Tee's room. I don't know whether to be pleased she's okay or angry she's snuggled up, blissfully unaware of the hell that's descended on the place.

Bev's about to open the door when it's apparent there's more than one set of snoring.

In unspoken agreement, we move back down the stairs, skulking off to the side of the building before speaking.

"Must be Lance, fallen asleep 'in' the job," says Bev, before slapping her hand over her mouth.

Whether this is to stop laughter or something more substantial, is anyone's guess.

"Crap! I didn't think of him. But won't he still be out in the bush with the others?" Ange gestures wildly with her rolling pin, narrowly missing Johnno's head. "I was thinking it's the kitchen crew in a food-for-favours kinda deal."

"Wonder if she's gone for the two-for-one offer?" This time there's no mistaking the laughter behind Bev's hand, with Ange and me quietly joining in.

"What if it's Anton?" snorts Bev.

This time Ange and I are powerless to stifle our laughter and not until I've got myself under control, do I answer. "Not gonna happen."

Bev looks from Ange to me and back again. "What do you mean?"

Before we can answer her, Hemi holds up his hand. "They friend or foe?" His voice, while low, is loud in the relative quiet.

Not wanting to further disrupt the stillness of the night, I answer with a shrug. He looks to Bev and Ange next, and they answer likewise. Even with the three of us discussing it whenever Tee wasn't around, we hadn't come to any conclusions.

We're collectively inching our way around to the front of the building when I see Horse step through the now-open door. I hadn't even seen him move, let alone heard the door unlatching.

The guy is more spectral than equine in his movements. He exits without a murmur from those in the room. He holds up three fingers before holding his flattened hand at waist height and bouncing it up and down.

*So it is the kitchen twins.*

"They're on the staff here," I whisper, before

looking towards the top of the property. "Not sure if they're in on everything else. I never spotted them up there." I calm my mind to think back, detached, the better to avoid bad memories. "Hang on, they must know about it, because one of them drugged the blasted coffee Chalky sucked me in with."

Horse nips back inside the room as quickly and quietly as he'd reappeared, with Hemi and Johnno close behind. I want to go in too, to assuage any fears Tee will have on waking to find three scary-looking men crowded around her bed. I'm miming this to Bev and Ange when the guys return.

Hemi and Johnno have a kitchen twin apiece, but the captives aren't offering up any protests; they're out cold. At least I hope they're out cold, and not on their way to simply being cold.

Hemi leans over as he passes with his quarry safely tucked under one meaty arm. "They'll be fine. Just gonna tie them up somewhere less obvious."

I take this at face value until Johnno's crow of "Yeah, right."

The kitchen twins on the way to their fate, I hustle into Tee's room to wake her so we can get the hell out of here. Bev and Ange are with me, shutting the door in Horse's face. If Tee is naked as I suspect, she won't want an audience – then again, there's no telling where Tee is concerned. If she'll screw that pair of weasels, there's no gauging what she'll stoop to.

We start by whispering her name but her snoring merely breaks its rhythm before settling down again. A gentle prod results in more of the same.

After checking all the curtains are pulled tight, we turn on the bedside lamp.

Ange presses a couple of fingers tight into the carotid artery in Tee's neck, ferreting around for a pulse. Not an easy task, thanks to the rolls of fat that have accumulated over the years. "She's gotta be drugged."

I know she's managed to locate a pulse when she angles the bedside clock and her lips move in silent counting. She takes her hand away and pats Tee on the shoulder before looking up. "It's fast, but that's to be expected, given her overall health."

Ange looking after Tee, I take time to open the wardrobe door, and find what I'm after. Tee's supply of clean Vale uniforms is stacked there and helping myself to a top and pants, I change quickly. They're too big, but they're better than running around covered in porridge and pork fat. The black uniform will also help me to blend into the night.

The other thing I notice at the bottom of the wardrobe is a couple of pairs of sneakers. Helping myself to a pair, I'm relieved to find they fit reasonably well. Tee has awfully small feet for such a large woman.

I'm rolling up the waistband of the pants so they don't fall down, when I see Bev pick up the jug of water off the dresser. I'm surprised when she doesn't grab the upside-down glass next to it.

*Don't tell me she's going to drink straight from the jug?*

None the clearer, I'm as astonished as Ange when Bev marches across the room and upends it over Tee's head.

It doesn't work, other than to modify the snoring to a muted gurgling.

"Geez, Bev, a glass would have done." Ange turns Tee's head to the side, and I'm alarmed to see water trickling out of the unconscious woman's mouth. "Any more and I'd have had to give her mouth-to-mouth."

"What the hell have they given her?" The water having failed, Bev puts the empty jug on the bedside table so she can give Tee a head-loosening shake. "A bloody horse tranquilliser?" She shakes Tee even harder, to no avail.

"Guys, we have to leave her here." Much as I want to save Tee, the longer we muck around, the more likely it is we'll be discovered. "We can't move her when she's doped to the eyeballs like this. We need to hide her."

Both Ange and Bev look at the plainly furnished room and then at me as though I've misplaced my marbles.

"Some of the best hiding places I had when I was a kid were those that were so obvious, people didn't think to look. If we roll her off the side of the bed, we can jam her between the bed and the wall. Flip the blankets over the top of her, it'll look like she's climbed out of bed and left it like that."

Bev looks at me and then down the side of the bed, gauging if Tee will even fit. Obviously deciding she can, Ange then nods at my rough-and-ready plan like a small dog on the parcel shelf of a 1960s sedan.

"She'll need to be on her side given how heavily she's sedated," says Ange. "Plus it'll stop her bloody snoring."

Tee as safe as we can make her, we leave her huddled under the folded-back blankets. Quietly pulling the door shut, I see Horse is no longer outside. Either he's morphed back into the bush or gone to join Johnno and Hemi at the top facility.

"Are you coming?" Ange waits for me on the bottom step. Bev is already a good way along the path.

"Not yet." If I can save myself the long walk into town, I will.

"Where are you off to?" Bev doesn't bother lowering her voice, eliciting a *shh* from Ange, that's even louder.

"If my bag's still in my room, I can get my spare phone."

Thankfully it isn't too far from Tee's. Especially so with us cutting cross-country, like something out of a *Pink Panther* movie. We're lucky we don't encounter anyone on our way, although we do hear squealing and grunting from the general direction of the cliff. This necessitates shaking my head to clear it of images of the wild pigs making a meal out of our enemy.

Oh, the disappointment when on opening the door I find my suitcase isn't there. More than that, there isn't any sign of me at all. I've been wiped off the face of the earth and the space given the full Mafia crime-scene treatment. I doubt I'd find any trace of myself, even armed with Luminol and a UV light.

Oh, the horror. Never mind the high-end luggage and the phone, there are two family-sized blocks of best quality dark chocolate MIA.

"What the hell's got you all riled?" Bev plays casual observer from her spot in the doorway.

"She muttered something about her phone." Ange pauses before grabbing me by my shoulders and spinning me in her direction. "What did you just say about chocolate?"

I nod emphatically, "Two bars. King size. Seventy percent." I twist free of her hold and continue searching. If ever I needed a hit of sugar and cocoa, it's now.

"Chocolate? Well, why didn't you say?" Bev storms into the room and proceeds to open and close every drawer and cupboard I've just searched – desperation blinding her to reality.

She's squinting into the dark of the bathroom, eyeing up the cabinet. She's even taken a step when I grab her by the scruff of her Vale top, yanking her backwards. "They're not here! They were hidden in the bottom of my suitcase." I wait for a beat. "There's also a chance the beam that activates the light triggers an alarm."

This more than me having a stranglehold on her top, rocks Bev back on her heels. "Those sneaky arseholes. I always thought the fan in my bathroom sounded too much like a zoom lens."

"Hah, yeah, right. As if anyone would be sick enough to pay to watch us using the bathroom." I shake my head to clear it of thoughts of what anyone spying on me in the bathroom would have seen. "No, it'll be because they wanted to see if we dumped that doped tea of theirs."

Bev tilts her head to the side before responding. "You sure about that, M?"

*Surely she can't be serious? How messed up would you have to be to pay to see people going ones or twos, or giving themselves an enema?*

I'm giving thought to the target market when Ange's, "I bet I know where we can find your bag," harnesses Bev's and my full attention.

"When we were scouting around up the top, I noticed a rubbish skip through a back window. They could have put your stuff in there."

*Damn it.*

I didn't want to go anywhere near that part of the complex, preferring to leave the dirty work to the guys. If I had my way, I'd be driving the Hummer down the road now, at speed and to hell with the paintwork. Shame the vehicle hadn't been in the small car park behind the Sleeping Beauty Suites.

"Come on," says Bev, "If we can find the phone, we can call for help."

"And if we find the phone, we find the chocolate," says Ange, a goofy expression dumbing down her features.

About halfway to the scene of my torture, I come to my senses. "What about the tofu munchers? Are they okay?"

"Checked out a few days back," says Bev, over her shoulder.

"Yeah, there for the afternoon yoga session, but didn't make it to dinner that night," adds Ange.

Bev stops without warning and Ange cannons into her, and I thump into Ange. "Remember, Chalky told us they were taking part in some meditation marathon."

"Crap." Ange swings around and retraces her steps, with Bev and me in hot pursuit.

There'll be no argument from me on this change of direction. Even if the tofu munchers were less than friendly, there's no way I'm not checking with the others. And heading away from the Sleeping Beauty Suites, rather than towards them, is a bonus.

## 23

It does indeed look like the mute vegans, the Megans, have checked out. That is until we get to the fourth room.

This sits in a duplex with the third, where I'm compelled me to get down on my hands and knees and check under the bed. Do I expect to find one of them hiding there? No. The bed is low to the floor so that skinny though they are, they still couldn't fit.

I do find contraband, flying in the face of my impression the Megans were holier than thou. Who'd have thought Vegan-friendly seaweed rice crackers would taste so good. Not us, but following a tentative nibble, we polish off the pack in no time.

This leaves one more room to check.

I turn the handle and push against it. "Damn, I think it's locked." I turn the handle the other way, but it still doesn't budge. It would appear Chalky can lock doors when it suits her.

"Give me a go." Bev muscles in next to me, with her superior strength, but it does no good.

"Guys," says Ange, crouched next to us and giving it her best shot to look under the door, "there's someone moving around inside."

I'm wondering what to do when Bev drops to her hands and knees next to Ange. She stuffs a hoarse "We're here to help," under the door like more contraband and is rewarded with a quiet reply. "We'll get you out in a jiffy," replies Bev through the gap, before scrambling to her feet. "They've locked her in there. We'll have to break the window."

Ange looks through the window, her face illuminated by the occupant opening the curtains. "Won't that be awfully loud?"

Bev is no longer next to me to ask how we're meant to proceed quietly. She isn't gone for long. Returning from the room next door, she's got a couple of pillows tucked under one arm and is carrying the drawer from the beside-table like a hard-sided suitcase.

"If you hold the pillows up against the glass, I'll smash it with the drawer."

It's a rough-and-ready plan, but it should work. All going well, the pillows will muffle the sounds of smashing glass and keep it from flying in our direction in the process. I get right up to the glass and explain to the captive what we're about to do. Her lips move in response, but I can't hear a thing. Either I've gone deaf, or she truly is mute.

Down on my hands and knees, I whisper hurried instructions under the door. Back on my feet, I'm reassured she's got the gist of it when she yanks the curtains closed as a barrier to glass flying into the room.

"Ready?" Bev stands a little back, drawer at the ready. Carrying it by the handle makes her look like a middle manager at a corporate retreat, and I have to stifle my laughter.

Ange and I push the pillows together, keeping

our hands well clear of the imaginary target dead centre of the square of Eiderdown and Egyptian cotton. Turning my head to the side to protect my face, I nod my readiness. Ange must have done the same, because next thing I know the glass is juddering and jarring under my hands. Knowing how strong Bev is, this surprises me.

Bev smacks the window even harder.

The glass doesn't budge.

"Screw this." Bev sends the drawer into the bushes at the side of the unit and grabs one of the chairs from the wrought-iron patio set, common to all the verandas. Hefting its weight to check its suitability, her nod alerts us she's ready for a second attempt.

There is no way the pillows will stop the racket this will make, and to hell with standing this close to all the action. In the world of Bed, Bath & Beyond, I'm opting for the third option, standing well clear of any potential shards of glass.

The safest place on offer is the room we've just searched and so I retreat with Ange, waiting for all hell to break loose outside. The unmistakable sound of heavy-duty patio furniture hitting even heavier-duty glass disappoints us when the large crash isn't followed by a tinkling of glass.

"You have got to be bloody kidding me?" Bev follows this with several quick breaths before we hear another resounding crash. Again, the delicate sounds of tinkling glass fails to ring out.

Stepping out onto the front veranda, I'm astounded to see the glass still holds. And this despite large patches of white where the chair has connected.

Bev stands to one side and using the chair in the

same way as she would a golf club, she takes another mighty swing at the window. It does no good. "Damn. This could take a while."

Half a dozen more of these and she's puffing alarmingly. Ange takes over, flaunting past tennis lessons.

"Ladies, stand back." I take a few practice swings with the cricket bat, imagining balls being fired at me by the captain of our first fifteen at school. That girl bowled with the best of them and even went on to be part of an under-16 team to take on Australia.

If the window hadn't been softened up by the other two, I hate to think what damage I would have done to my shoulder.

*The glass must surely be bulletproof.*

The jar to my body is bruising, forcing me to slow down with subsequent whacks.

It takes the combined efforts of the three of us to make a hole large enough for the vegan to clamber through. That she hugs each of us in turn is something of a surprise. All we've ever received from her and her mates are judgemental scowls.

"I thought you were them for a start. Coming for me."

"Where are the others?" I've got a fair idea, but it always pays to check.

"I don't know. Weird sounds coming from Gemma's room woke me late last night, and then a man's voice. He sounded angry, so I got up to see if she was okay, but my door was locked. When I opened the curtains, I saw them carrying her away."

The woman's next words catch in her throat and she gulps deeply before continuing. "She was limp, unconscious." A sob erupts and she's unable to continue with this thread. Eventually she adds, "There's been nothing since."

Ange, who's shoved her head through the gap, backs up and straightens. "You need to get out of here. Is there anything you need to take with you?"

"No. No, they took everything I own after the first week here. Said it was to purify my space."

"Arseholes," mutters Bev from beside me.

"Are you capable of walking out of here?" The woman looks to be in reasonably good shape, but this isn't something to take as a given. Just because you can pretzel yourself into all sorts of positions during a yoga class, doesn't mean you're fit. And it sure as hell doesn't mean you're capable of the very long walk down the hill to civilisation.

"If it means getting help for my friends, there's nothing I won't do." True to her word, she sits on the slightly worse-for-wear wrought-iron seat and tightens the laces on her running shoes. Standing, she zips up the front of her Vale-issue hoodie and stretches in preparation.

Before she can start out, Bev puts a hand on her shoulder. "You'll need to avoid the front gate when you leave. Even if there aren't any guards around, it could be alarmed."

Ange chimes in next. "Sneak into the bush. Dig under the fence. Exit down the road a bit. You should be okay."

Normally, I'd agree with this course of action. Now that I know what, or rather who, is lurking in the bush, I'm not so sure. "Probably best if you get out of the bush as soon as you can. If you run in the middle of the road, there'll be less chance of, ah, tripping."

"You'd better pace yourself," says Ange. "Last thing you want to do is pull something."

"Yes, slow and steady will be your best bet," adds Bev.

"It'll be good to stretch my legs and get back to my training."

"Training?" Maybe my impression that she's whippet-fit is on the money.

"I average three or four marathons a year. The trip into town will be nothing."

And with that she's off, the dark embracing her quickly, thanks to her all-black Vale ensemble. Soon, even the flashes from the reflective tape on her running shoes are lost to the night.

The Megan safely on her way to town, we nip back into the adjoining room and grab a drink from the jug on the dresser. The bed looks incredibly inviting, not having as much sleep as I'd like over the past two days.

While tempting, what was it they said about resting when you were dead? Given how close I've been to this state recently, even closing my eyes, albeit briefly, has flashbacks threatening to claim me.

As ready as we'll ever be, we assemble on the front veranda. "So let's get that suitcase of yours, shall we?" Ange looks at me expectantly.

Bev is also looking at me.

*What? They expect me to decide? Do I want the responsibility for all of us?*

I'm not even sure I like the responsibility of looking out for myself; it's easier to hand this over to others, courtesy of apathy.

"I guess we should check Chalky's office first." It doesn't take a couch and a chat with a counsellor to know why I'm opting for this. Anything is better than going within a bull's roar of the Sleeping Beauty Suites.

"Good idea. I'd like to get my handbag back if I can," says Ange.

Bev nods, and I find myself aping her action. It would be good to get hold of my pre-paid dummy phone, although chances of the battery having lasted this long are slim. Definitely worth a shot, though.

Skirting around the copse of shrubs and palms that back the administration building, we come up short.

*If the lights are on, then surely the cold-hearted bitch is in there, pawing through our handbags like a fat spider?*

My finger to my lips for quiet, I sneak up next to the portable structure until I'm right under the window by the sliding glass door.

Easing up on tiptoes and craning my head, I get an ear as close to the opening as I can. It's pointless; I can't hear a thing over the cicadas. Whether this is because Chalky isn't moving around or that I can't hear her moving around is up for debate. It's fifty-fifty.

Dropping back down, I turn to the others and shrug.

Bev jerks her head in the direction of the sliding door, backing this up by pointing at it with the lightweight frying pan.

Both sets of eyes widen and they melt back into the bushes. We have company. I do some melting of my own, first down onto my hands and knees, then under the hut as quietly, and efficiently, as I can. There'd better not be any weta – a New Zealand native akin to a grasshopper on steroids – under here. Even armed with the cricket bat, if I spot one of those, I won't stay hidden for long.

The outside lights flare into life, turning the gravel area out front into an arena of sorts. It also makes my hiding spot as good as useless. Throwing any caution about spiders and their mates to the winds, I slide the cricket bat along and under the steps and shuffle in after it.

Neatly tucked in behind the wide, wooden treads, I'm invisible to anyone not actively looking for me. It will have to do; the hut sits on a gentle rise, which means there's no escape out the back way, at least not without an excavator.

Two pairs of feet land heavily on the step right in front of my face and a squawk of alarm breaks free. It wasn't loud, but definitely audible. Dropping my body, I cover the pale wood of the cricket bat and face-plant the dirt in hopes my dark hair and black Vale uniform will blend into the gloom under the hut. My breathing is so shallow, as to be virtually non-existent. The loudest thing is my heartbeat, hammering away in my ears and threatening to deafen me.

One of the pair is Chalky, identifiable by those clunky white ankle boots of hers. As to who's with her, only time will tell.

I wait.

They wait.

"Musta been a pig."

*Lance!? Damn, if he's back, does that mean the other men have also returned to the compound?*

"Either that, or a possum." My scalp pings with a

weird mix of fear at being so close to him and relief he's unaware of my presence. Lance's voice makes my skin crawl far more than any weta could manage. I'm about to lift my head when something stops me. Maybe it's because they haven't moved since Lance spoke? I sink back down.

Lance jumps up and down on the stairs right above my head and I'm glad I'd stayed put. As it is, the dirt and detritus raining down on me smother my shout of alarm.

My stifled scream, when an enormous possum thunders past me and out into the night, will have been audible.

I don't think I've ever been so close to a shotgun going off, either.

"Dammit, missed the little fucker."

"There'll be more, darling."

*Darling? Chalky and Lance?*

The unmistakable sound of kissing follows.

I don't bother to take control of the shudder that traverses my frame. *As if anyone would put their mouth near that man, voluntarily. First chance I get, I'm rearranging his gonads. Watch the nasty bitch try to ride him then.*

"Did you and the men find any trace of our escapees in the bush?"

"Yeah, but that's all."

"But they have their instructions, right?"

"Yep, stick to the bush. Kill the lot of them. Leave their stinking carcasses for the pigs."

"Excellent. We've come too far for them to mess things up now."

The stairs creak under their combined weight as they walk down them, stopping briefly at the bottom to swap some more spit. As if this wasn't disgusting enough, Chalky fumbles with the front of Lance's jeans. I'm closing my eyes to block out this travesty when she speaks.

"Come now Lance, we'll need to get you harder than this to satisfy the client's request."

I'm still reeling at Chalky being the chief fluffer when they start up the boardwalk in the direction of the Sleeping Beauty Suites. A quick shufti at them, arm in arm, endorses that they're the ugliest 'beast with two backs' you've ever laid eyes on.

As soon as I'm confident they've truly gone, I throw my cricket bat out into the open and wriggle after it. Ange and Bev join me before I have a chance to get to my feet.

## 24

Inside the admin building, my spine crawls as I think about signing my life away with that damned contract. Everything looks as it did that morning, but with my new knowledge, it takes on a sinister air.

One thing that is the same as on the morning of my check-in is my Hermès handbag sitting on the credenza behind Chalky's desk. I close my eyes to picture when she'd drugged me.

*Nope, my bag wasn't there then. I'd sure as heck have said something if it was.*

Putting my cricket bat on her desk, I reclaim my handbag, worried to find it's a lot lighter than when I handed it over.

I'm relieved, therefore, to see my wallet is still in there. I open it, expecting to find it empty. It isn't, exactly. Instead the botoxed, expressionless tart stares back at me from my own blasted driving licence.

My hand stills before I unzip the internal pocket and shove my hand deep inside. Sure enough, when I open my passport, her face is next to my details.

*That bitch! She's making use of my identity and, no doubt, my bank balance.*

I'm unaware of muttering under my breath until Bev speaks. "What's got you so riled?" She doesn't look in my direction; she's too busy for that. Having dumped her frying pan on one of the visitor's chairs, she's pressing each wall panel at the end of the small room in turn. She's thorough, pushing once on each corner and again in the middle.

I stop searching my handbag for anything else with Chalky's name or mugshot on it to answer her. "That skinny old cow has been using my bag, and even my freaking identity." I wait for Bev to look in my direction, but her concentration on the wall panels is laser-like. "Ah, what are you hoping to find over there? It's the end wall."

"I noticed when we were hiding in the bushes that the windows don't go right to the corner, and yet they do in here. That means there's a gap behind this wall."

Ange, who's next to me, slams her rolling pin down on the credenza, doing a fair amount of damage. While she might be squeamish about hurting people, there appears to be no holding her back when it comes to furniture. Kneeling in front of Chalky's desk, she opens the top left-hand drawer and riffles through the contents.

I'd join them in their searches, but I'm too intent on checking my handbag to see what else Chalky's appropriated. Frustrated, I upend the contents onto the glass-topped desk, making a hell of a racket and eliciting a string of profanities from both Ange and Bev. Flicking through the pile of crap, I note everything is here, except my dummy, but still perfectly working, mobile phone.

*Damn!*

After gutting my wallet of all her paperwork, I stuff everything of mine back in the handbag.

Then I have second thoughts.

*What if some of these are her real documents and not just mine reimagined?*

Just in case, I scoop it all up and shove it in the side pocket of my bag, snapping the magnetic flap down securely.

"Bloody Norah, she must be trying to quit smoking or something." Ange pulls bag after bag of gummy bears from the second drawer down, piling them haphazardly on the desk.

She repeats the process with the third drawer and then the three on the other side until there's a veritable bear mountain in the middle of the desk. Sitting back on her heels, she stares contemplatively at them.

She rips open a bag and stuffs a couple of bears into her mouth, chewing contentedly while reading the back of the pack. "Sugar-free? Hah! I just got why she's so fricking skinny."

I also help myself to a couple. "Calories burned from all the chewing?" I say around the bears I'm beating into submission.

Ange stops chewing. "No. If you eat enough of these, it has a laxative effect. Like blow the back out your underpants." After tipping half a dozen onto the desk top, she closes the pack tight. As if to stop herself from being tempted, she grabs Chalky's stapler from the top drawer and staples it shut. "You should read some of the reviews online about this stuff. They're hysterical. Gross, but hysterical."

Spinning on her knees, she crawls over to the

credenza and slides the right-hand panel back. "Perfect."

She turns back and I see what is so perfect. It's a hideous orange carryall that wouldn't have been out of place in the seventies. On the plus side, it's large, and easily holds all the bags of gummy bears. Not too big, not too small, just right.

Bev stops pressing and prodding the back wall. "Seriously, you're nicking that evil bitch's gummy bears?"

"Hell, yes, I am. I want that cow as backed up as a 93-year-old who's been subsisting for months on a diet of overcooked meat!"

Ange's expression when she zips the bag closed is both delighted and grim in turn. I suspect her experience as a nurse means she knows precisely how backed up this truly is.

My evil thoughts of a constipated Chalky are interrupted by a loud click that's drowned out by Bev's yell of discovery. She swings the panel out into the room and we all crowd around for a better look.

We can't see a damned thing, so dark is the interior. Bev reaches inside the doorway and with an efficient slide up and down, finds the light switch.

Despite trying, there's no way we can all fit through the doorway at the same time. Bev, having discovered the room, is given first access, followed by Ange and then me. All three of us in there, it's best described as cosy. While the room measures about three metres square, with shelving lining every wall, the free space in the middle is half that.

The khaki paint coating every surface says The Vale's admin block has been on-site for a long time. That it was on site when the army was in residence is not in doubt. Silence descends on us like a smothering blanket as the consequences of what we see dawns.

I retrieve a gorgeous Givenchy handbag from the shelf in front of me. "There must be dozens of them."

"Yeah, and I doubt she's running a high-end leather goods importing business outta here." Bev picks up a bright yellow Louis Vuitton tote bag from the bottom shelf.

From the way it hangs from her hand, it's not empty.

"This is so much bigger than we thought." Ange turns to take in all the shelves, and keeps on turning, slowly, scanning them a second time. "So many women." She stills for a moment before shaking her head. "It doesn't make sense." Before Bev or I can ask what, she continues. "The number of bags in here is way out of whack with the bone pile."

Bev momentarily stops rummaging through the piles of handbags. "Too many, or not enough?"

"Too many. Far too many."

I stare absently at the shelves chock full of designer leatherwear. "So, more bodies to find?"

Ange nods; the tear trickling down her left cheek changes course. "A heap more."

Bev grabs a battered black leather handbag off a shelf on the right and hugs it tightly. "Here's mine!"

Soon after, Ange finds hers. It's white, but looks closer to pleather than leather.

*How was she planning to pay The Vale's exorbitant fees when it came time to check out?*

Then I have an *Aha!* moment. There won't be a check out in any fiscal sense. None of us will pay for our stay, other than courtesy of the counselling fees. Even if people noticed us missing, with all the cloak and dagger around check-in, there isn't a chance anyone could track us. We'd disappear without a trace, other than showing up when the sick wankers who'd forked out for the torture were replaying downloads.

*Dammit, if, no make that when, I get out of here, I'm going to throttle Lorraine for recommending this place.*

The grinding of my teeth rouses me from my nefarious thoughts.

*No, even she's not that nasty.*

It's more likely that the person she knew who'd been here was firmly in the celebrity camp. Hadn't they asked her to keep it quiet?

*Idiots if they thought that was happening with Lorraine involved.*

Hampered by their own handbags, they toss them into Chalky's office before we make short work of riffling through all the bags. We start with the middle shelf as the easiest to reach. Despite checking through a good fifty handbags between us, we don't come across a single mobile phone, android or otherwise.

Ange drops the handbag she's just searched back on the shelf in disgust. "Bitch probably has Lance flog them off at the local pub."

At first, I think it's my imagination. Dropping to my knees confirms it. "Do you feel that?"

Ange and Bev join me on the ground.

"Yep, there's definitely a breeze." Bev skims her hands over the boards in front of us.

"Guys," says Ange, as though explaining to newbie builders, "the building's up on stilts, of course there's a breeze."

"But this is a converted shipping container. So," I point down for emphasis, "There shouldn't be any gaps in the floorboards like this, and—"

"And the damned building is metal. There shouldn't be any gaps at all," Bev finishes for me at the same time as finding a ring-pull she'd been kneeling on.

I scramble away from a trapdoor that is now as plain as day and wait while she struggles to lift the slab of wood. There's nothing but black beyond.

Bev stares at it unseeing for a moment before speaking. "Hmm, this must have been how they got you from here up to the Sleeping Beauty Suites without us spotting you."

She's got a point, with part of me being very glad I'd been out cold at the time. The yawning hole at our feet gives me the heebies. I'm shuddering from that, when a bone-chilling cold oozes out of the depths before swirling around my ankles.

Scrambling to my feet, I jam myself hard up against the shelves, all while screaming, "Close it! Close it!"

## 25

I'm relieved Bev doesn't ask for an explanation. Without pause, she throws her considerable weight on the trapdoor, and while it starts to shut, she can't close it completely. Despite not being able to see why, I know what's behind it, or rather, who.

"It's her. It's Elizabeth Collins." Just saying the entity's name, I tremble uncontrollably, my hands crisscrossed protectively over my tummy. Much as I'd love a baby, I sure as hell don't want hers.

Ange scoots back, indicating she's also picked up on the other-worldly cold. She's lucky she's not frozen by it as I am. Leaning back into the office, she grabs the orange holdall of gummies off Chalky's desk. Poised and ready, the next time Elizabeth lifts the trapdoor, Ange shoves the bag through the gap.

I don't know if the laxative properties of the sugar-free sweets will stop Elizabeth in her quest to find a host for her ghost baby, but it works. The trapdoor slams down with a thundering crash.

The problem is, other than leaving Bev where she is, there is no way to keep it shut.

She gets to her feet, super careful to stay on the

side of the trapdoor away from the hinges. "Ladies, let's get a big ol' pile of handbags going."

Three seconds elapse before my synapses connect. Ange has no such problem and snatches handbags off the shelves, dumping them on top of the trapdoor. Bev gets those within arm's reach and drops them by her feet as she's bounced up and down.

The seeping cold held at bay, I'm able to help, thankful to find the majority of handbags on my side of the room are as over-stuffed as mine usually was. From the weight of some of them, they must be crammed with enough make-up to make a pig look attractive.

The middle of the floor is piled high with handbags before Bev is free to move.

"You smell that?" Bev sniffs the air frantically, giving her more than a passing resemblance to the chick in the movie *Polyester*.

Ange joins in, nodding in agreement.

I inhale deeply through my nose. "It's sweet, whatever it is."

"Not from sugar, it isn't." Ange's answer is garbled thanks to the gummy bear she's chewing on. A quick look at the desktop shows there are only a couple left.

Bev jerks her head towards Chalky's office. "Should we still be standing here, if the mother from hell has gobbled the lot?"

We get out as fast as we can, but we're not fast enough; the odour in the room changes from sugary to something altogether more organic. In the flare of a nostril, we're gagging.

"Looks like we're about to have our own gummy bear challenge," says Ange, before dry retching. I have no idea what she's talking about, but if we ever get out of here, I'm for sure Googling it.

Bev's shoves the panel shut, but it's too late. A stream of black shoots up through any gaps in the storeroom floor. It splatters the pile of handbags, the ceiling and Bev in turn. From the back, she looks fine, but when she turns, it's a different story.

"Bloody hell! It's like being on the geriatric ward all over again." Ange's comment is muffled because she has a hand firmly clasped across her mouth and nose.

The stink rolling off Bev in waves demands I do the same.

Bev doesn't speak. The whites of her eyes are all that's visible on her face; if she speaks, she'll get a mouthful.

"Chalky's room is the closest." Ange is already next to the door marked PRIVATE on the other side of Reception. She tries opening the door, but it doesn't budge.

"Stand back, I've got this." I don't bother trying to break the locking mechanism. greater satisfaction being gained by smashing through the paper-thin wall next to the door with my trusty cricket bat.

*Damn, I needed that.*

Bev follows me through the gap, not slowing until she's under the shower. She doesn't even wait for it to warm up. I can't say I blame her.

The water heating up does nothing to stop her shivering.

Leaving her to rinse off as best she can, Ange and I have a quick look around Chalky's room.

"Why on earth does she need a walk-in wardrobe? All she ever wears is those butt-ugly white shift dresses."

At this comment from Ange, I look up from where I'm riffling through the drawer in Chalky's bedside table. Apart from yet more gummy bears, there isn't anything else.

She's standing stock-still in front of the still closed wardrobe door. "Aren't you going to open it?"

Ange turns briefly in my direction. "No handle."

Grabbing my cricket bat off the end of the bed, I'm getting ready to swing it, when I realise the reason there's no handle is because it's a pocket door. Placing my palm flat against the wood, I slide it to the side.

Surprise, surprise, there isn't a white shift dress in sight. Instead, we're facing a bank of monitors and more switches and dials than would be required to run the Enterprise.

I stand shoulder-to-shoulder with Ange as we stare at the rows of small screens. She stabs her finger pointedly at the second screen in, on the middle row. "Damn it, that's my bathroom. See that chipped tile in the bottom of my shower?"

Next to this screen, I find a low-level shot of my bathroom, distinguishable by the small scratch on the bottom of the vanity door. There's only one reason they'd want a camera pointing in this direction.

*Sheesh, butt-hole-cam anyone?*

I drop into the office chair in front of the main control board. "Who on earth would pay to watch that?"

Ange sits on the nearest flat surface, not caring she's atop the keyboard that must be used to control things. While the first two rows of monitors show bathrooms, the bottom row shows the yoga studio,

Chalky's office and a few other rooms I'm unfamiliar with.

I experiment with turning a large dial on the right of the control board, rewarded with the low-level camera in my bathroom, zooming in for a close up. The focus is now such that any connoisseurs of arseholes paying for a looksee would be cross-eyed.

*Stuffed if I'll let that bitch use this set up to track our movements from here.* Jumping to my feet, I grab my cricket bat from beside the door. "Stand back, Ange. I'll take care of this lot."

"I'll go check on Bev."

With her safely out of the way, I make short work of smashing every screen, button and speaker in the control room. I even take out a few bits-and-pieces that do who knows what. My main aim is to ruin everything I can.

Never again will a bell ring when it's time for me to do number ones, and especially not number twos. Only when I've 'modified' everything to my liking do I re-join Ange and Bev.

The small bathroom is oppressively hot and full of steam. Despite this, Bev is still shivering.

*Not good. Not good at all.*

"We need to find Hemi, and fast. Bev, you stay under the hot water, we'll be back soon."

"I am not staying here on my own." Bev wrenches the shower off violently and the mixer comes free in her hand. She's still holding it when she steps dripping from the glass cubicle.

I take it gently from her hand, careful not to touch her, and drop it on the bathroom floor. "At least let's stop by Tee's room and get you dry clothes."

She nods shakily.

We grab our handbags and weapons and escort her to Tee's room. It's something that takes longer than it should with us having to scramble from hiding spot to hiding spot. I don't care that the majority of armed men are staked out in the bush; Lance might have finished and be back here somewhere. Even thinking about what his performance might have involved has me shaking in disgust.

On arrival at our friend's room, I smash all the cameras and motion sensors I can find. Something made easy now that I know what I'm looking for. Bev is then left to strip off and change in the bathroom.

While she's doing that, Ange and I check Tee is okay down the side of her bed. One plus with her current position is that it's stopped her snoring, lowering the odds of her being discovered.

We're flipping the blankets back over her when Bev joins us, and even though covered in several layers, she's still shivering.

"Are you sure you're okay walking?" Ange has her fingers on Bev's pulse, and I don't need to be a nurse to know Bev's is running fast. The woman is all but vibrating. Or is she trembling so hard, it looks that way?

A gravelly, "I said I was okay," sneaks out between her tightly clenched teeth.

"You don't look okay." This is an understatement; she looks like death before it was shoved in the microwave for a minute, on full.

There's no missing that Elizabeth has invaded her body, although the reason is lost on me.

*Didn't Bev say she couldn't have kids? If so, then why is Elizabeth claiming her as a host?*

*Dammit, why does Hemi have to be so far from where we are now?*

We've just made it down the front steps of Tee's room when the man himself marches around the side of the building and my heart does its best to burst through my chest. For a moment, I thought it was one of the mercenaries rather than the answer to my silent entreaty.

"Have you been back in the bush?" he says without slowing until he's in front of Bev.

"No!" Ange and I say in unison. Bev remains mute.

"Then how'd ya explain this?" Without waiting for an answer, he slams his hand hard against Bev's chest. There's nothing sexual about it. There's also nothing sexual about the scream that flies out of her wide-open mouth.

It has more of a birthing-suite quality to it. Fascinated and horrified in turn, I watch as black seeps out of Bev's skin before it drifts up to coalesce into human form. Indistinct as the apparition is, the period clothing and pregnant belly firmly identify the entity as the long-dead Elizabeth Collins.

Ousted from her most recent host, she looks around; her dead glare connecting with my startled gaze. She floats in my direction until Hemi blocks her path, both shielding me and obstructing my view.

There's no chance she'll take me by surprise again. I peer around Hemi's bulk, making damn sure I remain in his protective male aura. I'm shocked to see the woman's form is more distinct than just a moment ago. She's drawing energy from somewhere; I'm just glad it's not from me.

Her way blocked, she stops her advance, drifting

from side to side, seeking a way around him. Hemi's not having it, even going so far as to hold his arms out wide, increasing his perceived size.

Foiled, Elizabeth's ghastly visage stills, her gaze locked with mine. And when I drop my own to avoid hers, I'm faced with the gaping wound that mars her belly, something that was indistinct earlier.

Focussing, I see small hands grip the edges of the wound. Tiny fingers open and close, searching for comfort and a life outside that of Elizabeth's dead womb.

As disturbing as this is, it's nothing compared with the smile the woman bestows on me before streaking across the expanse of open ground and into the surrounding bush. It spoke of promises yet to be fulfilled by me.

I stare open-mouthed at the bush, even taking a few steps in that direction. I'm unable to rid myself of what I've just seen. Eventually, though, I turn to face Hemi. "Hell, did you see that?" I know he did; his face a mask of horror that I'm sure matches my own.

"See what?" says Ange, turning on the spot, looking anywhere and everywhere.

She didn't see what Hemi and I did. She's far too relaxed for that. "Nothing. I just need sleep. I'm seeing things."

I don't breathe out until she nods her acceptance of my lame excuse, which is good as I wouldn't know where to begin with the real deal. It might also be the less Ange knows about Elizabeth's true form, the better.

Turning away from her to check on Bev, I'm relieved to see she's with us again. Her eyes, while clouded with confusion, at least have a spark of sanity. "What the hell is going on? How in god's name did I get here?" She looks down at herself before running her hands over her Vale uniform. "And can someone explain why this butt-ugly outfit is now hanging off me?"

Despite filling her in, Bev isn't buying. "There is no way I could walk from Chalky's office to here and not remember it."

"Bev, it's the truth. You were invaded like I was. It must have happened when you got covered in her crap."

Bev swings away from Ange and stares at me. "Her what?"

"You don't remember?" Ange is as gobsmacked as I am that Bev has missed all the action.

It looks as if I'm alone in remembering the cold blackness when Elizabeth has me in her grip. I'd rather have gone down the amnesia route like Bev. As it is, I suspect the horrible sense of invasion will stay with me for life. Memories of this and Elizabeth's gaping belly reduce me to shivering.


"So it exploded?"

Bev's been badgering Ange and me with questions ever since she came back to her senses. She doesn't remember trying to push the trapdoor shut. She doesn't remember Ange shoving the bag of gummy bears through the gap. And she sure as hell doesn't remember that thing crapping itself all over the storage room and her.

Not until she's run out of questions do we realise Hemi's morphed into the night again.

"Dammit, we didn't even think to tell him to look

out for the tofu eaters." This is the first rational comment Bev's made since coming back to the here and now.

Ange screws up her nose. "Blast it. You know what that means?"

*So much for me avoiding the Sleeping Beauty Suites.*

It's as though I'm drawn to the place, and not in a good way. As much as we weigh up the pros and cons, we know that without us telling them, they won't look for the missing women.

*There's also the fact there's a working phone in my suitcase if we can find it.*

*Okay, and chocolate.*

A short discussion and we set off in that direction. We don't hurry.

"The thing I don't understand is them wanting the tofu brigade in the Sleeping Beauty Suites. It makes no sense. From the little I overheard, the guys are paying to watch overweight women being screwed and abused. Not skinny ones."

Stillness cloaks us as we ponder what's happening to them. If the pain and starvation inflicted on me is anything to go by, I don't like their chances.

*At least I had body fat in reserve.*

Despite recently reclaiming our handbags, there isn't a chance we're heading up to the top facility weighed down by them. We stuff them in the wardrobe in Tee's room before reluctantly leaving for the Sleeping Beauty Suites. Our reluctance is such that we're dawdling, barely moving forward. None of us wants to go back inside the top facility, voluntarily.

"We know they'll be there." Bev's voice is heavy with resignation.

"Much as I'd like to scarper into town, we can't leave them behind," says Ange.

"Once we let the guys know about them, we can leave." I all but cross my fingers behind my back.

"True." Bev peers in the general direction of the buildings obscured by the bush, "but we've gotta find 'em first."

"Why you all walking so slow?"

"*Arrrgh!*" I swing the cricket bat before I can stop myself. Luckily for Horse, not only can he move quietly, he can also move quickly when he's about to have his hair parted by a slab of willow. "Geez, Horse, don't sneak up like that."

Over her shock, Bev smacks him hard on the shoulder with her frying pan, and he takes an involuntary step to the side. "You stupid git."

Ange reins in her response to tutting and shaking her head.

My heart slowing, I turn fully to face him. "We were just coming to look for you. We found out there are three more women locked up. You'll need to look out for them."

"Where you gonna be?"

"We're walking into town," I say, already turning in that direction.

Horse sucks air in through his teeth. "I wouldn't be doing that if I were you. Road's a dangerous place at night. *Sheesh*, it's not even that safe during the day."

Bev's "*Pffft*," says she isn't buying this. "You're far safer on the road than you are in this place."

"Yeah, it's not as if there'll be any traffic at this time of night," says Ange.

Horse looks at the three of us in disbelief. "Cars are the least of ya worries."

## 26

Saliva is pooling in the bottom of my mouth before I find the words I'm after. "I thought Elizabeth stuck to the bush?"

"She used to, but she's getting stronger." Horse shakes his head, as if unable to believe what he's saying. "Man, she really wants that sprog of hers to live if she's prepared to leave the safety of the bush."

*If what he says is true, what are the odds of the woman we helped escape making it into town without Elizabeth getting to her? Let's hope she's infertile, or as fast as she says. If she fails on either count, the cavalry won't be arriving any time soon.*

Deep in thought, we fail to realise Horse is no longer next to us. I race to catch up with him and then stick to him like glue; the other two are likewise attached. None of us wants to roam too far from a friendly source of testosterone.

I can't believe how quietly he moves. Despite putting my feet exactly where he puts his, I make a racket in comparison and the other two are as loud. Of concern is the deep breath he takes before he parts the flax bushes to reveal the track up to the top facility. Is he expecting company? I hope not.

Meeting up with that dark mother-, ah, to-be, once in an evening is sufficient.

Horse stops without warning and I have to slam on the anchors to avoid crashing into him. Turning slightly, he whispers, "We need to hurry."

Hurry is an understatement. I haven't moved this fast since regional finals, or when Hemi carried me. Reaching the safety of the shadows afforded by the buildings that make up the Suites, my lungs are ready to explode from my chest. Listening to the other two, I know they're in a similar state.

"Give ... us ... a ... moment," pants Bev.

I'm unable to speak, more interested in getting as much air into my lungs as I can. Ange is in a similar position to me; bent double, hands on knees, gasping.

"Geez, you lot are unfit? Isn't that why you were here?"

None of us can respond, and Horse doesn't wait for a reply, and he doesn't wait for us. Rather, he nips along the wall and disappears inside the building.

Not until we've all caught our breath, do we follow. If the situation weren't so serious, I'd think it was funny, the way we're all running full-tilt while looking in every direction possible. Mind you, what we'll do if we run into any bad guys, lord alone knows.

We find out when on rounding the corner of the back entrance, we run straight into Hemi and Johnno. The sucker punch Bev dishes out to Johnno is impressive and Hemi just manages to stop Ange smacking him with her trusty rolling pin.

Ange and Bev's apologies follow with the same swiftness of their attack.

"Sorry, mate, thought you were someone else." Bev pats Johnno awkwardly on his back.

Ange spins her weapon of choice absently. "Yeah, sorry about that."

It's a few seconds before Johnno stands up straight. That must've been one hell of a blow Bev landed in his gut. His expression as he looks at her waivers between disgruntled and impressed.

"Geez lady, that's one hell of a right you've got."

Hemi looks sideways at Bev. "Have you always been that strong?"

Bev's so busy examining her fist it takes her a moment to answer. "Ah, no. I haven't. Don't get me wrong, I'm no wimp, but I've never had a bloke doubled over before."

It's an admission that gives me pause. Is it because of Hemi's male energy that we're stronger, or is it down to the possession itself?

Every time he's done that male energy thing, it's been as a result of her invasion. It's the same with Bev. It's therefore anyone's guess as to what's behind for our increased strength.

I file it, deciding it doesn't matter for now, so long as we're all stronger for the experience. Strength is your friend when you're facing an enemy the likes of Chalky and Co. "Where's Horse?"

"Bet the bastard's asleep somewhere," says Johnno, his longing for that state evident as he stares across the open to the bush.

I nudge him with the cricket bat. "But you must have seen him. He was right in front of us. He used this door." Looking at Johnno in the moonlight, his face is covered in sweat. Dropping my gaze, his shirt is stuck to his chest.

*What the hell has he been up to?*

Hemi is as dishevelled. The night isn't that hot. There's no way these two should be in this state without them having put in a serious effort.

"Ah, what have you been up to, to be all sweaty?" I wave my hands around like a game show hostess, rather than voice specifics.

"Had to get rid of a few, ah, problems." Hemi's expression is grim, leaving me well aware of what those problems were.

A month back, thoughts of people laid out would have upset me incredibly – apart from David, that is. Having been at the mercy of these people, I couldn't give a damn about their wellbeing.

Ange proves more squeamish, although she doesn't get very far on her whispered lecture on the sanctity of human life before she's interrupted by Hemi.

"Bill was a mate of mine. Them talking about killing you lot by slitting your throats and chucking you over the cliff like they did that poor old bloke, that did it for me, I snapped."

"So did they when they hit the bottom of the gully," chuckles Johnno.

"Pigs'll soon take care of 'em." Hemi's expression is forbidding and I don't rate the chances of anyone else we run into.

Before we're side-tracked further, I bring Hemi and Johnno up to speed regarding the three missing women. "That's three we know about, although the pile of handbags says there are more, like heaps more."

Hemi rubs his hands together. "Right, let's go get 'em."

I'm gripping my bat in readiness when I think of something. "Guys, Chalky talked about medical staff when she thought I was out cold. Probably best if you don't lob them off the cliff. We'll need them, for sure."

I'd rather we didn't, but remembering how skinny those tofu eaters had been to start with, who knew what state they'd be in now.

Voluntarily entering the Sleeping Beauty Suites has the flight part of my sympathetic nervous system yelling so loudly, I'm sure it's audible to more than me. It gets even louder when Johnno suggests we split up to cover more ground.

Unfortunately, he's right. The buildings are a veritable warren. The dodgy lighting doesn't help either, having a lot in common with the emergency lighting often seen in public buildings during a power cut.

Dimly lit passages meander haphazardly before finishing in dead ends, or rooms leading into yet more rooms. Grand Designs would describe the architecture as 'organic'. I'd describe it as creepy as all get out.

In the end, splitting up is an anti-climax. Staying rooted to the spot while the others wander off, I'm eventually on my own. Bev and Ange hadn't looked keen on splitting up either, but this didn't stop them from disappearing down their assigned hallways.

*Don't these people watch horror movies?*

*Don't they know splitting up like this is NOT a good idea?*

Shaking my head to rid it of every terrible scenario, I straighten my back and gawp down the hallway that's mine to explore. It's longer than it has a right to be given the overall size of the building.

Despite the doors being only on the left-hand side of the hallway, there are so many it's gonna take freaking ages to check them all. I pull myself up even straighter, take a deep breath, and double hand the bat above my head.

I don't know if this will make it quicker to deploy, but it sure as hell makes me feel safer at the ready like this. Unfortunately, it's a stance I can't maintain if I'm to open the first door.

My hand is already on the doorknob when I freeze. What if there's someone in there? I put my ear to the door, but all I can hear is the sea.

*Speed will be my friend, like ripping off a plaster.*

All going well, I'll have the element of surprise.

Getting as much air into my lungs as I'll need puts me in danger of hyperventilating. I bounce on my feet to stimulate the adrenaline. I'm as ready as I'll ever be.

Yanking on the handle, I storm into the room, cricket bat held aloft ready to brain someone if I have to.

It's a storage space.

Talk about anti-climax.

I'm about to leave the room when I twig what the neat piles are on the shelves that line the walls. Surgical scrubs, clean, freshly laundered surgical scrubs. There's nothing like blending in with everyone else, so I help myself to a set, pulling them on over Tee's Vale uniform. If anyone gets a glimpse of me, they'll think I'm the new girl, except for the cricket bat that is, it not being surgical quality and all.

To bolster my disguise, I nab a stethoscope from a tray to the right of the doorway, feeling very *Grey's Anatomy* when I clip it around my neck. It also means I can have a quick listen to what's going on in a room before I enter.

Freshly attired, I carry on searching my designated area. Out of one room and into another, and another. Empty of people but full to the gunnels with supplies. There's enough stuff in the rooms I've searched to keep a survivalist happy for a couple of years.

Given the clandestine nature of the place, they'd hardly want delivery trucks rolling up here every week. With this much in the way of supplies, you'd be lucky to see a delivery truck up here once a year.

Near the end of the hallway is a single door on the right, opposite the final one on the left. I've given up hyperventilating and holding the bat above my head in prep. This search-and-destroy mission is proving more like an end-of-year stocktake, and just as boring.

My approach to opening the final door on the left is casual. Not for long. The enormous chest freezer opposite where I'm standing rockets my heart into my mouth. The damned thing could easily hold all the missing women.

*There's one way to find out for sure.*

Grabbing the handle, I try lifting the lid, but it doesn't budge. As loath as I am, I put the cricket bat on the ground, freeing up both hands. It requires concerted effort on my part to fight the suction and the sheer weight of the lid to get it up and open as far as it'll go.

I don't know whether to laugh or cry when I see the contents.

If Tee were with me, she'd be beside herself with glee. The freezer contains hundreds of plastic bottles of that chocolate protein drink. But it's not this that grabs my attention; it's all the Vale-branded ready meals stacked in there.

Picking one up, I flip it over to check the nutritional panel on the back. On the face of it, the meal looks to be super healthy. The only thing not listed is what the meat is that I can see through the shrink-wrapped plastic top. Could this be what old Bill was on about with that scrawled message of his?

My next action is one of pure spite. Leaving the lid wide open, I slide my hand down the back and flick off the power before picking up my bat and leaving the room. "Smell that, Chalky."

There's now only one door left for me to check: the one facing the room I've just exited. Strangely, it's marked 'Linen'.

Given every other room I've entered that's held linen hasn't had a sign on the door, I smell a rat. The other thing that is odd about this door is that it opens out into the hallway unlike door every other.

*Surely it couldn't be this obvious?*

*But hey, if hiding in plain sight is working to conceal Tee, then it can work here.*

*They're hardly likely to have 'Torture Chamber' on the door, are they?*

Never mind the mundane nature of the search taking the edge off my nerves, there's no way I'll storm in there all gung-ho. I step over to the door and lay my stethoscope against it, listening for any signs of movement on the other side.

Nothing.

Checking my grip on the cricket bat, I slide my hand around the doorknob and turn it ever so slowly. It squeals loudly, and I yank my hand away as if the handle's red hot.

"Bloody hell!" I slap my hand over my mouth a second too late. I know I've been loud, the earlier shriek pale by comparison. But has it been audible enough for anyone on the other side to hear? I wait, my breathing shallow, my ears straining to the point I could hear a mouse fart, if one were nearby and had been eating beans.

Tight against the wall on the side of the door with hinges, I stay frozen until I deem it's safe to move again. This time I don't muck around turning the handle slowly; the faster I deal with it, the better it'll be.

Opening the door wide, I'm shocked.

It's a linen cupboard.

*Surely not?*

I step right up to the shelves, shoving my head inside as far as the piles of towels will allow.

I hold my breath.

*Music*? Actually, this isn't quite true. *Musak* would be a better description of what I can hear. Often found in elevators, but completely out of place here.

An experimental push on one of the shelves has the lot rolling away from me, revealing a sliver of what looks like a hallway beyond. It also means if there's anyone on the other side, they'll clock the shelves sticking out like a dog's balls.

*Well, that sucks the proverbial kumara.*

## 27

There's no way I'm going in there alone. If there's one thing Stephen King's taught me, it's that I need to find the others, and fast.

First, though, I need to move the shelves back to where they were. Much as I'd like to leave them as they are and shut the door, I can't. Last thing we need is for anyone to see them, if they already haven't.

"How many times do I need to tell you to push the shelves fully closed?" Chalky's nasal New York accent is close, and the spontaneous clenching of my sphincter and pelvic floor muscles is all that prevents me from losing everything consumed in the past three hours.

Luckily, they're still clenched when she shoves the shelving unit back into position. She does this with such venom, I'm nearly the recipient of an impromptu nose job and a heart attack.

Turning the handle as fast as I can generates the tiniest of squeaks and as I push the door fully closed, muttering comes from inside the cupboard. There's not a snowball's chance in hell I'll get away without being seen. Wasting no time, I nip to the side so the door will hide me if it opens. I wait. The cricket bat held aloft, I ready myself for action.

It's as if all my Christmases have come at once.

If it were a stranger, I'd think twice.

Unfortunately for Lance, he's had this coming since the first time he did the same.

He crumples to the floor without a peep, and all I want to do is smash away at him until I obliterate every image of him in my dreams. Make that nightmares.

Quietly closing the door, I make the most of him being out cold. Indulging in a boundary shot that will make sure he never rapes another woman, let alone pees straight. There's also the added plus that I've ruined Chalky's sex life for the foreseeable future.

I'm standing over him and even giving serious consideration into putting him out of *my* misery when I see Hemi steaming in my direction, scaring the crap out of me. Busy with my nefarious thoughts, I hadn't heard him coming. He and Horse move so quietly, I doubt I'd have heard him even if I were listening out.

He gets my mood immediately, making short work of taking the cricket bat away from me. Whether this is for Lance's peace of mind, or my own, he doesn't say.

"This creep give you any trouble?"

"Not today."

Seeing I'm calm, he hands the cricket bat back before bending down and grabbing hold of Lance's feet. He drags the creep down the hallway like a human wheelbarrow with me following in their wake. I don't want to stay next to the 'linen cupboard' on my own. We've rounded the corner and are a good way down the main corridor when I spot Horse and Johnno over Hemi's shoulder.

*Hah, so much for us all splitting up.*

Johnno nudges Lance none too gently with his foot. "Geez, looks like you decked this one good."

"Not me. Her."

I squirm under Horse and Johnno's scrutiny, both of them inspecting me, perhaps on the lookout for slipped cogs.

*Sure, I've got a few, but with good reason.*

Johnno breaks the silence. "Is this the bloke?"

I nod curtly and am pleased to see he doesn't so much nudge Lance this time, as put the boot in good and proper, with a satisfyingly fleshy thump.

"I'll take him from here," says Johnno.

Hemi drops the bastard's feet, allowing Johnno to drag Lance upright before bending and pitching him casually over one shoulder. He straightens and adjusts the weight of his captive before walking off with a laconic "Reckon he'll enjoy the view."

Despite knowing exactly what he means, I remain quiet. While the old me would have pleaded for leniency, the new me is a little more ambivalent about Lance's fate.

*Maybe him being dead will stop the night terrors?*

It's a chance I'm prepared to take.

No sooner has Johnno disappeared than Bev shows up, with Ange arriving soon after.

"Any sign of the tofu eaters?" I address this question to everyone.

Bev speaks up first. "The place is deserted, although I did find a room full of clothing and personal effects. Like a modern-day concentration camp." Her expression is one I share.

"I didn't find squat," confirms Ange.

Horse shrugs apologetically.

Hemi simply says, "Nope."

I turn back the way we'd come, beckoning with my finger for the others to follow. "I think I know where they are."

Back in front of the Narnia cupboard, I put a finger to my lips to stop anyone talking. For all the good it does.

Ange looks at the door, her brow wrinkled. "Ah, it says 'Linen Cupboard'."

I put my finger to my lips again before opening the door and pushing gently on the shelves.

Again all five shelves slide quietly away, before I pull them back into place. No one says a thing. They don't need to, their surprise evident.

Hemi shuts the door to the linen cupboard without a sound, with not even the squeaky handle daring to defy him. "If we're going through there, we need to wait for Johnno." He leans casually against the wall, a repose that shrieks of patience.

It's something I'm sadly lacking, with my desire to be rid of this place urging me to rush through everything. Of course, it makes sense that we should wait for Johnno, but does this make the waiting any easier to bear? Nope.

While waiting, I develop quite the eye twitch, and Bev and Ange fidget, all of us anxious to do something, anything. Mainly I want to run and never stop. In contrast, Horse has hunkered down against the wall, balancing on his toes. He does so with little to no movement; an achievement of note. Such a pose would see me in a heap on the floor.

Hemi is just as relaxed, leaning against the wall opposite, his eyes closed, his breathing slow and regular. I'm about to prod him, when he pushes himself away from the wall and re-opens the door to the linen cupboard.

"What?" I look at Hemi. There isn't a sign or even a sound of Johnno's return.

Hemi grins broadly before shoving the shelves through and out the other side, and with sufficient force to flatten anyone unlucky enough to be standing there.

Pity there isn't a welcoming committee on hand to greet us.

"Remember," I place my hand on his back to stop him, "don't hurt any doctors or nurses. If we find the missing women, they'll more than likely need medical help."

At least I hope they'll still need medical help because the evidence we've uncovered so far says no one leaves this place alive unless they're a celebrity, or they work here.

Nodding, he steps through the gap, followed by the now upright Horse, then Bev and lastly Ange, leaving me on my own again. I'm close to legging it and hiding out in the bottom of Tee's wardrobe, when Johnno turns up as Hemi has anticipated. The shame of running with an audience is too much for me, and so I hold my ground.

My questioning look is all he needs.

"The pigs'll eat well tonight."

Bile bubbles up in my throat, burning it and I struggle to hide my revulsion at how gleeful he sounds at the prospect.

I needn't have bothered because he looks past me at the linen cupboard, and through into the hallway. "They through there?"

I nod in answer, and unable to stall any longer, step into the cupboard, through the gap and out into a hallway on the other side, with Johnno right behind me. I'm following in the footsteps of the others when I realise he hasn't kept apace.

He's pushing the sliding shelves back into place, with the panel that backs them showing itself to be a perfect match to the wall.

Moving closer to him so I can keep my voice low. "Is there any point closing them?" It's not as if Hemi was quiet about opening the shelves.

Johnno shrugs before edging by me to join the others. His, "Who the hell knows?" as he passes by doesn't exactly inspire confidence.

This side of the operation appears as deserted as the side we've just come from, even though I know this isn't the case.

*Screw splitting up with Chalky at large.*

Seeing how ritzy this side is shouldn't come as a surprise. But really, that linen cupboard is The Vale equivalent of the wardrobe in Narnia. The facility we've entered smacks of an uber-expensive, private hospital, and is utterly at odds with where we've come from.

Looking down, I'm struck by the opulence of the decor. Rather than utilitarian linoleum, the floor is wall-to-wall marble tiles. Here the lighting is soft rather than dim.

*There's no way they're killing people over here. Not to a soundtrack of 'The girl from Ipanema', they're not.*

Hemi and the others had moved off down the hallway to our left. Strangely, my gut instinct was to go right, something to do with the psychology of shopping apparently. I don't know.

There isn't a chance I'm heading right on my own and I trail along behind the other five.

Eventually, I tap Johnno on his back, and we swap places.

The high-end finishes don't last past the first corner. Neither does the music, with a quick look up showing a scarcity of speakers. Here concrete floors and buzzing fluorescents replace the marble tiles and soft lighting. Even the windows cut into one side of the hall farther along are framed with uncoated aluminium. Not meant to be seen by celebrity clients from either inside or out.

I'm wondering what the view will be like when Hemi stops abruptly. He turns without a sound, puts a finger to his lips, and then drops quietly to his hands and knees.

For such a large man, he crawls with surprising speed and stealth.

We all follow suit.

As I crawl under the window, I understand the reason for our drop in altitude. Looking up through the Venetian blinds, I expect to see the night sky. Rather, there's a ceiling that features a couple of flickering fluorescent tubes. Even with the blinds angled as they are, anyone in the room could see us trooping past.

The temptation to pop my head up is overwhelming.

I don't know what I expected, but it's not this. I get a glimpse of large stainless-steel vats, more commonly seen in boutique breweries. The rest of the room it set up as a large industrial kitchen, one that's better equipped than that frequented by the laughing gnomes.

Temptation again gets the better of me, and I pop my head up to see more clearly into the room. There's no way I can pull my gaze away.

Perhaps it's that the glass gives the impression I'm watching a large television set.

A pity the scheduled programming is less *MasterChef* and more *Silence of the Lambs*. Johnno tugs me back down when a bloke in a white cap, overalls and gumboots appears.

I pop straight back up.

The guy is armed with a stainless-steel bucket that's chocker, if the way he's straining is any indicator. Mesmerised, I watch him upend the bucket of god knows what into the enormous bowl sitting under a floor-stand mixer in the middle of the room. Clanging the bucket down, he turns the knob on the side of the machine and the blades turn slowly.

I'm conscious Johnno is watching next to me. The others, safely past the window, have regained their feet and are already a good few metres down the hallway. Hemi disappears around a corner with Horse right behind him.

I'm about to continue crawling forward when another guy enters the room behind the glass and upends a similar bucket into the large bowl. The drone of the motor changes as it works harder on the extra load. When the new arrival speaks, I'm astounded at the clarity, proving the window is not double-glazed.

"I can't believe those fat bitches drink this crap."

"Hey, if those sad fuckers paying to see 'em get porked like 'em chunky, then this is the easiest way to make sure they stay that way."

I don't know what distresses me most. How casually they're talking about me and others being drugged and raped on a pay-per-view basis. Or watching how much cocoa powder and sugar they add to the mix?

*No wonder I'd had trouble losing any bloody weight.*

On the plus side, at least I can tell Tee what the recipe is. Actually, no, I can't, because I have no idea what the secret ingredient is that they've chucked in there by the bucket-load.

"Yeah, I'd love to see their faces if they knew they were on a steady diet of B-List celebs."

"That lot guzzling it down is sure as hell easier than us having to get rid of it."

They're laughing like drains when a third man arrives, also dressed from head to toe in white and carrying yet another stainless-steel bucket full to the brim.

"Mind your backs, more celebrity flab coming through." He upends another large bucket of the gelatinous sludge into the mixer.

"Bleeding hell, careful you don't overload the damned thing. Candy'll go ape-shit if we blow the motor again."

He's right about this warning. The motor sounds as distressed as I'm feeling. I don't know if it's my dry retching or Johnno's muttered oath that alerts them to our presence, but either way, we're busted.

## 28

So are the three guys when Hemi and Horse get to them. Again the two men startle me with their speed and stealth. They're in the room and the three guys out cold, without as much as a cry of alarm.

The guys stuff the unconscious men into the enormous metal vats that line the back wall, one criminal per vat, jammed in nice and tight. No need to tie them up; with them unconscious for the foreseeable future.

Ange and Bev join Hemi and Horse in the vat room, leaving Johnno and me in the hallway. He helps me to my feet looking as green as I'm sure I do. Not until my tummy has settled, do I walk along the hallway, around the corner, and into the room with the others. My last meal comes close to making a repeat appearance when I see Ange turn off the mixer and dip a finger in the lusciously dark chocolate smoothie.

I smack her hand away in time, but rather than thank me, she's pissed off and dips her finger back in the mix again. It's more than my stomach can take and I projectile vomit all over the mixer. A fair amount of this finds its way into the bowl itself, putting paid to anyone else sampling the brew.

Ange holds her hand in front of her mouth, unsure if she should lick it clean or not.

"You don't want to do that." Johnno takes hold of her hand and wipes it with a cloth he's found.

He hands me the cloth and I make short work of wiping my face with a clean corner. "He's right. We found out what the secret ingredient is."

After I run through the recipe, Bev and Ange throw up in concert, straight into the latest batch of The Vale's special brew. Like me, they're as upset by the vast quantities of sugar and cocoa as they are about the buckets of unwanted celebrity butt and gut.

One thing's for sure, from the sheer quantity we've seen thrown into the mixer, there's more than one liposuction operation taking place right now.

If I weren't feeling as sick as I am, it'd be funny to see how nauseated Horse and Hemi are when we explain what's in the mix. The last thing Hemi does before we leave the room is to rip the power cord free of the motor, putting an end to any more mixing in the foreseeable future.

Leaving the mixing room, we haven't gone much further when we enter a central hub. From here, three concrete tunnels spread out like the spokes of a wheel. A distinct downwards slant says we're entering the very hill itself.

*Army bunker anyone?*

Hemi looks stunned. "Hate to say it, as dangerous as it is, we're gonna need to split up again if we want to cover all the areas back here."

And, much as I too hate the idea of us going our separate ways, he's right. Bowie's labyrinth was straightforward compared with what we're looking at now. Other than unforgiving concrete making up their floors, walls and ceilings, these dark, dank spaces have something else in common. Each of them dog-legs off to the left after only three or four metres. As to what's around the corners – there's only one way to find out.

We pair up to cover each direction, with Johnno my assigned 'muscle'. I'd have preferred being with Hemi, who makes me feel safe, but to reject Johnno would look churlish and not be the best start to our partnership.

After fond goodbyes to the other two women, I follow in Johnno's wake. We're off down the tunnel to the left and have only just made it around the corner when we encounter two doors. They're dead opposite each other, in a pattern that's repeated at regular intervals for the length of the tunnel.

Johnno's hand is already on the first doorknob when I put my hand on his shoulder to stop him. His expression morphs from annoyed to understanding when I put the stethoscope to my ears and hold the chest piece against the door. A quick listen confirms there's no one breathing on the other side of the slab of wood. Johnno checks the room.

Actually, it's less of a room, and more of a cavern. Dug out of the hillside, the walls smeared with concrete to keep the worst of the damp at bay. Breathing out, I'm not surprised to see my breath cloud in the frigid air.

With the all-pervading damp it makes sense that the supplies crowding the space are double wrapped in clear plastic. As well as keeping things reasonably dry, it would also make it an easy task to find what you were looking for.

The room opposite is a mirror image.

I relax, thinking we're in the warehouse section of the complex.

Then I place the stethoscope against the next door.

There's no mistaking the sound of laboured breathing. Or the distinctive sound of leather hitting skin. I remove the stethoscope and hand it to Johnno. His face hardens; he gives the stethoscope back to me and retrieves his knife.

We storm the room, not getting far. I shake my head to clear it of what I'm seeing. I've been expecting a modern-day torture session, not what looks to be a 1950s classroom. It's perfect, right down to the chalkboard and obligatory apple sitting on the teacher's desk.

There, any similarities die; the 'teacher', one of the tofu eaters, is naked and hogtied across the desk next to the apple. The studio lights leave nothing to the imagination when it comes to her injuries.

Standing next to her with a horsewhip is a schoolboy. Well, he would have been thirty years ago. Now he's a pathetic excuse for a human being in a school uniform, one acting out some warped pay-per-view revenge fantasy. Maybe it's how ludicrous he looks, but both Johnno and I burst out laughing, breaking the tension that's frozen us.

The laughter dies in our throats when the idiot in the school uniform pulls a gun on us. He doesn't look confident with it, the piece wavering back and forth between Johnno and me. Eventually, he decides the scruffy bloke holding the big knife is the greater threat and concentrates his aim there.

His eyes skim above and behind where Johnno and I are standing. And there, right there, all those damned action movies David had forced me to watch come into play.

Sneaking a pink cardigan from a pile of clothing off the chair next to me, I flick it up and over the camera, blocking whoever's paying to watch. With luck, they'll simply think the connection has gone out.

The Axl Rose wannabe with that ludicrous school uniform of his swings the gun in my direction. I almost have an accident.

This is nothing like in the movies. It's scary as hell, but as a distraction, it's perfect.

In a scene straight out of *Crocodile Dundee*, Johnno throws his knife, and I watch, fascinated, as it buries itself up to the hilt in the schoolboy's throat. The handgun clatters to the ground, followed by its crumpled owner.

Three seconds tick by before I react. It's the first time I've seen someone killed right in front of me and shock wins out, followed closely by blackness.

Agonised screaming rouses me. My gaze landing on the heap of dead schoolboy lying next to me, I scramble to put some distance between us. As I regain my feet, I focus instead on the schoolteacher. Untied by Johnno but still draped over the desk and crying out in pain.

"What the hell do we do with her?" Johnno's brow wrinkles as he stares at the woman's flayed back and buttocks.

He's got a point. She can't get dressed with skin hanging off her back in strips.

"Let me think, let me think, let me think." This mantra is as much for my benefit as Johnno's;

repeating it helps my brain to focus on a solution. "I'll be back in a moment."

Leaving an open-mouthed Johnno, I stumble out into the tunnel, retracing our steps and opening the last storage cupboard we'd searched.

*Who could have imagined those first aid courses would pay off like this?*

Back in the classroom, I flick the apple to the side and stack my goodies on the desk next to the poor teacher. "This might hurt."

There's no point sugar coating it. Whatever I do, it'll hurt.

The woman has nerve endings open to the world.

I pat her awkwardly on the shoulder, the one bit of her back not shredded.

I rip open the industrial-sized container of cling wrap I've retrieved, pulling long lengths of it free and cutting it on the serrated edge of the box. With Johnno's help, we lay these down her back.

There's no need to pat them into place, the suction effect of all that blood and serum takes care of this. We repeat the process, going sideways until she's covered in a criss-cross of plastic from nape to thighs. We then cover her with another layer, making sure to go over her shoulders and around her stomach.

We've made it as secure as we can, but whether this makeshift covering will stay put when she stands is anyone's guess. Just as well I've got the very thing to help with this.

I've been so busy concentrating, I didn't realise she's stopped moaning. I place my hand gently on her shoulder and lean down "Are you okay?"

I get a brief nod in response.

"We'll need to bandage you. If we don't the cling wrap might not stay put." It doesn't matter that the plastic film is sucked in place; gravity might not be our friend. The extra layer will also help protect her from the cold with this cavern being no warmer than the storage rooms. I worry that some of her shivering is down to shock. "Are you ready?"

Again, I receive a tentative nod.

Taking a deep breath, I grab the bright blue fabric hand towel refill I'd found.

Johnno helps her slide backwards until her feet touch the ground, while she leans on the desk with her arms and shoulders. Her torso free, we wrap the towel around and around her until she resembles a mummy. Only then do we help her to stand, albeit very slowly.

I don't know her name but recognise her from meal times and yoga. She can barely stand, but there's no way we can carry her. It doesn't matter that Johnno is strong enough; stretching her back too much will cause more damage.

And perhaps even more important than this, Johnno needs his hands free in case we run into any of Chalky's team. No point being armed to the teeth if you're weighed down.

I dress her in an outfit that wouldn't look out of place on Miss Jean Brodie. Luckily, the waistband of the ankle-length tweed skirt is elasticated and loose and doesn't add too much to her pain.

Opening the room next door, we're confronted with a similar scene, although this time there's no schoolboy. The budget must only run to one. However, the tofu eater has already been stripped and tied to the desk, ready for appointment viewing. Luckily for her, she's in good shape and after throwing her clothes back on is up to helping her friend. After we find the third of the missing women, we leave the two who are able-bodied supporting their fast-drooping friend.

Armed with birch rods, horsewhips, and even Axl Rose's gun, they're ready to leave. There's no outward signs of damage to the firearm courtesy of Horse's earlier foray, so we decide it's safe for them to take it. As prepared as they'll ever be, we give the trio directions on how to get out. When they talk about walking back into town, Johnno holds his hand up, effectively stopping their gabble of incoherent thoughts.

"No! You don't leave the property. Barricade yourselves in a room and we'll get you when it's safe."

So forceful is he that they nod obediently, and in concert. We don't have time to warn them about Elizabeth and her foetus. They wouldn't believe us anyway.

*Hell, I don't believe it myself.*

We watch them shuffle down the tunnel, turn the corner and disappear.

I'd give anything to be going with them, but now I've committed to the search with Johnno, there isn't a chance I'm leaving. I regret this when Johnno opens the next door and the smell of death rolls out of the room like a living thing.

About to follow him into the room, my cricket bat aloft, he staggers back.

"What?" I croak.

Cobbling together his stuttered reply, the main word I take out of it is '*skinned*'.

## 29

I don't want to look into the room. I can't stop myself. I wish I had.

My dad had an electric planer like that, perfect for slicing through wood like butter, but devastating when used on the human body.

"But- but- but why?" I'm doing my best to stay conscious when I see what's lying on the floor in front of me.

Large chunks of skin, flayed from the poor sod still strapped to the metal bed frame in the centre in the room. Whoever did this to her was zealous: her femur bones are visible through what's left of the back of her thighs. Likewise, her shoulder blades sit proud of her ragged back, as though to fly her to safety.

All I can hope is that it was over quickly for her, that the pain allowed the poor woman to find the darkness as I had. Back out in the tunnel, I bend over and fight the desire to faint, knowing I need to stay strong.

*Why in god's name would somebody pay to see that done to another human being?*

Chalky truly has tapped into a vein of very sick

individuals. Of even more concern, is who'd do that to another human being? Anyone who's capable is certifiable and should be locked up, or better still, strung up.

Johnno's examination of the next room is as brief, his expression again one of revulsion. This time I don't give in to temptation. I accept his assertion that it's the worst home improvement show he's ever seen.

All the caverns checked, we establish there's no one left to save in this wing. Not even the sickos who've paid to see this carnage can be helped now, with victims and perpetrators alike beyond help.

I find it indescribably sad that this is the final resting place for these women, alone and unloved as they must have been in life, if no one has noticed they're gone. I sure don't remember hearing this many missing person reports on the telly.

*Do they even bother with those these days?*

Thoughts of them dropping off the face of the earth without so much as a whimper are closer to home than I'd like. If I do get out of this hole, I'm remedying that. No more hangers-on. No more being a hanger-on. True friends and family are what will be important.

*Hell, I'll even visit my mother in Invercargill. A couple of weeks each year should see both of us happy.*

The final door closed on its victim, the atmosphere in this wing is back to being innocuous. The only plus in all of this is that the caverns being as cold as they are, there's not much smell to deal with.

Spinning the cricket bat on its end, I grab the

handle before it can fall over. "We need to find the others."

"You got that right." Johnno shoves his knife back into the sheath on his leg and marches off the way we'd come and I scramble to catch up.

We haven't taken more than a step or two when Chalky's distinctive tones echo down the tunnel and around the corner. Much as I'd like to introduce that bitch to my cricket bat, I have no idea who she's talking to. For all we know, they're armed to the teeth.

Cricket bats and knives are useless against guns, although Johnno did okay against the schoolboy. He pulls out his knife and holds it up in readiness.

Tapping him on the shoulder, I form a gun with my hand and virtually pull the trigger right next to his head. He gets the message.

The one good thing about this section of the tunnel is that we aren't short of doors to disappear through. Selecting the one right behind us, I'm dismayed to see it's not a storage cupboard.

After the briefest glimpse of the dismembered body, I give the closed door more attention than it requires. Next to me, Johnno has no compunction about staring at the victim, *tsk*ing loudly and shaking his head.

A hand over my mouth, I desperately attempt to edit the images forever burned into my retinas. For one thing, I don't see that well-known Scandinavian chainsaw company listing this as a potential use on their bright-orange packaging.

Propping the cricket bat against the wall, I slide the stethoscope into my ears. The chest piece hard against the door, it's as if I'm in the tunnel next to Chalky. It takes every ounce of resolve not to yank the stethoscope free from my ears with her sounding as loud as if she were right next to me.

"Gawd dammit, Heath, move your sorry ass. I don't have all day. Start at the far end with the older ones."

At first, I can't work out the rhythmic quality of the squeaking. As it passes the door, I realise it's a trolley, presumably being pushed by Heath. Concentrating, I detect two more pairs of footsteps in his wake. Suddenly, I'm very happy to be on the side of the door with all the carnage.

I know Johnno's handy with his fists but I doubt he's that handy and if the guys are armed, we wouldn't have a hope in hell. And for all we know, Chalky is packing heat. Saying this inside my head paints such a ludicrous picture it's all I can do to stop the manic laughter threatening to erupt.

*Now what?*

Moving as close as I can to Johnno, I keep my eyes firmly locked on the door. Only when I'm hard up against him, do I speak. "Do we wait, or leg it?" I hold the stethoscope up to his mouth for him to whisper his reply.

"That tunnel goes on for bloody ages. Don't know about you, but I don't fancy an effing bullet in the back."

Even though he's kept his voice down, he's still loud, damn near blowing my eardrums.

I realise I've said something when he slaps his hand over my mouth, only taking it away when I nod. My hand shaking, I put the chest piece back against the door, listening for sounds of discovery. I even give up breathing for a heartbeat or two.

No sound. No footsteps. No one is talking.

They wait.

I wait.

Johnno, however, is restless to the point I hold my finger up to stop him from opening the door. I breathe again when the squeaking and footsteps resume in the tunnel. I can't relax completely. We've all watched that scene in movies and I'm damned if I'm getting sucked in.

Again, Johnno's hand strays to the door handle.

Again I stop him.

There are footsteps right outside our door and I point rapidly at it before putting my finger to my lips. Neither of us so much as blinks.

When the footsteps head back in the direction of Heath and Chalky, I slump against the door.

*Good thing we don't have any plans on leaving the room.*

*We can't.*

While waiting, it dawns on me that our hiding place isn't that safe after all. What the hell happens if the trolley they're pushing is capable of holding all the bodies?

I whisper this thought to Johnno and even in the dim red light of the room can see his eyes widen. A quick scan of the torture chamber shows that short of stacking up body parts, there's nowhere to hide. A quick tally confirms more than one person has died here.

*Can I be getting inured to this carnage so soon?*

Apparently so, if my mouth no longer flooding with saliva is to be taken at face value. I hope they took the victim's head off before they removed her breasts and disembowelled her with the chainsaw. I gulp hard to keep my stomach acid where it is.

Johnno has an ear pressed hard against the door,

his hand signalling to get the stethoscope back in place, and fast.

The sounds of the wheels have been replaced by grunting, painting a picture of a trolley stacked with bodies and spare parts. Hopefully too full for them to stop and empty the room we're in. Hearing grunting right outside our room, I let the stethoscope drop to hang around my neck and step to the side. Unable to tell what's going on, I raise my cricket bat in readiness to scone someone. Johnno positions himself next to me.

The door handle turns, the door is opened an inch, and we overhear Chalky say "Don't be an idiot, Heath. We're behind schedule already. You can come back for the others after we've butchered this lot." Slammed shut hard, the metal door shudders violently in its frame.

The stethoscope back against the door, I listen to Chalky's constant demands for the crew to move faster, sounding ever-fainter. Her dulcet tones no longer detectable, I indicate to Johnno that it's okay to open the door.

The smell that greets us is reminiscent of a butcher's shop; fresh meat. Even without the trail of blood bisecting the floor in a sick imitation of the wayfaring signage seen in hospitals, I'd know where they were heading.

Chalky having casually mentioned butchering the bodies, all I need do is close my eyes to see that row of meat hooks.

This begs the question as to where that room is, because I haven't seen it since being back in the Sleeping Beauty Suites. Neither have I caught sight of 'my room'. If I had, there'd be a lot of smashed camera equipment by now.

Without any conscious decision on our part, Johnno and I both keep well clear of the carnage in the middle of the tunnel. Pressed against the walls, we follow the bloodied footsteps of Chalky and her minions.

This takes us back to the hub where the three tunnels join up. The grunting of the trolley pushers no longer audible, we can clearly see where they've gone. The problem is whether we wait for the others or continue.

A hand slaps over my mouth from behind as I ponder this, successfully stifling my scream. Ange stands in front of me and gives me a thumbs-up before Horse removes his paw.

*How the hell did they sneak up on us like that?*

"Been waiting in that cupboard there." Ange's voice is so low, I'm tempted to put the stethoscope back in place and hold the chest piece up to her mouth.

Seconds later, Hemi and Bev round the corner at the end of the middle tunnel and march in our direction. Crowded around the blood-splattered floor, silence falls over the group, eventually broken by Hemi.

"As bad as it looks?"

He addresses this question to Johnno rather than me, as though as a woman, I'm incapable of answering.

*Well, to hell with that. I'd received too much of sort of treatment from David over the years.*

Not giving Johnno time to speak, I hold up my hand.

"That bitch is responsible for torture and full-on mass murder." I wait a beat before continuing. "With power tools. It was like HGTV had the rights to *Friday the 13th*." A giggle sneaks free, but the reactions from Ange and Bev stifle any further laughter.

After this, I don't bother going into my theory about what's happening to the bodies.

Hemi is also looking at me sideways but doesn't comment, before turning and following the trail of blood. We troop past the glass-fronted room with its stainless-steel vats and three unconscious lackeys tucked out of sight.

We file past the linen cupboard that would take us back to the Sleeping Beauty Suites. For some reason, I'd expected Chalky and the body retrieval team to exit through there. However, the trail of blood leads us in the direction I'd first wanted to head when we arrived.

We don't get far before we hit the T-junction at the end of the hallway. There are dead ends both to the left and right, which makes no sense at all. Perhaps even harder to understand is that the trail of blood has disappeared underneath a solid wall.

That is until Horse hunkers down and examines the skirting board, where he finds a couple of hairline cracks. They're sufficiently far apart you'd never suspect there was a door here. It must be at least two metres wide, if not more.

Waving my hand to get everyone's attention, I put my finger to my lips. Re-engaging the stethoscope, I place the chest piece against the wall, straining to hear what's happening on the other side. Chalky continues to berate the unfortunate porters, and I listen until their grunting is faint. Not until then do we risk opening up the wall.

Horse rises to his feet and pushes against the left-hand side of the panel.

Nothing.

Hemi pushes against the right-hand side.

*Bingo!*

The panel swings open on a central pivot, smacking into Johnno, who swears blind what an idiot his mate is. He's not quiet about it.

Waiting for all hell to break loose courtesy of his outburst, none of us speak, listening for a reaction. There isn't one and there should have been.

*Dammit, they've taken off on us.*

Johnno no longer playing the part of doorstop, the pivoting panel opens wide. The six of us march through, careful to dodge the trail of blood down the centre of this new hallway. On the bright side, with this Hansel and Gretel trail, at least we can find our way out again.

We know why Chalky and the porters didn't react to Johnno's outburst when we turn another corner and face yet another door. Hemi stops in front of it, puts his ear against it and holds his hand up for quiet. It's unnecessary, without as much as a peep out of us. Seeing him frown, I lean in and put the chest piece up to the slab of wood.

*That's odd.*

Even using the stethoscope, I can't hear anything either. This must be the mother of all doors. "What the hell is it made out of?"

Ange and Bev immediately shush me, but then Hemi talks in a normal voice, too. "No point keeping quiet. I reckon this door is solid steel." He examines the edges closely. "And airtight by the look of things."

Despite pushing it all over and looking for a mechanism in the wall on either side, we're stymied.

*Damn, now what?*

## 30

A nge looks at the blood trail at our feet, her brow creased. "That's not right."

"What isn't?" Hemi says.

"The blood leading up to the door is fresher. Look at the colour."

She's right. Retracing our steps, as the blood trail turns the corner, it goes from a darker red to a brighter hue. There's also there's a break in the pattern, with it changing from being irregular to something altogether more contrived.

"Those sneaky bastards," says Hemi, pushing against the wall next to the corner.

Sure enough, it opens.

Then all hell breaks loose.

Luckily for Ange, Bev and I, we're behind the men. Luckily for them, Horse had screwed up most of the guns in the place all those hours ago. Even luckier is Hemi's superhuman reflexes. When the guns explode, the panel has closed enough that we're not taken out as collateral damage.

However, the panel does nothing to save us from the noise, which is deafening. My ears are ringing so loudly, I almost miss the two dull thuds from the other side. Hemi turns and motions for us to stand back, something we scramble to obey.

He slams the wall panel open wide, smashing it hard against the wall opposite, and the guys storm into the breach. Storming isn't necessary: both guards are prostrate on the ground, their blood splattered over floor, walls and even the ceiling.

I don't want to look, but my gaze is lured by their twitching bodies. Who'd have believed a gun exploding in your face could do so much damage. These guys won't be using the fast lane at the airport again.

*Even using the slow lane will be a challenge.*

*If they survive at all.*

Stepping carefully over their convulsing bodies, we track the blood trail until I realise Hemi isn't right behind me. Instead, he's propped the disabled guards against the revolving panel, effectively stopping anyone from following us. Even on our side of the panel, the guards won't give us any trouble. Not with the remaining air in their lungs escaping through their windpipes in a sodden gurgle.

Pushing past me, Hemi joins Horse and Johnno, making sure all of our strength is upfront. Ange and Bev go next, while I bring up the rear in the safest position of all.

This doesn't stop me from checking back over my shoulder every few paces. As creepy as this place is, it wouldn't surprise me to see the guards in zombie form. Everyone knows a through-and-through head shot is best.

The layout of the hallway is anything but straightforward as it zigzags its way through this part of the complex. It brings back memories of a school trip to a local hospital where we were taken behind the scenes.

Without any conscious instruction, we all keep as quiet as we can. We sneak past a couple of operating theatres, the surgeons and nurses cocooned in a circle of light. Having watched more than a few episodes of *Botched*, I recognise the procedure as liposuction.

Over and over, the surgeon jams a knitting-needle type device into the arse of whoever they're working on, the offending lumps and bumps sucked out via a clear hose into a large stainless-steel bucket under the operating table.

In each case, the team's concentration is such they're unaware of having an audience. They're probably also unaware they're busy harvesting the main ingredient of The Vale's famous chocolate shake.

Reading the names on the boards outside each of the three theatres verifies we've been fed Grade-A leavings. I'm suddenly feeling that little bit closer to Hollywood.

The one operation we haven't seen yet is the very one that prompted me to book in here in the first place.

*What the hell were these women thinking, undergoing surgery in a backwater like this, all for the sake of privacy?*

*Crazy.*

It isn't as though these stars fool the paparazzi when they rock up to an event, minus their love handles. Sure Spanx are good and all, but not *that* good.

*What if something went wrong? You'd be screwed. Didn't that famous author Olivia Whatshername die of complications from plastic surgery? Not while she was on the table, but later when things settled.*

A hand slapped over my face shocks me out of my reverie. This time it's foe, not friend, and much as I'd like to fight, the feel of hard steel in the middle of my back guarantees my compliance.

Even if the gun is one damaged by Horse, misfiring would still do irreparable damage. Not a risk I'm prepared to take. I do, however, allow the cricket bat to slip from my fingers, breaking its fall with my foot.

I hope the others see it.

The gun jammed hard against my spine, my assailant drags me backwards into a room. Even without the whiff of familiar perfume, I'd know who's behind the firearm.

People protest our presence and I swivel my eyes to see we're in an operating theatre. This one doesn't have a glass viewing panel.

Confident of my obedience, Chalky takes her hand away from my mouth. The gun stays exactly where it is. Using her free hand, she slides the bolts shut on the entry panel.

There's no way the others can get to me, although I soon hear their attempts. Much as I'd love to cry out, "I'm in here," all I manage is a faint whimper. Although not so faint that those in the operating theatre don't hear.

The surgeon voices his disapproval about us contaminating a sterile area. Chalky waves the gun briefly in his direction, silencing any further complaints. Shoving a gel implant into the cavity of whichever starlet it is, his eyes above the bright green mask are dark with anger.

Forced to watch the rest of the boob job, I rethink the procedure.

*If I get out of here alive, a push-up bra will suffice.*

However, making it out in one piece is looking less likely all the time. Big tits lose their appeal when you won't be around to flaunt them.

The surgery takes forever, to the point the scrabbling of my friends on the other side of the wall stops. Chalky even gives up on jamming the gun into my back. Eventually, the medics leave through double doors opposite where Chalky and I wait. They push the patient before them, casting filthy looks in our direction.

The swinging doors have barely settled when Chalky shoves me towards the operating table, blathering about what she's about to do to me. If she's doing all that, she'll need to have her hands free. Faking a stumble into the trolley of discarded surgical items, I grab hold of a scalpel.

Meanwhile, Chalky flips aside the sheet covering the operating table to reveal manacles on the corners of the table. I'm in deep do-do if she gets them in place. Resistance I haven't experienced in a long time rears its head. This time my throat doesn't close on me and I yell my lungs out, hoping my friends are still nearby.

Pistol-whipped for my efforts, I drop the scalpel and get a reaction from Chalky I'd rather avoid.

"You bitch!" She raises her arm to whack me with the gun again. Still woozy from the first hit, I grab blindly at whatever comes to hand on the trolley next to the operating table and fire it in her direction.

If she's too busy fending off surgical equipment, she's too busy to clobber me. It's obvious she doesn't plan on shooting me. No demand for that, apparently.

It's a lame plan, but it's all I've got.

My hand rests on a stainless-steel kidney dish; I grab it, rear up and smash it into her face. Bloodied swabs fire all over the show, followed by the gun.

*Dammit, I haven't knocked her out, just slowed her down.*

Even so, it gives me time to grab yet more items and throw them at her.

But she keeps coming.

A glance in the direction of the bolts holding the panel in place suggests I don't need to hold out much longer. It'll be close, especially with Chalky on her hands and knees, scrabbling for the gun.

*Oh, no, you don't.*

Falling to the ground next to her, I grab the scalpel I dropped earlier. I bury it in the back of her hand, stopping her manicured fingers from closing around the handle of the gun. But, rather than scream as I expect – hell, I've even relaxed a little – she slams me with a dead glare, calmly pulls the scalpel free, and then flings it negligently across the room.

*Oh, hell.*

All that's available for protection now, is the trolley itself. Summoning strength I didn't know I had, I grab it by two legs and swing it, flattening Chalky in the process. This time she yells a string of obscenities.

I struggle with her, even winning, when a familiar cold slithers near me. Twisting my head, I watch in horror as a cloud of black drifts up through the drain in the middle of the floor. It glides across the lino like dry ice, getting closer. Any closer and I could reach out and touch it.

*So not gonna happen.*

If this weren't terrifying on its own, Elizabeth's face morphs in and out of focus amid this black mist. Her gaze locked with mine, the anticipation in those dead orbs unequivocal: she's come to collect.

Or implant.

Or even take me over body and soul so she can experience the birth.

Try as hard as I might to avoid it while fighting Chalky, the cloud covers me. It's cold, clammy embrace cradling me from neck to womb.

Chalky pulls away, putting as much distance as she can between us.

Desperate to roll up into a tight protective ball, I'm frozen and rigid.

Flat on my back.

Unable to move.

Unable to think past the bone-deep terror that is Elizabeth Collins.

The bitter blackness invades my brain, chilling my thoughts as the wall splinters and Hemi storms through. I can't call for help; the cold squeezing my throat makes speech impossible. All I can do is communicate with my eyes. Hoping I'm understood.

*Need ... more ... air ...*

*Blacking ... out ...*

The last thing I'm aware of is Hemi flooding my system with enough testosterone I'm in danger of sprouting chest hair. I can only hope it's enough to save me yet again.

## 31

Opening my eyes, the now-dead operating theatre light stares down at me. Moving my arms and legs, it's a relief to find I'm not manacled in place.

Of greater relief is that I'm no longer cold. My hand strays from my side, splaying across my tummy, which is warm to the touch. Not what I expected, not with mum-to-be Elizabeth having just invaded me.

Swivelling my head, I see that only Ange and Bev are with me.

"Where's Chalky? And the others? Did they get her?"

Bev struggles to find the right words, her face a mask of concentration as if deciding what to tell me.

"No sugar coating, please." I take stock of my wellbeing before continuing. "Give it to me straight. I can take it."

It's all the encouragement Ange needs to share everything in excruciating detail, her verbal shorthand making this faster than if Bev had answered.

"Horse and Johnno grabbed Chalky. Hemi worked to get rid of Lizzie. You started screaming."

Bev shivers. "Only it wasn't you. It was her."

There's no need for Bev to confirm for me which *her* she means. "You can relax, she's gone now. There's not a trace left, so far as I can tell."

Ange wrings her hands in a motion I equate with her and stress. "Oh, we know that."

My gaze swings back and forth between the two women. "What aren't you telling me?"

Between them, they update me on everything since I lost consciousness. Part of me wishes I was still unconscious.

"Hang on, why on earth would Elizabeth latch onto Chalky? She wouldn't be up to carrying a kid." They know my theory about the the woman's likely age; I don't need to go into the state of the her uterus.

It's Bev who answers. "Turns out if a woman is evil to the core, Elizabeth can come and go as she likes. And while she's in residence, the host is as strong as an ox. That's how Chalky escaped."

Thinking back to my fight with Chalky earlier, I wonder if Elizabeth was on board then.

*No, that can't be right. Chalky might be an evil, cold-hearted cow, but the woman had been warm to the touch when we were fighting.*

"Here's hoping they catch her and soon." This last sentiment is as much for my benefit as the others. Thoughts of the already evil Chalky imbued with the power of a malevolent spirit don't bear thinking about.

Ange takes my pulse again, with a bemused expression on her face. "If I hadn't seen it for myself, I'd never have believed it?"

"Believed what?"

Bev lubricates her mouth to speak. "Your pulse. It was so faint that Ange couldn't even find it earlier."

I, on the other hand, feel amazing post Hemi's infusion of male energy. Stitch that, I feel borderline invincible, well, apart from the prospect of running into a possessed Chalky. That aside, I jump unaided off the operating table, a definite spring in my step.

"Let's get the hell out of here and find my phone."

The tofu eaters located and safe for now, there's nothing to keep us on this side of the linen cupboard. There's also the small matter of the king-size bars of 70% dark chocolate hidden alongside my phone.

Bev and Ange are already at the double doors the surgical team left through earlier when I come to my senses. "Ah, I don't think it's a good idea going that way. You never know who, or what, we'll run into."

The women stop, unspoken questions in each of their expressions.

"If we go back the way we've come, we know where we're going."

Also if we retrace our steps, anyone we meet will either be comatose, or in the case of the guards whose guns exploded, plain old dead.

Convinced of my strategy, they nod. When they move in my direction, I receive the ultimate confirmation that my plan is sound.

Walking through the hole smashed through the wall, I'm pleased to see my cricket bat lying where I left it, a marker to my location as intended. It's good to be in control of it again and, without my late husband to hold me back, I'm going to resume play.

*Surely there's a Master's League I can join?*

Before retracing our steps, I look down the hallway as it disappears off to the right. I know the trolley with its pile of bodies went that way because of the drying trail of blood. A shudder wracks my frame at thoughts of those poor women being butchered. Memories of that horrible concrete room are destined to haunt me for the rest of my days.

"Did you find anything before you twigged I was missing?"

Bev shakes her head before putting her answer into words. "Nah, they disappeared through another one of those panels."

Logic says if we follow the trail of blood to its conclusion, we'll find what we're looking for. Common sense says we don't do that without the guys being with us. Waiting suits me; with those unfortunate women long past help.

We reach the fake linen cupboard without encountering a soul. Even the guards whose guns blew up are missing, although matching red streaks along the hallway say this hasn't been under their own steam.

As the one in the lead, I've already grabbed hold of the decorative moulding on the back of the sliding shelving unit when the whole thing moves of its own volition.

This means one thing. Swinging back to the others, I put my finger to my lips before double-handing the cricket bat high above my head.

I don't have the luxury of knowing who it is before I act. All I know is that it's not one of our saviours and whoever it is, he's wearing camo. That's fine by me. The cricket bat stoves in his cranium with a sickening crunch and he drops to the ground, not knowing what hit him.

Rolling him over with my foot, I recognise Piers and I'm tempted to give him a frontal lobotomy to go with that dent in the back of his skull. I can't quite bring myself to hammer him. "Here, take my bat." I hold it out and Bev grabs it, an inquisitive look in her eye.

Grabbing hold of one of Pier's feet, I wait for Ange to grab the other and between us, we drag him in the direction of the mixing room, not stopping until we're next to the vat full of chocolate drink and vomit. I drop his leg and grab an arm. Ange also drops her leg, although she isn't as quick to grab Pier's other arm.

I'm about to speak when a moan comes from one of the vats at the back of the room.

*Damn, I was hoping the technicians would still be down for the count after being dealt with by Horse and Hemi earlier.*

I point at the vat before laying my finger across my lips – it's far better for us to keep our voices low. If the guards do make it out of here in one piece, the less they know about who's responsible for what's about to happen, the better.

Looking at the unconscious man, Ange wipes her hands down the side of her pants before moving closer to me so she can keep her voice low. "What do you have planned?"

"Drowning. Apparently, it's a really relaxing way to go."

"I don't, ah, no. I can't do that," she stutters out, not bothering to keep her voice low. She stumbles back, looking at me like I've got two heads.

"Ange, they skinned women back there," I hiss at her. "They chopped them up with chainsaws. They drilled holes in them. I don't think they did it to them after they'd died of natural causes. This prick," I take time to kick him in the stomach, "used a loaded gun on me without being directed to by Chalky." I kick him in the balls even harder. "And he made sure it hurt."

Despite this, Ange is reticent about physically taking someone out.

Bev has no qualms. After a barely audible, "Here, hold these." She hands Ange my cricket bat, along with her frying pan. She doesn't need any help to heft the now-moaning Piers up and over the top of the mixing bowl. She pushes him forward until he's buried up to his shoulders in the gloop.

It takes our combined strength to keep him under until he stops struggling.

While not a whole lot of fun, it's preferable to any of us taking him and Lance to court for rape and us being on trial as much as they were.

Hell, if they got a good defence lawyer, they'd try to spin it that because none of us fought back that we were 'asking for it.' It wouldn't matter that we were drugged or tied down. No way am I putting myself through that.

Back in the hallway, I make sure I have both Ange and Bev's attention before I speak. "Remember, what happens at fat camp stays at fat camp? Okay?"

Neither of them argues the point, nor is it discussed on our way back to the linen cupboard. Far better we concentrate on checking whether anyone is around, than arguing the right or wrong of what just happened.

Closing the door to the cupboard, I bemoan the fact there's no key. There isn't even anything we can use to jam it shut. Distance will be our friend in this case, and we waste no time in scarpering.

We leave using the same door we'd entered through earlier. The difference now is that rather than being the dead of night, the sun's made an appearance over the hills that back the spa.

*It's funny how things seem less evil in daylight.*

"Let's check on Tee," says Ange, not waiting to see if Bev and I are in agreement. She's off through the flax bushes, leaving us to follow as best we can. It's as though she's trying to distance herself from us.

"I don't think she liked seeing someone murdered," says Bev, as we scurry to catch up.

"If she'd seen what I'd seen, she wouldn't be so squeamish. Anyway, it wasn't murder, it was a well-deserved execution."

I thought we'd spoken quietly until Ange stops in her tracks and spins to face us. "Okay, you two freaked me out. Cold-blooded murder freaks me out. I've spent the last twenty years of my life devoted to keeping people alive. I can't flip a switch."

"Even when they're truly evil?" Bev looks genuinely intrigued.

"Yeah, when they've murdered people in cold blood for money?" I add.

"I get that it's not straightforward. Just don't ask me to help. Okay?"

She gets nods from both Bev and me.

My last rational thought is that even Hemi can't save me from Elizabeth this time.

Everything's white. Funny, I expected hell to be redder. I also didn't expect Ange to be there with me, in a nurse's uniform.

"What happened?" I remember being taken out by the mother of all spectres, her cold dread filling me and flooding every fibre of my being. I can't feel her presence. Rather than be cold, I'm cocooned by a warm, peaceful calm. Everything's pink and fluffy in my world right now.

*Must be drugs involved. Lots of them.*

"It's been touch and go." Ange looks away from me to check the readings on what appears to be state-of-the-art monitoring equipment. "I was so relieved we managed to stabilise you."

"We?"

"Horse, ah, strong-armed one of The Vale doctors into assisting Hemi and me."

"We're still here!" How agitated I am is reflected on the monitor, with more red buttons flashing than is recommended by healthcare professionals or even the manufacturers.

Ange is doing her best to calm me when Hemi and a man I've never seen before burst through the door. Bev follows soon after.

The guy I think must be the doctor checks the monitoring equipment, while Hemi slams his hand down on my forehead, pushing my head back into the pillow. My forehead is immediately flushed with heat, leaving Hemi somewhat confused. "She's not there."

"I know. I'm all lovely and warm."

The doctor peers at the monitor. "There must be something wrong with it." In the medical equivalent of the method used by IT departments the world over, he flips the machine off and back on again. For a second, every light on the device glows brightly before normal transmission resumes.

Hemi takes his hand away, leaving my forehead cold and bereft. "You sure you're okay? Why'd the machine go off its rocker?"

Embracing my inner drama queen, I admit my reaction was to the news we're still at The Vale.

A tide of red suffuses Hemi's face. "We couldn't risk moving you."

"What? I was that close to death?" No one answers, with every one of them, even the doctor, looking anywhere but at me. "Guys, I deserve to know."

Eventually, the silence is broken by Bev, who's sitting in the visitor's chair, which I doubt gets much use this far out in the boonies. "You didn't just get close to death, you died."

"But I'm okay now. So that's the main thing?"

*Hah, who am I kidding? Being told you've been on the wrong side of life is disconcerting.* Of more concern is that none of them backs up my assertion that I'm okay.

Again, I look at the doctor, unsure of how much he knows about what's been going on. I take a moment to formulate my next question, making it sound more innocuous than it is. "But, Elizabeth, she left, right?"

Again, I have to wait for a response with no one keen on giving it.

Hemi shuffles his feet, appearing unsettled for

Not giving Bev a chance to answer, her gaze swings in my direction, scanning my new, thinner self, before dropping to the cricket bat I'm in control of again. "Didn't you check out?"

"Hah, I damn near did. Get dressed and we'll tell you all about it."

While waiting for Tee, we sit on the veranda admiring the view, although this is interrupted when Johnno and Horse cross the vista, a struggling guard slung between them. Even though I'm not familiar with him, there's no remorse as I watch them pitch him over the cliff without a second glance. Ange, however, stifles a cry of distress.

"Right," says Tee, walking out of her room, "you want to tell me what the hell is going on?" We don't have the chance to, before she adds, "We should have been called for breakfast by now."

"Trust me, when we tell you what's been going on, you won't be so keen on eating." Ange's tone gives the impression it'll be a while before she drinks another smoothie, unless she's prepared it herself.

Tee looks longingly at the dining room. "Don't bet on it. I'm not easily put off my grub."

Rather than wait for us, she takes off to get to the dining hall as soon as she can, not bothering to keep to the raised boardwalk. Her tummy is rumbling loudly, so that even a good couple of metres back, I can hear it.

"We need to get there before her, otherwise she'll be headfirst into the fridge and hoover whatever's on hand." Bev accelerates after her, with Ange and me not far behind. Tee will never forgive us if we don't tell her about the secret ingredient in those big-arse smoothies. Whether this will stop her from drinking one is anyone's bet.

The four of us are close to the doors to the dining room, when Anton explodes through them, with Hemi in pursuit.

"Run, Anton, run!" says Ange, in a fair *Forrest Gump* parody.

I think she's kidding around until I see she's wringing her hands.

Tee looks from Anton – who's close to being caught by Hemi – and back to Ange. There's bafflement writ large on her face. "Why?"

Bev looks at the pursuit that, while potentially deadly in nature, has taken on a comedic air, with Hemi and Anton's physiques representing both extremes of the bell curve. "Because if Hemi gets hold of him, he'll send him over the cliff, as with all the others."

"You're joking." For once, Tee looks away from the source of food.

Ange continues to wring her hands. "Unfortunately not."

"No, he's sodding isn't!" roars Tee.

She moves surprisingly quickly for such a big woman, and Hemi is no match for her when she slams sideways into him. She takes him off his feet, landing squarely on top of him; the *oomph* of air escaping confirms she's winded him.

"I'd better go see if he's okay," says Ange, already jogging in their direction.

Anton, making the most of Tee's diversion, legs it in the direction of the Sleeping Beauty Suites.

"Hell, I've just thought of something!" I don't bother explaining before taking off after him.

I'm gaining when he as good as disappears right

in front of me. At the row of flax that borders the dense bush, I see the gap. I shoot through it without slowing down and am rewarded with seeing Anton not too far in front of me. Thinking he was safe, he's slowed.

*Big mistake.*

Sneaking up behind him, I'm aware I'm moving as quietly as Horse. This works in my favour, because I slam a hand on his shoulder before he knows what the hell's going on.

"Take me to your car!"

The words are menacing, even if inside my head they sound in a, "Take me to your leader" voice. Wrenching free of my grip, he spins to face me, his expression changing from terror to humour in a heartbeat. That is until I raise the cricket bat.

"Hell's bells, okay, lady."

"You don't even know my name?"

He shrugs. "What's the point?"

Much as I'd like to part his hair with my cricket bat, I stop myself. I don't know if he's saying this because he knows this is where fat women come to die. Or is it there are so many moving through the place, that remembering their names is impossible. For his sake, I hope it's the latter.

"Your car?" I indicate up the track with the cricket bat, before prodding him hard. I'm surprised when he staggers back a step or two. So strong.

He turns and storms off, leaving me there for a couple of seconds until my legs catch up with my brain and him. The car park is miles away. No wonder I'd never seen any cars other than the Hummer on the property.

Eventually, we clear the bush into a large gravel car park, home to at least a dozen high-end vehicles and a large shed; the latter most likely a chop shop. Sure, a few of the cars will belong to the medical staff and Chalky, but the rest must belong to ex-residents.

"Go!"

Anton doesn't need telling twice. He sprints over to a hot pink Mazda convertible and jumps in without bothering to open the doors. He starts the car, leaving in a spray of gravel.

There's a crunch of gravel behind me and I turn, expecting the others to have caught up with me.

Chalky's white smock is no longer pristine. It's ripped, shredded and smeared with dirt and leaf litter. The rest of her isn't looking too hot, either. At the slightest movement, her right eyeball bounces against her cheek courtesy of an overly tenacious optic nerve. And yet despite this, she looks remarkably healthy for someone who's just been introduced to the bottom of a cliff the hard way.

Held in place by the dead glare of the eye that remains in its socket, I do nothing, waiting to make my move. She perseveres in her examination of me as she staggers drunkenly around, thanks to a broken tibia poking through the side of her calf muscle. "Well, well, well, Marilyn, it's not often I'm surprised."

*Why the hell is she surprised? That I've lost weight? That I'm alive? That she's alive? Could I even tell with that botoxed deadpan expression of hers?*

"What will it take for me to get back what you've taken from me?"

"Me, taken from you?" This is followed by a jumble of thoughts I don't have a chance to make sense of. Is she talking about me screwing up her little money-making pay-per-view enterprise, or the power Elizabeth had temporarily given her? If the crazy bitch is talking about Lance, then I can't help her there.

"I will take it back." So conversational is her promise, that it takes a moment for my foetus to understand we've been threatened. A surge of power races through my system. Catching sight of the large hunting knife she's holding behind her back is all the encouragement I need.

There's no time to think, just act.

S winging the bat hard, I shatter her knife hand and, following a full rotation, connect the bat – hard – with the side of her head. She drops to her knees and pitches forward without a peep.

Tossing the bat to one side, I lean down and grab the knife off the ground before turning her over by shoving at her inert form with my foot. There's one way I can stop this evil cow, and one way only.

Slashing her jugular, I'm sprayed with a satisfying amount of blood. I lick my lips clean, thanking my lucky stars the tracksuit I'm wearing is black.

*Who has time to pre-soak at a time like this?*

A couple more goes with the knife and stamping on what's left of her spine, I hold her head aloft by her inky black hair.

At the sound of the others coming through the bush, I turn, holding her noggin aloft like The Vale's version of an 'Immunity Idol'. It's too much for Ange who faints, while Bev raises an eyebrow. Tee, at the rear, and still not au fait with everything that's been going on, looks confused.

The guys, however, are all action. Grabbing Chalky's hair, Hemi prises my fingers away. He makes short work of shot-putting the head off into the bush to be enjoyed by the local wildlife.

Johnno and Horse have already grabbed Chalky by her arms and legs when I spot something. "Hang on a second." While they wait, I make short work of removing my Rolex from her twig-like wrist. "Okay, now you can get rid of her."

Johnno and Horse turn wheel around, ready to retrace their steps. Using the knife, I point at the area of bush where the bitch's head landed. "Why don't you just chuck her in there too?"

"Nah," says Hemi. "The farther apart the bits are, the safer it is."

"Bits?" cries out Ange, before fainting again. For a nurse, she sure is squeamish.

Johnno and Horse off to various drop points, Hemi stays with us. Bev and Tee take care of Ange, while he and I check the cars. Our goal is one with keys in the ignition and, more importantly, a full tank. Even a half tank would get us back to town.

I'm next to a Range Rover when I hear something that shouldn't be possible. Deep within the bush where Chalky's head lies, comes chanting, 'What's yours is mine. What's mine is yours!' Exactly as she did before Johnno shoulder-pressed her off the cliff.

*Could it be Elizabeth is trying for another baby?*

I'm unsure what to do. A lack of power surge says that other than the ick factor, the baby isn't under threat from either Chalky or Elizabeth. It's confirmed when a now-familiar English voice sounds inside my head. "I will protect my own."

What happens next says the spectre isn't playing

with a full deck. I sure as hell don't feel protected. My body no longer under my control, I double over, wailing in pain with my hands pressed tight against my abdomen, as if to protect the baby.

"You bitch!" I scream, forced to the ground by an unseen force. There I curl in on myself instinctively as a means of protection.

I don't stop screaming until Hemi crouches down and gently slides his hand close to my tummy, but without touching it. "I ... I think she's gone."

His words are tentative and for a minute, I think he's talking about the baby. I don't need to be an expert in body language to know he's relieved by this. *Would I be feeling the same way if I were in his boots?*

Placing my hand protectively across my stomach, I'm surprised by what I sense, finding it hard to comprehend.

So what if the conception was thanks to a deadly combo of Lance, or Piers, and the spectre that was Elizabeth? With one of them chucked over a cliff, and the other dead in a vat of chocolate shake, all connections to the living have been lost.

Tears roll down my face and Bev pulls me into a motherly embrace. "It's over, Marilyn. We can all get back on with our lives now."

Ange, who's conscious again, crawls over and joins in the group hug. "Yep, a bit of counselling and a bucket-load of chocolate and this will all be a nasty memory."

While I admire their confidence that life will return to normal, I know it'll never be the same again. I have Elizabeth to thank for that.

# EPILOGUE

A month has passed since we escaped The Vale. After finding my case Tee, Bev and Ange had made short work of demolishing the chocolate. I'd tried a piece, but had to spit it out. It reminded me too much of those chocolate shakes for me to fully enjoy it.

The battery on my phone had been close to dying before we could convince the cops it wasn't a prank call. No sooner had the first police car pulled up than Hemi, Johnno and Horse muttered about the pigs and disappeared into the bush.

From what they'd said while we were waiting, Johnno was off to a forestry contract down south, Horse was returning to his city lifestyle, and Hemi would lie low at his place further up the coast.

The only evidence they hadn't been a figment of my imagination was Hemi's phone number programmed into mine. I couldn't blame them scarpering. An absence of hunting licences was reason enough not to hang around. Add to this the sheer number of corpses they'd left on the property and they were better off getting the hell out of it.

The rescue helicopter took the tofu eater with

the flayed back to Auckland hospital, while the rest of us were taken by ambulance to Thames hospital. This left the place to a forensic team that looked as if all its Christmases had come at once. Whether this was down to the mess they needed to sort through, or the chance to meet celebrities was anyone's guess.

Part of me was pleased to know the medical staff had no idea what was going on as it made it easier for us to keep to our story.

My first week of freedom, was spent in hospital with the two remaining tofu eaters, Tee, Bev and Ange. Rather than be left to convalesce, we were prodded, poked and tested for STDs.

In between these indignities, we were grilled by the cops, with them asking us the same questions over and over.

Even in my first interview, I could tell they weren't buying our story. But, with all of us spouting the same narrative, they had no option but to believe us.

That the tofu eater undergoing skin grafts at Auckland hospital backed up our version of events, helped immensely. Sadly, the member of their group who'd run into town for help, never made it. The cops scoured the bushes on either side of the road, but no trace of her was ever found.

*I'll bet Elizabeth Collins knows where she is.*

I'd tell the cops my theory but doubt they'd believe it.

The one thing in all of this that I point-blank refused was a pregnancy test.

*I didn't need a slip of paper to tell me what I already knew.*

I couldn't face returning to the city. Instead I'd caught a bus back up to Coromandel to collect the Lexus before taking Bev up on her offer to stay with her in the country. The hardest part of grabbing my car was getting away without being given the third degree by Gary at the petrol station. And if that wasn't enough, Colin had been in there filling up.

In the end, I'd said I wasn't allowed to talk about it because it was an ongoing police investigation. Anything to stop the multitude of questions they fired at me. My refusal to speak had Colin close to tears.

Hemi had checked in via text, asking how I was doing. Even though this was in general terms, I knew what he was after. But, I wasn't sharing, instead keeping my responses brief and deliberately vague.

This had worked for a while, before his enquiries became more pointed. I don't know how much longer I can keep him in the dark. All I need is a couple more months before it'll be too late.

Unable to stay with Bev and Sid indefinitely, I'm back in the city. I haven't committed to a house or even an apartment, and am staying in an upmarket B&B close to my old haunts. Deciding what I want to do with my life is taking more energy than I'd have thought possible.

Being close to death has changed my priorities, with lunching and constant clothes shopping barely making the list. Today, however, I'm catching up with my girlfriends. I'd be a self-confessed idiot not to understand this has more to do with them wanting the dirt on The Vale than any concerns about my wellbeing.

Stepping out of the shower, I make short work of drying myself. I don't bother blow-waving my hair into submission. I finger-comb some mousse through its much shorter – and blonder – length. In a final show of defiance, I mess it up until it's a riot of curls. So many hours wasted over the years, maintaining the smooth, helmet-like bob David had preferred.

My clothes readied before my shower, I'm dressed in minutes. Thanks to the tan I acquired on my daily walk at Bev's place, I leave my make-up at mascara and lipstick.

I'm so much 'lower maintenance' than I used to be, and I love it. I'm nothing like the corporate wife who'd left town. I'm thinner, healthier and generally happier in my skin. The only dark clouds that remain are those clogging the part of my brain devoted to memories.

The restaurant isn't far. Rather than drive and waste ten minutes looking for a parking space, I walk. Winter hasn't quite got us in her icy grip and the sun is warm. I've also eschewed heels for sneakers bought from a surf shop that'll allow me to walk at a good clip. It was the sort of place I'd never have entered in my old life.

Lorraine's strident tones greet me before I even

see her, flying like birds of prey over the high wall that surrounds the alfresco part of the restaurant. "Has anyone seen her since she got back to town?"

It wouldn't take Einstein to know she's talking about me and my steps slow of their own accord when she gets a volley of "No" in response. Rooted to the spot, I wait to listen to what else the nasty piece of work will say.

"Twenty says she hasn't lost an ounce." I don't need to see Lorraine to know spite is fighting her facelift for supremacy.

*Why did I ever bother with her before? That's right, our husbands did business together.*

I walk in briskly.

A dozen steps and I'm next to their table, although it takes a few seconds for my presence to be registered.

"Yes?" Lorraine looks both up at me and down her nose simultaneously. Just this one word and I have to fight my Pavlovian response to cower. I want to make myself smaller, to apologise, even though I haven't done anything wrong. That is until I'm swamped by the new and now-familiar surge of power.

The old me would have ignored the bitchy comments I'd overheard on arrival. The new me has no compunction about prodding the elephant sitting in the middle of the large round table.

"As you can see, Lorraine, I have lost more than an ounce."

"Marilyn, is that you?" Deidre, albeit as shocked as Lorraine, hasn't been called out as being a spiteful bitch. She has no trouble asking me, if I am indeed, me.

Meanwhile, the skinny orange cow sporting the

obviously fake boobs is still mute. Even thinking this about the nasty piece of work, a smile breaks out.

*Imagine if I said it?*

Rather than answer Deidre, I hold my arms wide and turn slowly. My body has changed dramatically and so has my wardrobe. Gone are the designer outfits David insisted I wear and that are still favoured by these women. They've been replaced with jeans, a long-sleeved T-shirt and a weathered leather jacket.

I know damned well I look good, with more than one guy trying to catch my eye on the walk here. Backing this up, the expression of pure hatred on Lorraine's face says it all.

"I'd love to join you for lunch, but I've got packing to take care of."

"Packing?" says Claire. "Are you off on holiday?"

"Nope. I'm moving. Away from here. Away from all the bad memories." I pause, making sure I've got Lorraine's attention. "Away from skinny orange cows with poached-egg tits."

*Oooh, now that felt good.*

I don't bother to wait for a response, and swing around and leave the way I came in. I'm on the other side of the high wall before Lorraine puts voice to her anger.

"Well, I've never been so insulted in all my life!"

"She did look good though, didn't she?" says one of the others.

"Yes, thank you, Audrey. If I wanted your opinion, I'd have asked for it."

A magnificent grin makes itself at home as I stride off along the footpath. Back to finish packing for my new life in the country. Finding vacant land at the back of Coromandel Township was easy when money was no object. I've also bought a relocatable home which, all going well, will be on-site tomorrow.

While many might think I'm moving to the back of beyond to work on the psychological scars inflicted on me by The Vale, they'd be wrong. I believe it's important for a little one to be born near both her birth and surrogate mothers. The biggest challenge I'll face when I move is making sure Hemi doesn't see me until well after the birth.

My hand on my gently rounded tummy, my grin gets even wider. For once in my life, I'm happy to be putting on weight.


THE END

# THANK YOU

First off, a bloody high-five to my critique partners, and fellow authors, Kirsten McKenzie and Madeleine Eskedahl for their unwavering support and input.

Without our weekly catch-ups over the lockdown, I'd have been smacking my head against the nearest wall. You truly kept me sane in what were trying times.

Next I'd like to thank Jayne Southern, my editor. I've been working with Jayne since I was first published in 2014 and am still gobsmacked at what a steel trap that woman's mind is. Any errors you find will be because I tinkered with the manuscript after she signed off on it.

Lightning Source UK Ltd.
Milton Keynes UK
UKHW021321210322
400383UK00011B/2866

9 780995 141636